ATON

Almost a god—
Very much a man!

From the lost chronicles of pre-history, Irving A. Greenfield again creates a larger-than-life hero whose battle for a way of being drives him to the limits of human endurance. This is thunderous entertainment and moving human drama on a scale of epic proportions, matching Greenfield's creation of Ronstrum in THE ANCIENT OF DAYS and Ibanez in A PLAY OF DARKNESS.

Avon Books by
Irving A. Greenfield

A PLAY OF DARKNESS	19877	$1.50
THE ANCIENT OF DAYS	14860	$1.50

ATON

IRVING A. GREENFIELD

AVON
PUBLISHERS OF BARD, CAMELOT, DISCUS, EQUINOX AND FLARE BOOKS

ATON is an original publication of Avon Books. This work has never before appeared in any form.

AVON BOOKS
A division of
The Hearst Corporation
959 Eighth Avenue
New York, New York 10019

ISBN: 0-380-00374-0

First Avon Printing, July, 1975

AVON TRADEMARK REG. U.S. PAT. OFF. AND
FOREIGN COUNTRIES, REGISTERED TRADEMARK—
MARCA REGISTRADA, HECHO EN CHICAGO, U.S.A.

Printed in the U.S.A.

ATON

Part I

FATHER AND SON

1

ONLY THE MEREST CRACK in the dark sky glowed red like the flames of the huge fire in Nempie's camp, around which his people were gathered. Some stood and others squatted on their haunches.

Nempie was a tall, broad-shouldered man. His black beard was streaked with gray, and his bushy eyebrows overhung penetrating black eyes. He said nothing as he three times circled the man at the stake. Still silent, he moved closer to the fire, where the wavering light from its flames made his eyes glisten like bits of black rock.

Nempie was feared by everyone as a hunter of great skill and strength. Even Aton, his eldest son, at whom he peered through the flickering light of the fire, feared him.

Aton was dressed in skins. He was as broad and tall as his father though his beard was not as large, and his eyes were gray rather than black.

Ordinarily, Aton, like his brothers who were old enough to sit at the fire, dared not look directly at his father lest he incur his wrath and become the object of his pitiless jibes or receiver of the blows which would be delivered with big clublike hands.

In the past, if Aton had seen the menacing curl of Nempie's lips, he might have trembled with fear. But since he had not looked directly at his father he had not seen it—or perhaps he had pretended not to see it?

This night was different from all the others that had passed since Aton had taken his place at the fire with the rest of the men who hunted for the people of the camp. Now Aton had no game to match with the kills of the other hunters. This night Aton had returned with a man—a stranger from a different people. In the past Nempie had been the only hunter to have returned to camp with a man they could eat.

Other peoples who hunted close by would not hesitate to eat the flesh of a man even if he were dead before he was brought to their camp.

They were less than Nempie, his people, and all the leaders of the people before him. As far back as any of the old men could remember, no one was allowed to eat the flesh of man other than one who had been brought to them alive, as this one had been.

People who ate the flesh of a dead man never gained his strength and were changed into vultures or jackals when their spirits separated from their bodies. So said the old men in the camp.

But the man whom Aton had brought back to camp was alive. Some of the blood was dried and matted in his brown beard from the wound on the right side of his head where Aton had struck him with his club. He was stripped of his skins, and the light from the fire revealed a sheen of sweat.

By returning to camp with a live man, Aton's hunting skill now equaled his father's.

Nempie's looks were black and he said in a voice loud enough to carry across the crackling of the fire, "Aton, you have hunted well today."

"I was not afraid," Aton answered, looking at his father.

"The heart is yours," Nempie told him.

Aton circled the fire and with his stone knife in his hand went to the man at the stake.

Some of the bolder women began to shout to be allowed to play with the man, make his organ throb with the expectation of having a woman, and then force it to spend itself, wasting his fluid to guard the women of the camp against being raped by other men of his people. It was always done before a man was eaten.

Their cries stayed Aton's movement and he glanced at Nempie.

"It is always done," Nempie told him.

Aton was close enough to the man to look into his eyes. He saw no fear in them.

"It is our right," one of the women shrilled. A second and a third agreed with her.

The man, though he could not understand the women, seemed to know what they wanted. His eyes went wide with fear as he pressed himself back against the stake. He began to speak, his lips hardly moving.

Aton tried to make out what was said but could not understand the tongue of the stranger. All men were strangers and they were always less than the men in Nempie's camp. But the women taken in raids on the camps of other people were not strangers; they were women and were used.

The women's demands grew louder and in a chorus they called out, "Give us what is ours. Give us what is ours, Aton, son of Nempie. Give us his fluid."

Aton felt a sudden tightening in his own groin. Springing forward, he plunged his knife into the man's chest. Even as the man screamed, Aton tore the still throbbing heart from the man's bloody chest and, skewering it on his knife, dashed to the fire where he let the flames sear it until the scent of roasting flesh reached his nostrils. Then he brought the still bloody meat to his mouth and began eating.

The people rushed at the body of the man. Each cut pieces from it to roast in the fire until the bones lay drenched in blood at the foot of the stake and the smell of burnt flesh hung like a dark cloud above the flames of the fire.

Nempie waited until later, while the people were busy devouring the small deer he had brought back from the day's hunting, to call out to Aton, who had resumed his place on the other side of the fire, "Aton, what will you give the women in exchange for what you denied them?"

"Nothing," Aton answered.

Nempie cocked his head to one side. "Surely they deserve something," he said.

Aton shrugged.

"It has always been the custom," Nempie told him, "to allow the women to protect themselves——"

"He was a brave man, Nempie," Aton said. "He fought well."

Nempie mimicked his son's answer and then asked, "Is that all you have to say?"

Aton remained silent; his heart began to race.

"What, no words to tell us of your skill?" Nempie challenged. "No words to boast that you will soon wear the tusks of Pula, the black boar?"

Aton clenched his jaws, afraid that he might give way to his own anger and come to blows with his father. He would not take another beating from him without fighting back.

"It is better you say nothing," Nempie said with a harsh laugh, "much better to say nothing." Then he stood up, called to Bisha, his favorite woman, and stalked off to his shelter. "The matter will be settled soon."

Aton picked up a piece of deer meat and began to chew on it; he no longer had a taste for it.

Gens, who was dropped from a different mother than he but was his brother through Nempie, leaned close to Aton and said, "Someday you will fight him."

"I would lose now," Aton responded.

"I am not so sure you would," Gens said. "And if Nempie was sure he would be the winner he would have confronted you before."

"I would lose now," Aton repeated.

"Not if we fought him together," Gens whispered.

Aton glanced at his brother. If the two of them fought they might have a chance. Gens, too, was strong, a good hunter, and skilled in the use of a spear or a club.

"Out of spite," Gens said, "Nempie will not give you the woman you ask for."

"I have taken those I have wanted," Aton answered.

"And should you want Bisha," Gens questioned, "would he give her to you?"

"You want her?"

"Yes. But he will not give her to me out of spite. I do not want to wait until he tires of her. I have already lain with her——"

"He would kill both of you if he knew!"

Gens nodded and said, "So now you understand why I must kill him first."

"And what do you want besides Bisha?" Aton asked.

"Half of all that comes to us."

Aton looked into the fire and said, "If I killed him myself I would take all that was left. I would become the leader of the people as Nempie did when he slew his father."

"But you are not sure you would win," Gens continued.

"And if I did——"

"I would try to kill you, Aton."

"I will think about it," Aton said, getting to his feet. Gens nodded and reminded him that part of something was better than nothing. "It would even be better," he added, "than having to fight me."

"I said I will think about it," Aton answered. "But now I am tired and need sleep."

"Do not think on it too long, brother," Gens said.

Aton started away from the fire and then, struck by a sudden thought, turned back. "And if I should decide to do nothing, what will you do, Gens?"

"Then I will have to wait until our father's anger forces the fight on you," Gens replied, "as you know it will. . . ."

Aton's shelter was made of boughs and rushes. It was large enough to hold him and Rika, the woman he took the previous summer.

Rika had, as all the women in the tribe, first belonged to Nempie. He had her when her blood had first started to flow, and she had borne him several children before he had given her to Dabo, the arrow maker. But then Dabo's spirit had been taken from him, and Nempie had given her to Aton.

Rika's breasts were no longer firm, and her body was not as lithe as some of the women who had not yet borne so many children; but she was skilled in the ways of pleasing a man.

Aton stretched out next to Rika on a pallet of skins, under which she had placed a great many pine boughs.

The bottom of her covering was pulled up and exposed her sex for him to use if he should want to.

Aton was not interested. With his hands behind his head and the sharp scent of pine in his nostrils he stared at the top of the shelter, where the smoke from a small fire rose into the clear night sky.

He thought about Gens. Of all of Nempie's sons he was closest to him. Each of them were dropped on the same day. Nempie did not keep either woman with him very long. From what others in the camp told him Aton knew that his mother's spirit had left her body soon after he had come out of her. Nempie had traded Gens' mother to the leader of another people for a hunting dog.

Often he and Gens had eaten from the same bowl or had torn meat from the same chunk. They had even shared their first woman. When they became hunters, each knew that some day one of them would have to try to kill their father.

Rika whispered, "You will feel easier if you mount me." And she reached out to stroke his manhood.

He pushed her hand away.

"You should not have brought the man back to camp," she said. "Nempie is jealous."

Aton gave a snort of disdain.

"There can only be one great hunter in the camp, Aton," Rika said, "and he must be the tribe's leader. Already the people are whispering that you are better than he."

"Then they are fools!" he exclaimed angrily.

"They have eyes, Aton," she told him.

"Then let them use them," he answered. "I do not want to talk about Nempie any more."

"Aton," Rika whispered after awhile, "I would give you pleasure if it pleased you."

"Yes," he answered with a deep sigh, "it would please me." And reaching out, he took hold of her hand and placed it on his manhood.

Gens stayed at the fire until after everyone had left. Excepting guards around the camp, the rest of the tribe was asleep. Gens thought about his talk with Aton. He had told his brother everything Nempie wanted him to and now there was nothing either of them could do until Aton came back with an answer.

Gens heard the footfall before he saw the dark form come out of the shadows on the other side of the fire. He stood up and moved toward it.

"What did he say?" Nempie asked.

"That he would think about it."

"And you told him everything?"

"All that you instructed," Gens said.

Nempie pulled on his black beard. Then he put one of his huge hands on Gens's shoulder and said, "Aton is not like other men. He will not do what other men do."

Gens nodded.

"What else did he say?" Nempie asked.

"That he would lose," Gens told him, "if he fought you."

"Then we must get him to fight me."

"As soon as he gives me his answer, I will tell you."

"Press him for it."

"I will."

Nempie took his hand off Gens's shoulder and said, "Bisha waits for you. . . ."

2

NEMPIE'S SLEEP was restless. When the first light, coming up over the mountains out of whose insides the sun broke free each day, drove the night creatures from their work, he ventured outside his shelter.

There was a chill in the air and a grayness lay over the land.

Nempie rubbed his arms to put some warmth in them. His eyes moved from the edges of the clearing to the various shelters where his people lived. Each beehivelike shelter was no more than boughs of wood covered with a matting of rushes garnered by the women from the banks of the river flowing beside the camp.

He sniffed the air. It was filled with the scent of people and the sharp smell of smoke from the smoldering night fires.

His eyes went to where the bones of the man lay. They were strewn about the stake, which someone had topped with the victim's skull. It seemed to look at Nempie as he viewed it. Soon the crows would come to eat out of its eyeless eyes and gaping mouth while the dogs chewed the rest of its bones.

That Aton had brought a man back to camp was sign enough to Nempie that he must somehow force a fight between them before Aton's strength surpassed his. When that would happen, he, like his father, would not survive.

Nempie moved his eyes from the skull to the river, which was already changing from black to gray and would change again from gray to green as the sun crawled out of the mountains and began its journey across the sky.

A white bird suddenly took wing! Nempie looked up and followed its flight. It soared high above the river and seemed to remain aloft without even using its wings. Suddenly it plummeted, dropping like a stone into the water of the river and sinking from view only to leap back into the air with a fish in its beak.

Nempie shook his head.

The white bird could be another sign of Aton's threat, hovering over him in wait for the opportunity to strike. Aton was not like any of his other sons, some of whom he had fought and killed when they had challenged him and others he had beaten so badly that they pleaded for their lives, promising even to let him walk over them if he would let them live. No, Aton was different from all of them. He was even different from Gens, for whom he held some regard. Gens was similar to the others, though more cunning. Like those before him, Gens was willing to risk death to have possession of a woman or to become the leader of the people. Aton, though, seemed to be satisfied with Rika and showed little or no direct interest in becoming the leader of the people.

Suddenly he remembered what Aton had done the previous night and his brow furrowed with anger. Not giving the women the chance to take the fluid from the man's organ was Aton's way of challenging him. Nempie was sure that Aton did it to anger him. Aton hunted the same way, always equaling or surpassing his kill.

Nempie glared at his son's shelter and, growling low in his throat, he was ready to let that growl become a blood cry, a challenge that would bring Aton into the open where he would kill him!

But Nempie balled his fist and forced it into his mouth. No more than he could stop the wind from blowing out of the great desert or make water flow where there was none, could he challenge Aton. The challenge had to come from Aton. The people expected it to happen that way. Even he, their leader, could not change the way it had always been between father and son.

So great was his anger that Nempie's teeth sank deep into the fingers of his hand, filling his mouth with the warm, sharp taste of his own blood. He licked the gashes until the blood stopped and, turning to look at the skull once more, saw that the crows were busy at it.

From the beginning, when Aton was dropped from his mother, Nempie had been warned by Tesu, the seer, that the boy would cause him trouble.

Tesu had foretold it all and the child's mother, before her spirit separated from her body, had said, "I have brought forth a man amongst men, Nempie ... a man better than all others."

"And then the bitch gave up her spirit," Nempie growled low in his throat, "without another word."

He moved closer to the impaled skull. The crows chattered amongst themselves. Some of their kind were posted as guards in the saplings nearby or on the roofs of the shelters nearest to the stake.

The skull grinned at him. It seemed that death was something to laugh about. Nempie spat.

Spitting did not help Nempie and, sighing wearily, he uttered Aton's name. Almost immediately, the skull spoke his son's name.

Nempie leaped back, causing the crows to take wing with a sudden burst of cawing. He spoke again, keeping his voice low.

The skull was silent.

Nempie circled the stake.

The crows returned and chattered even more than they did before.

Nempie stood before the skull and, looking up at it, repeated Aton's name.

The skull again spoke Aton's name.

Nempie drew back. His heart thumped in his chest. He heard the throbbing boom of the warning drum, though from where he stood he could see that no one was even near the huge hollowed-out tree trunk.

"Aton," the skull said.

Nempie screamed wordlessly. The crows whirled into the air, their black wings turning gray in the bright sunlight and their cawing mingling with the excited cries of his people, who burst forth from their shelters and ran to where he stood.

"The stranger spoke," he told them, pointing up at the skull.

Gens pushed his way forward and asked, "What did it say?"

Nempie shook his head but his eyes searched out and found Aton.

"Tell us what it said?" Gens pressed, realizing his father's gaze was on Aton and there was some connection between the words of the skull and his brother.

"It must have said something!" exclaimed one of the women who had wanted to play with the stranger's organ before he was eaten.

And another woman, who saw Nempie look at Aton, cried out, "It is angry with Aton for having killed him before he gave us his fluid."

Many of the women shouted agreement.

Nempie cocked his head to one side and, looking at his son, asked, "Are they right, Aton?"

"I do not know," Aton answered. "You were the only one who heard him speak, Father."

Nempie scowled.

One of the women called, "Let Aton give us what he would not let us take from the man."

Aton stepped away from Rika, who had been standing at his side. His knife was in his hand and he quietly said, "She who will come to me to do what would have been done to the stranger will die."

No woman moved.

"Let my father," Aton said, his voice a whisper, "tell us the words of the skull."

Nempie shook his head. "They were words I did not understand." Again pointing to the skull he said, "Since it was Aton who brought the man here, he will gather his bones together and, together with the skull, he will bury them in the forest."

Everyone agreed with Nempie's instructions.

"And I myself," Nempie added, "will seek out a bull whose hot blood will satisfy the stranger's spirit and in whose liver Tesu will see the future."

Aton returned his knife to his skin belt and, going to the foot of the stake, began to gather the bones of the man in his arms. The people silently watched him. When his arms were full, he asked Nempie to reach up and take the skull from the stake. "Put it on top of the rest of his bones," he said.

Nempie did not move.

Aton asked Rika to do what Nempie would not and she carefully placed the skull on top of all the other bones.

Aton carried the bones to a place in the forest where the cedar trees grew sparsely and the earth was strewn with boulders glittering in the sunlight.

Using a large rock with a tapered edge, he began to scrape out a shallow grave. He paused occasionally to wipe the sweat from his brow. The ground where he dug was not as soft as it was in the forest and to make the opening large enough to hold all of the bones he had to chop away at the hardpan that lay below the top soil.

The sun was high when Aton was finally satisfied with the depth of the depression. He dropped the bones into the shallow pit and then picked up the man's skull.

He had no doubt that it had spoken to Nempie; such things often happened. He had often heard voices, whisperings that he could not understand. All of his people had similar experiences.

Aton glanced quickly around him. Wherever a man went, there were spirits; everyone knew that.

He looked again at the skull and tried to remember what the face had looked like. It was not much different from his own. For a stranger he had fought almost as well as himself.

Aton closed his eyes, savoring the memory of the combat that had taken place between them. He had come on the man where the forest was thick with trees and the river became narrow.

The man was looking at the river's white water and listening to its roar. A many-colored band hung in the mist above the rushing water.

Aton crept forward, stopped, and crept forward again. The breeze came from the river, giving him the advantage. The scent of the man was sharp and strange. There was a sweetness to it. Sunlight glinted off his brown body.

Aton loosed a war cry. Leaping out of the brush in which he had hid himself and brandishing his club, he rushed at the stranger.

The man whirled around and brought up his spear. He, too, shouted the war cry. With violent thrusts he held his attacker off.

Aton circled him and, swinging his club, missed his mark.

The man screamed.

Aton clenched his teeth and continued to move around the man, looking for a place to land a telling blow. He came too close and the stranger's spear raked his chest, drawing a thin line of blood. Aton leapt backward and lost his footing.

The stranger screamed again and hurled his spear.

Aton rolled to one side and grabbed hold of his club.

The man's spear whirred through the air and thundered into the soft earth.

Vaulting to his feet, Aton expected the man to turn and flee. But the man faced him and, with a shout of defiance, charged. With a single blow to the side of his head, Aton dropped the stranger at his feet. . . .

He opened his eyes. The skull was still in his hand, and he might have spoken to it if for no other reason than to praise the man, whose head it had been, for not running away, but the warmth of the sun suddenly left him.

Looking up, he saw a huge cloud in front of the sun. The darkness of the cloud spread a grayness over the land. A wind came up, blowing, it seemed, from everywhere at once. The trees swayed, first one way and then another.

"Is this your doing?" Aton asked, holding the skull at arm's length. "Is this your work?"

The skull remained silent.

"You spoke to Nempie," Aton charged. "Why not speak to me?"

No voice came from the skull but in the sound of the wind was the mournful wail of the man's spirit.

"You fought well," Aton shouted.

The wail became a shriek.

Aton, afraid he would never escape from the stranger's spirit, threw the skull into the pit, turned, and began to run.

He ran as far as the edge of the glen when he suddenly stopped. To leave the pit open and the man's bones uncovered would make it easier for him to roam the forest and do harm to the people who devoured him. The stranger's spirit would know each of them because part of his body was now also part of their bodies. Even he himself might be taken by the stranger's spirit.

To protect the people of Nempie's camp Aton rushed back to the pit and hastily pushed dirt over the bones. He could not cover the man's skull and, reaching into the pit, snatched it up. When the grave was mounded over and covered with slabs of rock to prevent the wild dogs from scratching their way to the bones, Aton broke the bough of a nearby sapling and, thrusting it into the earth, shaped the end of it to a point and mounted the skull on top of it.

His work done, Aton realized the wind had diminished and he was again bathed in the light of the sun.

He stepped away from the grave and, with a nod at the grinning skull, turned and walked slowly back to camp. He knew something strange had happened to him but was unable to understand it.

Just as he was about to enter the forest, he glanced back at the skull. A breeze passed over him, carrying with it his name, "Aton . . . Aton . . . Aton. . . ."

Tesu was a tall thin man. Tufts of white hair were scattered throughout his scraggy beard. His eyes were deep set and, though he was not a hunter, his stride equaled Nempie's. He said nothing until they came within sight of the herd, which grazed on a large grassy knoll. Then he whispered, "They know we have come for one of them."

Nempie glanced at him.

"It is why they are here," Tesu said. "There is a purpose for everything. They give us the light to see into the past, a path for the future, and meat for our stomachs, not blood to slake the thirst of the spirits. I even wear their skins on my body. They are special animals, Nempie. They are always here waiting for us."

"Yes, they are always here," Nempie agreed.

Whenever they came to take one of the herd, whether it was a bull, from whose liver the future could be foretold, or a cow, in whose entrails Tesu's eyes could see deeply into the past, he always said the same thing.

For Nempie, the killing of a cow or bull lacked the excitement of hunting other game; there was hardly ever a chase. The cows died easily, making gasping sounds as their spirits separated from their bodies. The most the bulls ever did was charge. Any good hunter could avoid the thrust of their horns. The cows and bulls alike stank and seemed to do nothing more than stand and switch their tails to keep the flies away from them.

"We must go for the white bull," Tesu said, pointing to the animal on the far side of the herd near the top of the knoll. "He stands away from the rest."

Nempie preferred a closer bull, but the seer always chose the animal he would use.

"It would be best to get him," Tesu said, "before the sun makes his shadow too small."

"I will have to go around the herd," Nempie explained, moving his hand in the direction he would go.

Tesu shrugged, for now his work was done. Later, when the bull was brought back to camp he would have much work to do. "I will wait there," he said, gesturing to where the trees of the forest began. Turning his back on the herd he walked slowly away.

Nempie made a wide circle of the knoll where the cows and bulls were grazing. He eased his way toward the white bull.

The animal caught his scent and threw up his head, shook it, and began to snort. The herd milled.

Nempie hefted his spear.

The bull's snorting became louder as he pawed the ground in front of him.

Nempie shouted a blood cry and, rushing forward, heaved his spear at the animal's chest.

As the spearhead entered the bull's body the sun vanished behind a dark cloud.

Nempie ran forward and pulled the spear from the bull's chest, only to drive it into his neck. Torrents of blood gushed from the two wounds, staining the white chest red.

The bull died with its angry eyes looking at Nempie and its tongue hanging out of his gaping mouth.

The sun was high in the sky when many men dragged the carcass of the bull into Nempie's camp.

Tesu, wearing a bull-horned headpiece, stood ready at the fire pit with his cutting knife. As soon as the men placed the body of the bull where he wanted it, he began to chant.

"Bull, bull, tell us what you will . . . Bull, bull,
whisper your secrets . . .
Bull, bull, do not hide anything from us . . . Bull,
bull, there is none better than you. . . ."

The people joined their voices to that of Tesu's.

As they sang, Tesu's knife sank into the animal's chest. He worked swiftly, cutting away the forelegs and ribs, making bowls of the chest and stomach into which poured the beast's warm blood.

Tesu paused. It was hot work, and already green flies swarmed over him and the dead bull.

One by one the people came and dipped their gourds into the bloody well of the bull's chest and drank their fill while Aton drenched the earth around the stake with the hot blood to satisfy the thirst of the dead man.

Tesu cut away the back legs, pushing each in turn

down to the ground. Then he severed the bull's genitals from the rest of the carcass.

He tossed the bloody remnant to the young men, who immediately cut it into pieces, eating it raw to gain the strength to mount many women, in the manner of bulls mounting other cows.

And then Tesu let go of his knife and, thrusting his hand into the bloody stomach cavity, pulled the dark liver from the animal. He carried the liver a short distance from the carcass. Setting it down on a flat stone, he poured water over it.

When the excess blood was washed free he bent over the liver and, with a frown on his brow, looked hard at it.

"Tell us what you see," Nempie called. "Tell us, Tesu, what the future holds."

The seer began to rock back and forth. Several times his right hand passed over the red flesh, as though he were removing something from the top of it. But the people could see no more than the flies that hurriedly took wing with each of Tesu's movements, only to settle down again when his hand became still.

Again Nempie called out, "What are the signs, Tesu? Tell us what are the signs?"

Tesu's right hand moved over the bloody meat, sending a cloud of flies above the heads of the people gathered around him. With his finger he followed a line on the liver. "There will be a temptation," Tesu said. "We will move against another people and be victorious, but we will lose some of our young men in the fight."

"And what of the skull that spoke?" Nempie questioned.

With a shake of his head Tesu answered, "Nempie will be the leader of the people."

"And what of my sons?" Nempie asked, already satisfied with Tesu's words.

"Their future is not here."

"Nothing?" Nempie questioned.

"Nothing," Tesu replied with a shake of his head. "Their future does not show here."

Nempie nodded and though his lips did not spread in a smile there was laughter in his glittering black eyes when he looked at Aton and then at Gens.

Suddenly Tesu began to rock back and forth. His eyes rolled up until they were white. Spittle leaked from his trembling lips.

The people drew back.

Tesu leaned over the liver and laid his trembling hands on the bloody flesh. With a bull-like snort he shook his head. And in a voice louder than his own he shouted, "Aton!" Then he pitched forward, bruising his head against the rock that held the liver.

The laughter left Nempie's eyes. The heat of anger and the dark shadow of fear spread over his face.

3

Tesu's prophecy mystified the people and strengthened Nempie's determination to provoke Aton's challenge. Aton would not be moved, though at the end of each day his kill would equal or exceed Nempie's. At night, after he and Rika left the great fire and went to their shelter, he seldom had the appetite for her that men have for women.

Often Aton would stare up at the small smoke hole in the overlay of the woven matting of rushes and look at the small circle of the dark sky. Once he had said to Rika, "I would challenge Nempie, but that would give him what he wants." With a chuckle he added, "I could not do that."

"If he could challenge you," she answered, pressing close to him, "he would."

"That is because he fears and hates me," Aton whispered, touching her breasts.

"And do you not——"

"No. I do not hate or fear him."

"But you are afraid of losing if you fight him?"

"I would lose," he told her again.

"But how could you be so sure?"

"Because," he said, removing his hand from her breast, "it is something I know. It is something I feel deep inside me, even as I feel that the fight between us will come."

"And you will lose?" she cried questioningly.

"Yes, Rika, I will lose."

She began to sob. "And Nempie will separate your spirit from your body?"

Aton shrugged and, stroking the back of her head, replied, "That is what I do not know. That is really what I do not know."

When the morning light came into the sky it was neither the pale pink of dawn nor the familiar yellow of the sun as it rose out of the insides of the mountains in the east. The gray light lay over the land as far as anyone in Nempie's camp could see.

The air was so still and heavy that none of the leaves on the trees or bushes moved. Dogs in the camp bared their teeth and growled low in their throats. Birds flew in strange patterns over the river and the forest, and the high shrill chatters of the crows made every mother clutch her child to her breast.

As one sign after another was noted, the people became more and more frightened. Some of them, especially the women who would have taken the stranger's fluid if Aton had not killed him first, complained that the spirit of the man was against them and that the blood Aton had poured on the ground around the stake had not satisfied it.

Nempie listened to the accusations and called Aton to answer them.

"And how can I do that?" Aton responded. "How can any man speak for the spirit of another?"

"But it was you," one of the women charged, "who

killed him before he knew the pleasure of our touch, before we took from him what was ours to take."

Aton shrugged.

"To do what you did," a second woman shouted, "was against the way of our people. Now the spirit will stalk the women of our camp and rape those who are not fast enough to run from him or strong enough to fight him off. And even the men from his people will be able to rape us because of what you did."

"He fought well," Aton said. "And when I brought him here it was not to be made the plaything of women. If his spirit is angry, it will seek me out. I alone will answer for my actions to it."

Aton's voice in the still heavy air was more like the low roll of distant thunder than a sound familiar to the people. Even Rika did not recognize it. Gens was puzzled by it.

Nempie, scowling with anger, realized that his son was far craftier than he had thought him to be. Gens was openly cunning and everyone knew it, but Aton was more wily, even to the changing of his voice to make more of his words than they deserved. Nempie waved his hand and said, "Aton has taken the spirit's anger to himself. You have heard him say so and the spirit has also heard him."

The women who spoke out against Aton murmured amongst themselves but did not dare dispute Nempie.

As the harangue between Aton and the women took place, the sky in the west, where the great desert lay, began to change from gray to brownish-yellow. They then knew that the hot wind of death would soon blow on them.

The women began to wail and the children, hearing the cries of their mothers, cried, too. Old men wept. Nempie ordered the warning drum at the edge of the camp, near the river, to be sounded with the hope that the noise would drive off the wind.

Aton and the other hunters formed a line facing the

direction from where the wind would come. Each of them was armed with a spear and a bow and a case full of arrows with which they hoped to wound the wind, if not to kill it. Even the boys, who were not yet old enough to be hunters, and the girls, whose blood would soon begin to flow, gathered rocks to stone the oncoming wind.

The brownish-yellow of the sky came toward them. To breathe became an effort. Lips became dry, split, and finally bled. Everyone's throats were parched, but no amount of water would bring an end to the thirst.

Nempie's people waited. The women ceased their wailing and the children stopped crying. The old men no longer wept and gathered behind the young boys who were not yet old enough to become hunters and threw rocks at the wind.

Aton looked toward Tesu, who stood with Nempie near the stake, and called out, "Where was the foretelling of this in the liver of the bull?"

"All I saw," Tesu answered, "I told."

"Perhaps you should have looked harder," Aton commented. "Perhaps you did not see this because you were too busy looking for other things."

"I was the one who asked the questions," Nempie shouted.

"As is your right but——"

A hot gust of wind suddenly blew against Aton. And he called out, "It comes. It comes. It comes. . . ."

His cry was taken up by everyone in the camp.

The hot wind rushed down on them, and the hunters loosed their spears at it. The wind shrieked in agony but still it blew, bringing with it the sting of sand and dust.

Arrows shot into the wind were hurled to the ground. Thrown rocks were brushed aside and the booming of the warning drum did not frighten it.

Without spears, arrows, or rocks, the people stood helplessly in the path of the hot wind. They watched the green leaves wither to brown and saw the water of the river vanish before their eyes until it was no more than a trickle. Birds fell from the air. All around the camp, animals cried in agony.

The wind blew through many days and many nights, and night or day it was hot. Some of the old men gave up their spirits before the end of the first day, while others were able to cling to life a few days longer.

Many children, too, gave up their spirits, even while still suckling at their mother's teat.

The wind passed over the camp and the land, leaving in its wake the fearful prospect of starvation for those who survived its withering blast. With the wind and sand gone, the sun shone in a blue sky; the land beneath it was all but dead.

Aton and other hunters sought game but there was none. Those animals that could not flee from the hot wind had died and already their bodies were swollen with rot. But even these were dragged into the camp to feed the people.

Day after day the hunters searched for game, but none was found.

More people died; their stomachs swelled from hunger, and then their spirits separated from their bodies. Many holes were dug for the bodies, lest their spirits do spite to the living.

Nempie waited for a sign, something that would show that the game would come back, that the leaves would once more grow on the trees and bushes and that the river would flow as it had in the past, but he saw nothing. The land and all that was on it was like a woman in whose body the fluid of one man or many became nothing.

Tesu scolded, exhorted, and wept to coax the game back, but the animals remained deaf to his pleas.

Aton, too, looked at the land and the trees on it and knew that many more of Nempie's people would die before there would be meat again, before the leaves came back to the trees and bushes and before the river flowed.

The people pulled the lizards from the mud of the river and ate them. They caught and ate snakes, rats, and grubs whenever they could find them.

On the day that dark clouds filled the sky up over the mountains, the people gathered at the great fire pit in the center of the camp. Tesu's shrill voice rose above the others and they beckoned the clouds to come and pour their water over the land. The clouds did not come, not even when the great drum was sounded to answer their thunder with a booming plea for water.

Late one afternoon the people demanded that Nempie end their misery.

Tesu told him, "Something is against us, some spirit holds the water back, frightens the game from our land, and keeps the leaves from the trees. Such a spirit will do us harm until there is not one of us left. All that will remain of Nempie's people will be the bleached bones of the last to die."

"It is the spirit of the man Aton killed," shrieked one of the women. "His spirit has brought hunger and death to us."

Nempie looked at Tesu.

"Aton did not let the women use him according to our way," the seer answered.

Ready to defend his life, Aton drew his knife.

"Give the spirit a woman," Tesu said.

"Aton's woman," the other women cried. "Give him Aton's woman. She is wise in the ways of pleasing men."

Aton started toward Rika but several of the men grabbed hold of him and though he fought with them, he was no match for their combined strength.

The women seized Rika and dragged her to the stake, where she was bound and then stripped of her covering.

Aton struggled to free himself but was held fast.

Tesu began to chant, and many of the men threw faggots on the previous night's smoldering fire.

"Do not let them do it, Nempie," Aton shouted. "She——"

"The spirit must be satisfied," Nempie answered. "If you were any other man but my son you would be in her place, but such is the way of our people that you must live until one of us kills or subdues the other. Challenge me here, Aton, and should you be the victor, Rika and any other woman in the camp would be yours."

"No," Rika screamed. "No, Aton, do not——"

But her scream was but a whisper against the sudden war cry that broke over the camp.

Aton and the other men scrambled for their weapons.

Already the arrows of the attackers had found marks. Several men dropped as soon as they had started to run.

Aton and Nempie led the other hunters, who ran toward the attackers and hurled themselves on them. Many of Nempie's men died impaled on spears, but those who were left continued to fight.

Aton's spear was stained with blood. Blood smeared his hands and chest, too.

Nempie's men fought and killed many of those who came running out of the forest.

Aton's spear was shattered and he was forced to grapple with a man who tried to plunge his knife into him, but Aton gouged out the man's eye. He dropped his knife while Aton strangled him, breaking the man's windpipe with his hands.

The attackers were driven back toward the forest, leaving many wounded behind.

Aton and some of the other hunters followed them into the forest, killing as many as they could before they gave up the chase and returned to the camp.

Wet with sweat and streaked with blood, Aton went

to Rika and wordlessly cut her down. Pointing to the captives, he said, "Use them as you will but you will not have her." Gathering Rika's naked body in his arms, he carried her to their shelter. No one stopped him; even Nempie was afraid to try.

4

TESU CLAIMED it was the blood of the captives that finally satisfied the spirit that had brought so much misfortune to the people.

Each night for the space of seven nights a man was tied naked to the stake and the women coaxed his member to give forth its fluid. Aton did not interfere, though he did eat his share of the meat taken from each of the men. Those who ate of the brave men added to their own courage.

After the last of them was sacrificed, the dark clouds rolled down from the top of the mountain and brought with them the rain.

The dry earth sucked up the water more greedily than a child sucks milk from its mother's teats.

The people, filled with joy, let the rain fall upon them and opened their mouths to take the drops into their bodies.

The trickle of water in the bed of the river soon became a stream, and the stream became a rushing torrent. Everyone knew it would soon become a river again.

Nempie called his people together at the great fire, which could not be kept burning because of the rain, and said to them, his voice louder than the drumming of the rain, "We will be as before the hot wind came. The game will come back. The river even now begins to flow and the leaves once again will come on the trees and bushes."

His words became those of the people and they repeated them to each other over and over again.

Then Nempie said, "And our hunters will once again stalk Pula, the black boar."

And all of those who brought meat to the camp shouted Pula's name and stamped their feet.

"The hunter who kills him," Nempie told his people, "will be the mightiest hunter of all camps. Of the beasts in the forest he is the only one who is named, even as each of us are."

Nempie waved his hand toward the forest and said, "He will soon be back, for this is his place. All of us have seen him. He is bigger than a bull, blacker than a stormy night, and moves like a shadow."

The hunters agreed, and each one spoke of where he had seen Pula and how he had hurled his spear or shot his arrow at the beast only to discover that his spear or arrow had dropped harmlessly to the ground.

Nempie once told the other hunters of the camp that he was the only one whose arrow had ever wounded Pula. But that had happened many, many seasons ago as Aton and Gens had become old enough to hunt on their own. The people now remembered it and believed that some day Nempie would kill the black boar and wear his thrice-circled, spear-pointed, tusks on his arms, so that none would ever dispute his hunting skill.

Many of the hunters called out, "Your arrow will find him again, Nempie, and you will bring his carcass back to camp."

"I will do that," Nempie answered, "and we will put his skull on a stake so that all will know that it was Nempie who killed him, who separated his spirit from his body."

"And with Pula's skull there," Tesu said, "our strength will be as his was."

The people shouted for the skull of Pula, the black boar.

"I will bring it to you," Nempie told them. "I will bring it to you."

The rain continued for many days and nights. The river's water, dark with the death that had been on the land for so long, began wildly churning, taking with it part of the banks and the trees that lived on them.

But then the sun rose out of the insides of the mountains, and Nempie's words came to be: the game returned, the leaves clothed the trees and bushes again, and the river's rage subsided until it flowed as it had before.

Everything was as it had been, and Nempie's feelings toward Aton were, if not the same, stronger than before death's hot wind came.

Nempie knew that Aton had killed even more of those who had attacked the camp than he. And Nempie also knew that when Aton cut Rika down from the stake he did it to challenge him—perhaps even to challenge Tesu, whom he had taken to task for not having foreseen the coming of the hot wind of death in the liver of the bull.

All these things Nempie knew; they filled his head with the smoke of his anger whenever he saw his son.

But Aton seemed less affected by Nempie's wrath. At night, when all the hunters sat around the great fire, Aton spoke to his father only if Nempie spoke first.

There was a change in Aton that Nempie could not fail to notice. Aton no longer kept his eyes averted

33

from his father. Each night he gazed at him through the wavering light of the fire. He looked for something, though he himself did not know what it was.

On the days Aton did not hunt, he sought out Tesu, offering him a choice cut of meat from the previous day's kill. He said, "It was wrong of me to blame you for not seeing the hot wind of death in the liver of the bull; with this meat I hope to restore the good feelings that we once had."

Flattered by Aton's words and placated by his gift, Tesu was eager to be on friendly terms with Nempie's son, who could become the leader of the people.

"Let us walk," Aton suggested the first day.

"To the river?" Tesu asked.

"If it would please you."

Tesu realized that though Aton was a skilled hunter he was also a skillful speaker.

When they stood on the riverbank, Aton lifted a stone and, hurling it toward the opposite bank, made it leap three times before it finally sank beneath the water. "Last night," Aton said, looking from the river to Tesu, "my mother's spirit came to me."

"It is the way with a mother's spirit to do that," the seer said. "I am sure she meant you no harm."

Aton picked up another rock and made it leap four times before it sank into the river. With a shrug of his shoulders he said, "I do not know. Her spirit separated from her body soon after she dropped me."

Tesu nodded.

"Tell me about her." Aton looked at the seer again.

"She was pleasing to look at," Tesu responded.

"Where did she come from?"

"Nempie took her in a raid."

Aton faced the river again and asked, "Why would she come to me now?"

"Are you sure it was your mother's spirit?" Tesu questioned.

"She said she was," Aton answered, knowing how much he was baiting the seer with his words.

"Did she say anything else?" Tesu asked.

Aton hesitated.

"She was the daughter of the leader of the camp that Nempie raided. She fought beside her father."

"Yes," Aton responded, "she told me that and. . . ."

"And what?"

Aton shrugged and said, "Her voice began to fade. . . . She came to me too close to the coming of the first light."

Tesu pursed his lips and, leaning close to Aton, said, "She might have tried to tell you what she told Nempie before her spirit left her body."

"Do you know what she told my father?"

Tesu nodded and said, "I was there when she said, 'I have brought forth a man amongst men, Nempie, a man better than all others.' Those were her words."

"That was what I thought I heard," Aton said. "But who could be sure of what a spirit says?"

"If it is the spirit of a mother or father," Tesu answered, "a child can always be sure."

In the days following Aton's first walk with Tesu to the river, he went other places with the seer, even to the grassy knoll where the bulls and the cows grazed.

There Aton asked, "Tell me, friend, how is it you are able to see the future in the liver of a bull or the past in the entrails of a cow? Yet when I look at them I see nothing of the future or past. I see only what they are."

Tesu smiled and, clapping his hand on Aton's shoulder, said, "As you were taught to know the signs of animals from their tracks, the way they ate of the leaves on the trail, or even by the spoor they left, I too was taught to know the signs in the liver of a bull and the entrails of a cow. Though there is no need for it, since Nempie has no trust in it, I can also tell the future from other signs, though I will not tell you which ones."

"You are a wise man, Tesu," Aton told him.

But he too, like Nempie, found the stink of the bulls and cows offensive.

The seer smiled and, nodding his head, he pointed to a brownish-red bull and said, "He will be the one whose liver will next reveal the future."

"Why him?" Aton asked.

"Because I saw him in the liver of the white bull," Tesu explained. "One always reveals another."

"The way men do?"

"Yes," Tesu said and added, "If you have learned that, Aton, you have learned more than most men."

Aton smiled and said, "I am sure I have always known it."

That Aton was spending whole days with Tesu gave Nempie a reason to jibe at his son more than he usually did. To him it was a possible sign that Aton was weakening and that the battle to the death between them might yet be avoided. Each night when the people gathered around the great fire Nempie attempted to prove he was better.

"Is Aton trying to become a seer?" Nempie questioned with a laugh.

"No, Father," Aton answered, looking straight at him through the flickering light of the fire.

Nempie pulled on his beard. His son's answers shut off other questions.

"Have you lost your taste for the chase?" Nempie asked.

"No, Father," Aton replied.

Angered by Aton's simple replies, Nempie stood, questioning, "Or is it that you think a seer is better than a hunter?"

"Neither better nor worse," Aton told him.

Nempie paced before the fire and, suddenly whirling

around, said to Aton, "You are a hunter. Though a seer is needed, a hunter is needed more. A hunter is a man."

"Even as I am *a man amongst men*, Father," Aton responded.

The breath caught in Nempie's throat, and he began to cough. "I tell you this, Aton," he said, forcing out the words between fits of coughing. "You will hunt tomorrow and you will hunt the next day and the day after that. You will hunt because it is not enough that you bring meat for yourself and Rika. There are others in the camp who also must be fed."

"I will hunt, Father," Aton answered. "I will hunt; none, not even you, will ever again question my skill."

Nempie said nothing. He alone understood Aton's challenge and could not answer it, for as always it was never with words he wanted to hear but with others that he could not call him to account for.

Gens leaned close to Aton and whispered in his brother's ear, "He would kill you now if he could."

Aton shrugged and answered, "He will not. Our fight is yet to come, Gens. He knows that and so do I."

5

EACH DAY ATON HUNTED, killing only enough to feed him and Rika and bring a gift of meat to Tesu every third day. Though he did not spend whole days with the seer, he often walked with him in the evening when the light was still in the sky over the great desert.

On one such evening, before the great fire was set ablaze in the center of the camp, Tesu said, "The people whisper about you, Aton."

"And what they say," Aton answered, "is as meaningless as the breeze when it whispers through the leaves of the trees."

"They say you have lost your hunting skill."

Aton shrugged.

"And they say that you are afraid of your father."

Aton smiled and said, "I told you that their whisperings were meaningless. Come, Tesu, the people are already moving toward the fire to share the meat from the day's kill."

Several days passed before Aton mentioned anything

about his talks with Tesu to Rika. They lay side by side, breathing heavily after exchanging pleasure. When Aton could speak he said, "Do not be afraid, Rika, that I have lost my hunting skill."

"I do not fear that," she responded.

"What is it that you do fear?"

"I do not know, but it is strange for a hunter and a seer to go as you go with Tesu."

Aton rolled away from Rika's naked body and, staring up at the small circle of the sky that showed through the smoke hole he said, "Tesu has told me many things, things about my mother held from me by Nempie, things about what he sees in the liver of a bull or the entrails of a cow."

"And," she whispered, "you are not now as you were. There is a distance between you and all that is around you."

Aton nodded but did not speak. How could he possibly tell her of the things in his head? Between himself and his own understanding there was a mist far thicker than that which often hung over the river, obscuring the other bank from view. Like the river mist, it often moved just enough to let him see what lay behind it. He turned his head toward Rika and said, *I am a man amongst men.*

"I knew that, Aton, when you cut me down from the stake; no other man would have done that."

He uttered a deep sigh. She did not understand what he had told her. He did not blame her. He himself was not sure what it meant to be *a man amongst men.*

"Aton," she questioned, "will you be taking another woman soon?"

"No, Rika," he replied, stroking her bare arm, "I do not think so."

Nempie's camp was on the bank of a river, and Pula, the black boar, lived nearby, preferring, it seemed, to be close to the company of men over his own kind.

Many of the hunters saw Pula, and a few even shot arrows or hurled their spears at him. As before the hot wind of the desert came, none of their weapons ever found their mark. When a hunter went to retrieve them, he always found his arrows or spear on the ground or lodged in the trunk of a tree.

One afternoon when the sun was already well past its highest place in the sky Aton caught a glimpse of Pula and, laying aside the deer he had already killed, immediately began to track the beast.

Pula went into heavy underbrush and Aton, dropping on his hands and knees, followed. The wind favored Aton and he was able to crawl very close to Pula.

With his heart pounding, Aton crawled even closer.

Pula was very big and black.

From where Aton lay, Pula's back blotted out a portion of the sky. His tusks had three curls and were tapered to a sharp point.

Pula moved slightly, bringing his huge head to one side, and fixed his beady eyes on his pursuer.

Aton stopped. His heart thumped louder than the warning drum. He smelled the stink of the animal. His stink was more like the stench of death than anything else Aton could recall. In the close confines of the thick underbrush it made him feel as if he was falling into a huge pit filled with rotting flesh. In the beast's eyes he saw the look of recognition.

Pula suddenly snorted and pawed the ground. Spittle poured from the edges of his mouth.

Aton sucked in his breath, expecting Pula to charge and knowing that he would not be able to escape the beast's spear-pointed tusks.

Suddenly Pula snorted again, turned, and crashed through the heavy underbrush.

Aton scrambled after him.

Despite his size, Pula moved quickly.

Aton could not lessen the distance between the two, but still he ran. He ran until he was choked for breath, until his chest ached, until it seemed he could run no more.

Filled with the strange feeling that he was bounding over hills and leaping wide rivers, Aton continued the chase without knowing whether it was day or night.

When Aton faltered, Pula looked back. With a snort he called to him. Aton ran faster.

The chase took him farther and farther from camp, farther than he ordinarily would have traveled for game. The more he ran after Pula the more he realized that Pula was not just another animal to hunt down. In the running he felt something between them that he had never before felt between himself and his quarry.

It almost seemed that Pula forced him to run.

They reached a clump of willows and Pula rushed into it. Wet with sweat and with his chest heaving, Aton stopped. He would not repeat the mistake he had made earlier and go into the willows for Pula as he had gone into the thick undergrowth.

"I will let you come to me, Pula," Aton called out and, circling around the trees, he went down to the river, where a forest of rushes grew in brackish water. He found a place and knelt to wait until Pula came to the river to drink.

For awhile Aton looked intently at the willow, expecting the beast to amble forth and make his way down to the river. Then he wondered if he had made a mistake by calling out to Pula, especially since he had already felt there was a bond between them?

Though his gaze remained fixed on the trees, Aton began to think about the conversation he had had with Gens about Nempie. There was much to be said for what his brother offered. Though he had reached this conclusion several days ago, he had not ventured to speak to his brother about it.

The hum of insect wings attracted Aton's attention and he saw that the creatures of the night were already beginning to weave the cloak of darkness behind the willows, making their light green leaves deeper-hued as they wove more and more of it.

He glanced over his right shoulder. The sun was far down in the sky. It would soon drop into the pit at the end of the great desert. Already the clouds were on fire there.

He looked back at the willows. Nothing moved, though the leaves were several shades darker.

A frog croaked and another answered. A crow called out to argue noisily with another crow. Aton saw neither of them. A water snake slithered by, its body moving sinuously through the still water.

Aton became frightened. No man moved about without the light from a torch to keep away the spirits of the dead who always prowled around at night looking for a living person. The spirit of a woman would entice a man to lay with her, and then she would enter his body and rob him of his manhood. The spirit of a man sought to rape a woman, but a woman could stop herself from being raped if she wanted to by clamping her thighs together. There was nothing a man could do to protect himself against the wiles of a female spirit.

Perhaps Pula had lured him to that place to make it easier for a spirit to get at him?

A breeze rose and riffled the flowers topping the rushes. Then Pula snorted and walked out of the willows.

In the fading light the beast was blacker than the oncoming darkness that surrounded it, and its tusks were very white.

Aton strung his bow, drew an arrow, mocking it, and waited. Again his heart raced and the blood sounded in his ears.

Pula moved, stopped, snorted, and moved again.

Aton sucked in his breath. As Pula stopped to snort

he loosed an arrow. The bow twanged and the arrow hissed before it slipped into the neck of the beast.

Pula grunted with rage.

Aton sent another arrow hissing toward his quarry.

Pula reared up on his hind legs. With two front paws he tore the first arrow from its bloody wound.

Aton shot again and missed his mark.

Pula snorted and pawed the ground. His neck was red with blood.

Aton grasped his spear. With a wild shout he ran at the beast.

Pula grunted, lowered his head and charged.

Pula was no more than a huge dark mass coming straight at Aton. He hurled his spear and almost instantly knew he had missed. Aton drew his knife and breathlessly waited for Pula to come close enough for him to leap aside and slash at the animal.

Suddenly, when Pula was nearly upon him, the beast dropped to the earth.

Aton leaped up and, running, fell upon the hard-breathing animal. He slashed its throat. Hot blood gushed from the cut, bathing Aton's arm in its sudden steaming flow.

Aton stood up and, looking at Pula, said aloud, "The wind favored me, Pula, and kept my scent from you."

The beast snorted several times; his spirit separated from his body.

Quickly Aton took Pula's tusks and slipped them on his arms, so that all who saw them would know that it was he who had slain Pula the black boar.

When Aton returned to the camp in the morning, the people saw the thrice-circled tusks on his forearms and knew he had slain Pula, the black boar.

Now they did not doubt that Aton's hunting skill was equal to Nempie's, perhaps even greater.

Nempie said, looking at his son in the full brilliance of the morning sun, "I do not see Pula, the black boar.

I only see thrice-circled tusks. Have you brought his carcass back?"

"No, Nempie," Aton answered, looking straight at his father.

"Then surely you brought his head?"

"No," Aton said.

Nempie roared with laughter and, pointing to his son, he questioned, "No carcass and no head, yet you expect me to believe that you slew Pula, the black boar?"

Aton nodded.

Still pointing to his son, Nempie shouted for all to hear, "He would make fools of us by gaining our praise for something he has not done, for something no man could do. Those tusks on his arms, he tells us, came from Pula the black boar. That is what he tells us. But has he brought Pula's head to show us?"

Suddenly Aton shouted, "I slew him, Nempie, I, Aton, *a man amongst men* slew Pula, the black boar."

In a fury, Nempie lifted his hand to strike Aton.

But Gens called out, "Nempie, let Aton take us to where the carcass is." And he pushed his way to where his father and brother confronted each other.

Nempie's anger was so great that he could not speak, but he did not strike Aton. Slowly he lowered his hand.

Aton said nothing and immediately he started off.

Gens fell in beside him and said, "I did not expect you to come back."

Aton looked at him questioningly.

"Nempie said that you had probably joined some other people or——"

"But why should he have said that?" Aton asked. "I was only gone part of yesterday and last night."

"Aton," Gens told him, "you were gone for many days and many nights."

Aton almost lost his footing but Gens grabbed his arm and held him steady. He did not understand how part of a day and a night could have been many days and many nights to Gens? But even as he pondered this puzzle, Nempie called out from behind him, demanding to know how much farther they would have to go before they came to the place where they would see Pula's carcass?

Aton could not answer.

And Nempie jibed, "Is your hunting skill so great, Aton, that it has made you forget where you separated Pula's spirit from his body?"

The sun moved higher into the sky and the ground shimmered in front of them.

Aton and those who followed were wet with sweat and covered with dust.

Suddenly Nempie shouted, "I have had enough, Aton. Enough! Rushing at his son, he struck him to the ground. "If you were any man but my son," he said, holding his spear to Aton's chest, "I would kill you here and now. Say that you did not kill——"

Aton's eyes went to slits.

"I will drive this spear into you," Nempie threatened, his voice filled with grinding anger.

"These tusks are Pula's," Aton said. "To get them I slew him."

With a howl of rage, Nempie lifted his spear high over his head and thrust it down toward his son's chest. But Aton rolled to one side and the head of the spear sank deep into the earth.

Aton sprang to his feet.

Nempie, seeing his son's face was set for killing, swallowed his own anger and, with a forced laugh, said, "Lead us to where you slew Pula."

But Aton did not move.

"It was a test," Nempie told him.

"None was needed," Aton answered flatly.

"Then lead us——"

"No," Aton said.

The false smile left Nempie's face. His brow furrowed and rage once again showed itself.

Aton crossed his arms and, touching each of the tusks with his forefinger, said in his strange thunderlike voice, "These are enough. There is no need for you, Nempie, or any of the others, to see more than these. All of you know from where they came. Most of you have tried to slay Pula, the black boar, so you know of his kind. He was the only one whose tusks were thrice circled."

"His carcass," Nempie shouted. "Show us his carcass!"

Aton answered, his voice sounding even more like thunder than before, "It lies beyond the reach of men's eyes. It lies in a willow grove, where it was meant to lie."

"His head," Nempie screamed. "Bring his head!"

"It was not mine to take," Aton said and, walking slowly past his father, returned to the encampment.

That he had been gone from the encampment for three days and three nights astounded Aton, and he sought out Tesu to speak to him about it. They walked by the river, as they had when Aton told him about his mother.

Aton told Tesu all that had happened between him and Pula, the black boar, even how he thought the beast had summoned him to follow.

The seer listened without interrupting.

Finally Aton said, "As soon as I separated his spirit from his body, Tesu, I took these tusks I wear on my forearms."

"What is it that you want from me?" the man asked.

"I was away for the space of three days and three nights but to me it was no more than one night and part of a day."

Tesu made a clicking sound with his tongue. In a low voice he said, "There are some things that no one understands, but this I know: Pula, the black boar, was not like the rest of his kind. He was different, Aton, even as you yourself are different from the rest of Nempie's sons, even from the rest of the men in the camp. If you were not different, you would not have slain Pula. Perhaps, Aton, he was placed here in this forest for you to kill him."

"But why?"

Tesu pointed toward the mountain over which the dark storm clouds gathered and he asked, "Whose voice is it in the thunder and who knows what it says?"

Aton looked toward the mountains and with a nod he said, "I have often wondered about that myself."

"Perhaps some day you will know," Tesu suggested.

Aton shrugged. He was not interested in whose voice was in the thunder or what it said when its roll shook the earth. He was having enough trouble understanding what had happened to him when he had chased Pula, the black boar, and no one could tell him.

Now when Aton walked through the camp he realized the people looked at him and then quickly turned away.

When he asked Rika about it she said, "They are afraid of you, Aton. They say you are not like other men. Some say it is because of me——"

"What?"

"They say that any other young man would want a younger woman," she told him as they sat in their shelter.

"They are fools," Aton grumbled.

"Do you want a younger woman?" Rika asked.

Aton shook his head.

"Another man would——"

"I am not any other man," he told her. "I am *a man amongst men*. I will do what I must do."

"And what is it that you must do?"

He touched the thrice-curved tusks of Pula and

whispered, "When it must be done, Rika, I will know it."

In the nights following Aton's return to the camp the spirit of Pula, the black boar, came to Nempie and mocked him until sleeping or waking he could not forget that his son wore the thrice-curved tusks of the beast he had told his people he would kill. And he knew he would not be able to draw Aton into a fight; even his plan with Gens had gotten nowhere.

Nempie stared into the fire and through its wavering curtain of flames he saw Aton. More and more it seemed to him that Pula's tusks glowed with a fire of their own, and he wondered if his people saw it, too.

The days passed and each evening Aton's kill was as great as Nempie's. Often it was greater and then Nempie would be angry at everyone, including Bisha, whom he no longer gave to Gens to lay with.

Nempie was on the verge of challenging Aton before everyone, but that was against the way of the people and even as the words were on his tongue he stopped himself.

Then one night as Nempie stared into the fire and looked at Aton different words came to him. With a smile he said, "Aton, the thrice-curved tusks you wear prove that you are a great hunter, for though all of us tried, only you succeeded in slaying Pula, the black boar."

Aton nodded and said nothing.

And Gens poked his brother in the ribs, whispering, "He is set upon something."

"Some of our young men," Nempie said, stirring the fire with a long stick, "are in sore need of women and you yourself Aton have one that will soon cease to give you any pleasure." With a laugh he continued, "Oh how well I know the difference between mounting a young one and one as old as your Rika." And reaching out, he fondled Bisha's breasts. "These are full and hard; her nipples are quick to come alive. Bisha, take off your tunic and let Aton see the difference between the body of a young woman and that of one that has been used by many."

Bisha stood up; her covering fell.

The light of the fire danced over her nakedness and Aton found himself moved by the sight of her.

"I would give her to you," Nempie said, "but for now she is my favorite. Of any of the women we capture, you will take the one you want, even before I myself choose."

"Make him give more," Gens whispered.

"There is another people in a valley three days' journey from here," Nempie said. "They too are hunters, but we are stronger than they. I have watched them hunt and found them not as skillful as ourselves. But their women are pleasing to look at, some as pleasing as Bisha." And he reached up to place his hand between her naked thighs. "I think they would squirm with delight, even as this one now squirms to my touch."

Gens gnashed his teeth and told Aton, "I swear by my manhood that I will kill him!"

"Father!" Aton called out. "Bisha's nakedness has inflamed all of us. Would that I could stroke her even as you now do."

Nempie laughed and said, "Then you see the pleasure that will be yours?"

"But I would have two for my prize," Aton told him.

Nempie's laughter stopped. He said, "But I offered one, one even before I make my choice."

"Two, Father," Aton said. "Two before you make your choice, Father."

Nempie pulled at his beard. His first feeling was to deny the request but then he nodded and told Aton, "You will have the two of your choice. And now the sight and touch of Bisha has so inflamed me that I must use her for my pleasure." Nempie lifted Bisha into his arms and carried her to his shelter.

"I will give you any one of the two I choose," Aton said to Gens.

And his brother answered, "I want Bisha."

Aton cautioned, "He would kill you rather than give her up."

"I will kill him," Gens said tightly.

Aton stood up and without saying anything more walked slowly to his shelter, where Rika awaited him.

"I did not know," she whispered when he lay down next to her, "that you wanted a younger woman."

"I am content with you, Rika," he said.

"Then why——"

"Because," Aton told her, "it must be, Rika. It must be."

"Do not be fooled by Nempie," she said.

"I am not," Aton answered.

Rika lifted the bottom of her tunic and spread her bare thighs. "Mount me, Aton," she pleaded and when she felt him in her body she pressed his head to her breasts and whispered in a cry of passion, "I fear for you Aton, I fear for you."

6

FROM HIS EARLY DAYS when coarse black hair began to sprout around his manhood and he felt the need for a woman, Aton took part in his father's raids, whether they were to chase another people from their hunting grounds so that his people would have more meat, or whether they were to capture women for the men, or just for the pleasure of killing.

And Aton had killed many men, separating their spirits from their bodies with a thrust of his spear or with a well-placed arrow. Sometimes the outcome of the contest between himself and his opponent seemed doubtful. From those hard-won victories his body bore many scars.

Perhaps it was the prospect of being so close to death, or perhaps it was the feeling of strength that comes to a man when he takes the life of another man, or perhaps it was the prospect of rape that excited the men in Nempie's camp. All of them were eager to go on the raid. Weapons were put in order, new arrows were made; spearheads were fitted to straight shafts, and the blades of swords were honed to a fine edge.

The women worked to set provisions aside. Smoked goat's meat, skins of water, and dried fruit were placed in wrappings of woven rushes.

Scouts went out to keep track of the people and when they returned Nempie listened carefully to everything they said. Often he repeated to Aton what the scouts had told him. To the many who would go on the raid it was obvious that Nempie favored Aton above all the other men. He began to boast that Aton would kill more men than anyone else.

"He will drive them before him," Nempie said while sitting at the fire one night. "The way the wind drives the leaves, the sand or the snow, the strength of Pula, the black boar, is with him. I have seen it all in my sleep. Am I not right, my son?"

"You have seen more than I have," Aton answered.

Nempie laughed and, slapping his thigh, said, "The meaning of what I saw is clear, Aton. You will drive many before you but you will fight and kill their leader. Because he fought hard against you we will celebrate your victory by eating his heart, for that is the place of a man's courage."

The men of the camp shouted approval.

"I will try to do all I did in your dream," Aton answered.

"No father," Nempie responded, "could ask more of his son than that."

Aton remained silent. He was deeply troubled by Nempie's attitude toward him. His own feelings were voiced by Gens, who asked in a whisper, "Do you trust him?"

"No," Aton answered after a considerable pause.

"And what he just said," Gens asked. "Do you believe that?"

"No."

"Then why are you letting him make a fool of you?"

Aton rubbed his hand over his short beard and said, "I can not help you, Gens."

"If you fought him——"

"I would lose," Aton said.

"But you would not lose," Gens told him, "if we fought him together."

"That is what you have already told me," Aton responded.

"And that is what I believe," Gens told him.

"But I do not," Aton replied. "Do not be deceived by Pula's tusks. Yes, I took them from him, but I did no more than he wanted me to do."

"I do not understand," Gens said.

"Nor I," Aton admitted, and he proceeded to tell his brother how he slew the black boar.

"But surely that was a sign," Gens maintained.

Aton shrugged and asked, "From whom and for what, Gens?"

Gens did not answer.

"And what of the days I was away?" Aton questioned. "How could part of an afternoon and a night to me be many days and nights to you?"

"I do not know," Gens whispered.

"And why do I feel that what Nempie is doing is something that must be?"

"Is that what you think?"

"It is what I feel," Aton answered.

And after a short silence Gens ventured to ask Aton, "Did you lay with a female spirit?"

Aton shook his head.

And Nempie, who was watching his two sons from the other side of the fire, suddenly remembered how he and his elder brother, Kez, schemed to kill Aga, their father. "What are the two of you talking about?" he called out.

And Aton answered, "Such things, Father, that would anger you."

Nempie forced himself to laugh and asked, "What could you be talking about that would do that?"

"I would not anger you, Father, by telling you," Aton replied.

Rough Nempie's anger roared through him the way a fire roars through a summer-dried wood, but he kept a smile on his face. "You are wise, my son, not to anger me—wise beyond your summers." To himself Nempie said, *You will not play me for a fool much longer, my son, not much longer*.

"You were foolish to anger him," Gens told Aton after Nempie left the fire.

"Less foolish, brother," Aton answered, "than to fight him and lose."

"Then why anger him?"

"The words come," Aton answered. "I know not from where. They come and I must speak them."

The sky was green and tinged with streaks of yellow the morning that Nempie led his men out of the encampment. Nempie moved swiftly, almost at a trot, and insisted that Aton remain at his side.

Through the morning the color of the sky had changed to the brown of dust and a hot wind began to blow out of the western desert.

But Nempie called to the men, urging them to keep his pace and telling them that they were stronger by far than any people and that they would soon enjoy the spoils of the raid.

As the sun slipped down the western side of the sky, the wind was so hot that even Nempie had to stop to wet his parched lips with water. After they began to move again, the sand storm struck, forcing them to halt and seek whatever protection the land afforded. The sand clogged their ears, their noses, and caked in their mouths. The howling wind drove the sand against them until every man suffered from raw and bleeding wounds.

Aton and Gens shared the scant protection offered by a large boulder. The wind screamed around them.

When night came the spirits of the dead added their shrill cries to the sound of the wailing wind.

By morning the wind was gone; the sun shone brightly in a blue sky, and, except for the covering of brown sand all around them, there was no sign of the storm.

Nempie quickly organized the men for the day's march. After eating some smoked meat and dried fruit, they were on their way again.

Soon they had made up the distance they had lost. While sitting around small fires at nightfall, they spoke quietly about the next day's fighting.

According to Nempie, the camp was in a small valley. There were two large hills on either side of it and one small one at its rear.

"We will have men," Nempie said, "on all three hills. I will stay on the one behind the camp and Aton will take some men and attack the camp from the front. The people will go to the hills but we will be there to meet them." As he spoke he made marks in the dusty earth to show where each of the hills stood in relation to the camp.

Satisfied with Nempie's plan, Aton was excited by the prospect of the coming battle. He was sure that he would kill many. Afterward, he would hold Nempie to his word and take the two women he wanted.

Though Aton could see almost every part of what would happen the following day inside his head, he could not see himself with either of the women he would choose. The more he tried to see it the darker that portion of his vision became.

Later he mentioned it to Gens who said, "Let he who puts words into your mouth, Aton, also answer your questions."

"I did not know you were angry," Aton said.

Gens snorted. "If you had any eyes you would see not only that I am angry but what Nempie is doing."

"Why are you angry?" Aton asked.

"You well know why."

Aton heaved a weary sigh but did not speak. He knew his brother was past understanding words.

"All this," Gens said with a wave of his hand, "is for you, Aton. Nempie is doing this for you."

Aton shook his head.

"It is, Aton," Gens told him. "He wants you dead, Aton, and for whatever reasons he has, he can not kill you himself. Perhaps he is afraid of you or perhaps he does not want to risk your spirit coming to him at night. I do not know, but I do know that he wants you to die tomorrow."

"Then he will have to kill me himself," Aton said. "No one will do it for him, not even those I fight—of that I am sure."

For awhile neither of them spoke. Then Gens asked, "What will you do, Aton, if Nempie goes back on his word?"

"Then I will fight him."

"And I will join you," Gens responded eagerly.

"But I do not think that even Nempie would go back on his word," Aton commented.

"Each of us will take half of the people and——"

"There will be time enough for such talk should we slay Nempie," Aton said.

"I want Bisha."

Aton did not answer.

"I want Bisha," Gens repeated.

"I can not give what is not mine to give," Aton answered.

Gens suddenly reached out and, grabbing hold of Aton, said in a low harsh voice, "I want your word, Aton, that I will have Bisha."

With a swift movement Aton broke from Gens' hold and said, "You press too hard, Gens, even me you press too hard. I will not give my word about Bisha or anything else. And take heed, brother: I will not fight

Nempie unless I am forced to; but then I will—with or without you."

"I will be with you," Gens said. "I will be with you to kill him."

Aton rolled over and, closing his eyes, hoped sleep would soon come to cool his anger.

When Gens was sure that Aton slept, he crawled away from his fire and sought out Nempie, saying, "I have done what you have asked."

"It will not be necessary," Nempie said with a knowing smile.

"Are you certain he will fall?"

"He and those with him will have a hard fight," Nempie said.

"Aton will not fall."

Nempie looked at him questioningly.

"If you go back on your word," Gens told him, "he will fight you."

"Is that what he said?"

Gens nodded and added, "He does not think he will win."

"If it should come to pass as you say," Nempie said, "I will give you what you want."

"Bisha?"

"Bisha," Nempie answered.

Gens nodded and crawled back to the fire where Aton slept.

Aton led his men into the wide-mouthed valley that narrowed considerably. They moved deeper into it and closer to where the camp lay. On either side the hills were brown, rocky, and very steep. The air was still. It was hot for early morning.

Aton paused. The ground before him was strewn with boulders, and he ordered his men to go from one to another.

He began to move again, seeking the cover of the huge stones that lay on the floor of the valley. High in the blue sky he saw the slow circling flight of a vulture—first one, and then another, and then many. They seemed to know when there would be carrion for them to gorge on.

Aton wiped his brow and, dashing from one huge rock to another, waved to his men to follow. He paused before running forward again to scan the tops of the hills where Nempie and the other would soon be.

That Gens had suddenly decided to go with Nempie rather than with him surprised Aton. Gens was a strong fighter.

Aton shrugged and scurried for the next stone. Quickly, he ran until he could see the smoke from the fires in the camp stand straight up in the still air as if they were the slender trunks of tall trees.

Soon Aton was close enough to hear the shouts of women and children. From behind a large boulder he studied the camp which was similar to that of his people. The shelters were covered with skins or boughs of saplings; some were thatched and a few had sides of rocks piled on top of one another. Nearby two men stood guard, facing away from him.

Aton silently beckoned to one of his men and pointed to the guards, indicating he wanted the man to kill one guard with an arrow, he would do the same to the other.

The man nodded.

Aton strung his bow and, notching an arrow, looked toward the men, who waited for his signal. He nodded and two arrows hummed in the still air.

The guards, hearing the sound and knowing its meaning, tried to flee. Even as they moved, the arrows entered their backs with a sudden thudding wharp. Each staggered from the blow. Blood poured down their backs.

Aton nodded again, and his and the other man's arrow whizzed through the air. Each of them found their mark.

The guards fell face forward. One gasped as his spirit separated from his body, and the other clawed at the hard brown earth of the valley before his spirit left his body.

Aton set down his bow and case of arrows. They would not be needed in the rest of the fighting. He picked up his spear, hefted it, made sure his sword and knife were secure in a belt of animal skins, and looked behind him to see if his men were ready. They, too, held their spears.

Aton looked toward the camp and, sucking in his breath, he leaped up and rushed toward the camp.

As his shrill whoop slashed the heavy stillness in the valley and the cries of his followers rent the air, Aton saw the men suddenly appearing on the narrow ledges above the camp and below the tops of the hills. If able, he would have bolted his charge or diverted some of his men to attack those on the ledges, but the force of his charge swept his followers into the camp. They were met with a hail of stones and rocks from above and a shower of spears from in front. Several of his men lay dead or dying.

More rocks spilled from the ledges. The head of a man close to Aton split open, showering him with brains and blood.

Several of the men broke away and ran to the side of the hills at a command by Aton, who, with the other warriors, ran screaming at the camp's defenders who stood before them.

Aton hacked and cut his way through the lines of men. His body was covered with sweat and his chest heaved with each breath he took. He fought through a third line. His men followed, but he alone killed and killed and killed until his spear was dyed red and his hands were, even to his forearms, covered with blood.

Spears gave way to killing knives, where each man struggled with his opponent to bury the blade of a knife into each other's body. Some fought only to die locked in each other's arms.

Aton reached the far end of the camp and saw that his men had fought their way to the ledges and were already killing those who but a short while before had rained death on them.

Here and there the fighting raged and Aton, picking up a spear, rushed back into the melee. Now he was in a blood rage and in his eyes the valley and the hills around it were red. He killed, spearing his victims and tossing their writhing bodies over his shoulder as though they were not men.

Suddenly, those who fought against Aton and his men broke from the fight and ran toward the hills.

Breathing hard, Aton looked about him, nodded and ordered the women and children to be rounded up. Then he turned and watched Nempie and his men kill with flights of arrows all those who ran.

When the weeping, frightened women and children were herded together in the center of the encampment, the boys were torn from their screaming mothers and were riven by the killing knives and spears. No more were left alive with the seed of their people.

The women whose sons were taken from them ceased their screaming and whimpered softly while those left with daughters or those too young to bear children themselves, waited in frightened expectation of what would happen to them.

Aton looked toward the low hill at the far side of the camp. Nempie was running down its steep slope. Gens was close behind him, and all the others followed according to their strength as runners.

Aton wiped a bloody hand against his bloody brow and walked slowly around the cowering women. His eyes moved from one to the other. He did not say, *I choose that one or this one*. He looked and said nothing. When he knew that Nempie was close by, he turned and said, "I am ready to make my choice."

Nempie stopped. His eyes went to Gens, who nodded.

"My choice," Aton said, "is to let the men who fought here with me in the valley to choose the women they want and then I will choose."

Aton's men yelled their approval.

Nempie's shouted *no* brought a sudden silence to the valley.

"My choice!" Aton roared.

Nempie glared at him.

"I will forego a second choice," Aton said, "to have the first."

"No," Nempie bellowed. "I will choose my women first."

"That is not what you said," Aton told him.

"It will be——"

Aton grabbed a spear from the clutch of a dead man and said, "I do not want this fight, Father."

Nempie's spear was already in his hand.

Gens flung his spear down and, drawing his killing knife shouted, "Aton, go at him from the other side while I——"

Nempie rushed at Gens and plunged his weapon so deep into Gens' stomach that he could not pull it free.

Gens screamed and fell to the bloody earth, trying to do what his father with all his strength could not.

Nempie picked up a war club and, flailing the air with it, drove Aton back, never giving him a chance to thrust at him with the spear.

Suddenly Aton's back was against the rock side of a shelter. Nempie's face, twisted by anger and hate, was in front of him. He struck at it but a terrible pain exploded in Aton's head and Nempie's face broke into bits and pieces. A black wind whirled in front of Aton's eyes, hurling him into nothingness.

7

ATON HAD NEVER ENCOUNTERED such blackness. It was darker than those terrible nights when the hot wind of death blew over the land withering all that lay in its path.

The heavy darkness was never still. It swirled and rushed around him the way a river's waters whirled around those rocks that lived in the narrow gorge, where the bank of one side and the bank of the other are within throwing distance of a hunter's spear.

Though at first it seemed the blackness was around him, that he was no more than a swimmer in its flow, Aton soon came to realize that the darkness was also inside him, as if he were dead.

He felt nothing, not his limbs nor any other part of him—nothing except the blackness.

Was this what it was like when the spirit left the body? What would happen?

Aton did not want to die. If there were any hope he could somehow force the darkness from him he would, like a swimmer suddenly caught in a strong river current, struggle against it.

The more he strove to free himself from the blackness the heavier it became and more difficult became his battle. He would not pause; he would not let his spirit leave his body without fighting hard to keep it!

When his strength seemed gone the blackness began to lessen as if it too lacked the vigor to continue the struggle between them.

Though the darkness remained, Aton sensed a difference. It did not hold him as tightly as before, nor did it give him the feeling that it was sucking at him when he moved through it. There was in its deepness a peculiar kind of light allowing him to see into it.

With the eyes of a hunter Aton looked about. There was only the strangely glowing darkness through which he began to move, not knowing whether he was going deeper into it or making his way out of it. He moved through what seemed more and more like a huge cave.

Aton saw other presences hovering overhead or moving toward to him.

Suddenly the darkness gave way and there was light, a circle of it in which there were two people—a man and a woman.

"Aton comes," the man announced. "We must begin our play."

Aton stopped short of the circle of light. The presences hidden by the darkness now were revealed as the spirits of the people and the animals he had killed. They ringed him as he stood and watched the players.

Aton recognized the man, the stranger he had brought to Nempie's camp and whose heart he had eaten. Aton did not know the woman, though she could not have been older than he.

They squatted down and played stones as children do. Each was intent on the game.

Other than the short sharp crack made as a stone struck another, the great cave was silent.

For the children who played it, the game of stones was less a contest than the beginning of a hunter's training. To win, a player must hit all of his opponent's stones. There were as many as ten of them.

The man hit three and missed his fourth shot.

The woman played exceedingly well, taking all but three of the man's stones.

The man shot again and missed.

The woman took her turn and she, too, missed.

Neither seemed able to take more of his opponent's stones.

Suddenly the man struck his fourth stone and quickly took his fifth and sixth before his aim went off.

Aton watched the woman. Though he did not recognize her, there was something familiar about her, something to make him feel he knew her.

She smiled at him, fired the stone with her thumb, and missed.

In succession, the man took two more stones. "I will win," he said.

"No," the woman answered.

The man shot again, and his stone glanced off hers.

The woman moaned.

"I have won your son," the man said.

"No," she cried. "No!"

The man turned.

Aton saw the stranger as he had been when the people of Nempie's camp had eaten him.

"Run, Aton," his mother shouted. "Run to the right. Oh, my son, run!"

Aton ran through the darkness. Behind him shrieked the spirit of the man he had brought to Nempie's camp. He ran. Following behind were the spirits of all the animals he had ever slain.

Aton ran and after him came his mother's words, "I have given to you, Nempie, *a man amongst men.*"

He ran to the right, and the huge cave became smaller and smaller until Aton found himself in a narrow passageway. He forced himself into it, and passing between the two walls of stone, he suddenly realized he had stopped running, that he was listening to the flapping of great wings and that the air was filled with the stench of rotting flesh.

Aton took a deep breath and began to cough.

Again he heard the sound of flapping wings. He opened his eyes and found himself lying face down in the dust. Slowly Aton moved his head to the right. Within an arm's length a great black vulture stretched its red skinny neck toward him.

"Ahga!" he shouted, waving his arm.

The bird screeched and hopped back.

Aton lifted himself on to his knees and, reaching for a spear, hurled it at the vulture. The bird became a mass of screaming blood and feathers.

The sun blazed hot. The stench robbed him of breath. His vision blurred, and he felt like dropping down into the dust again, but there were other vultures waiting. These were wise enough to keep farther away from him than the one he had killed.

He remembered the attack on the camp and his fight with Nempie. He looked over his shoulders. Nearby lay what was left of Gens.

The vultures had picked at the wound made by Nempie's knife, torn his entrails out, and pulled them around the body like a great blue snake.

"Nempie," shouted Aton, shaking his fist at the sky, "Nempie, I will kill you. I will kill you."

Each word was caught by the spirits in the valley and repeated over and over again until Aton was forced to clap his hands over his ears lest he hear nothing else for the rest of his life.

When the spirits were silent, Aton crawled toward the water hole. It was slow, difficult work. He was wet with sweat and aware that the vultures were following. Several times he blundered into a swollen body that burst, spewing its stinking insides all over him.

The water hole was befouled with the bodies of several boys. He sat down and, holding his head in his hands, tried to stop the pain from ripping it apart.

When the booming inside his skull stopped, he crawled to gather a spear and a killing knife. Looking up at the sun, Aton judged he would be able to reach the top of the hill before the creatures of the night fully wove the cloak of night over the land.

Moving slowly, he left a trail of blood from his torn knees and bleeding hands. On all fours he made it halfway up the hill, paused until the vultures became daring enough to come close, so close to him that he thrust his spear into another bird and watched the others of its kind tear it to pieces.

His spear supporting him, he got to his feet and took several faltering steps up the gentle slope. His shadow lay long in front of him. Over his shoulder he saw the sun was low in the sky, hanging over the huge pit that lay beyond the great western desert.

Aton's eyes moved to the top of the hill; already the creatures of the night had begun their weaving.

"Nempie!" he exclaimed and forced himself to take several more steps. Each time he spoke his father's name he forced himself to move higher and higher up the slope to the crest of the hill.

Aton burned with hate. This fire seemed to hold the vultures away from him. He knew his father had never intended to keep his word, that the raid on the camp was nothing more than a plan to kill him and Gens.

Gens thought he could be more cunning than Nempie, or that he could fight him. Gens was a foolish man!

Aton always knew that he would lose when the fight between him and Nempie came. . . .

"But the next fight, Nempie," he shouted at the crest of the hill, "the next one you will lose!" The spirits took his words again. Clapping his hands over his ears, Aton pitched forward and rolled down the other side of the hill.

Part II

KEZ

8

THE TANNED, BEARDED MEN came across the low hills on small shaggy horses. Armed with a case of arrows, a bow, and a spear, they were led by Kez, on whose right side hung a short metal sword.

They rode toward the long valley and when they reached the crest of a nearby ridge Kez ordered a halt. The stench of death came on the wind from over the top of a hill, across the shallow, rock-strewn valley to their ridge.

The men and their mounts sniffed at the foul scent. The horses nervously pawed the hard dusty earth while the riders looked questioningly at each other.

"It has been a long ride for nothing," one of the men said.

Kez turned and, glowering at him, said, "I can not undo what has been done here. We will find slaves somewhere else. There are many bands of people whom we will be able to capture and bring back to our camp—many." He swung his arm in a wide arc to indicate the dimensions of the land and the many people they could take from it. As he gestured across the shallow valley that lay before him, he saw the figure of a man stumble over the top of the distant hill and then pitch forward. Crying "Aaah!" Kez slammed his heels into the flanks of his mount. The horse bolted forward into a gallop!

His men, too, shouted and charged after him. Soon the shallow valley was filled with the thunder of galloping horses and wild cries of "Ayah ... Ayah ... Ayah ..." as each rider urged his mount to run faster.

Kez was the first to reach the fallen man, who lay below the crest of the hill. Reining in his mount, he brought the animal to such an abrupt halt that it reared up, snorting wildly. Kez pulled harder at the reins and fought the rebellious horse under control. He leaped from the back of the trembling animal and stood over the fallen man as his riders crowded around.

Kez put his foot under the man and rolled him over.

"Is he alive?" one of the riders asked.

"Yes," Kez answered. "But from the looks of him he has been badly battered." With his skin boot he pointed to the dried blood on the side of the man's head. "That was probably made by a club and this one on his shoulder, is the result of a spear thrust." He bent over the prostrate form and studied him. "He is not from this camp. His markings are different and he wears the tusks of a boar. The men from this camp would hunt nothing more ferocious than a deer. They were like women that way."

The riders laughed.

Kez straightened up and glanced at his men. When his eyes found the man who had complained he said, "So, Bal, we did find something after all?"

"Yes, Kez, we did," Bal answered, his cheeks hot with anger under his brown beard. Kez had promised the capture of more than one man, though.

"It stinks here," one of the riders complained.

The other men agreed.

"There is still enough light left for us to go beyond the smell of this place," Kez said. Then he reached down, lifted the man in his arms, and slung him over the back of his horse. As soon as Kez was mounted he gestured toward the deepening darkness and told his men, "We will ride until the smell has left the wind."

Aton gagged on the water coursing down his throat. He opened his eyes.

A blazing fire settled first into his vision. Then the surrounding darkness registered. Finally, in the wavering reddish light of the fire, he saw the faces of several men looking down at him.

Aton sniffed; these were not his people. He tried to move, only to find that his hands and feet were bound.

The men near Aton had an animal odor about them. The whole camp stank of the same thing. Then his eyes moved off to the side where the light of the fire flowed into the darkness. There he saw many animals, a small herd of the kind he had once chased but could not get close enough to kill.

"This one is a hunter," Kez said.

Aton looked at the man who spoke. He did not understand him, but his eyes immediately went from the man's face, which was not much different from his own, to the dull sheen of his long, strange-looking knife.

"And he would like to get his hand on this," Kez said, grabbing the weapon's hilt. "Better bring him some meat."

A man held a partially cooked chunk of meat on a spit of wood in front of Aton, who thrust his face to it and began tearing at it with his teeth.

The men watched; the man who had spoken before said, "Give him something to drink too."

Aton looked at him again. He was to these men what Nempie was to his people.

71

A second man held a water skin in front of Aton, and he tilted his head back to let the water fill his mouth. When his thirst was satisfied, he pulled his head away.

Looking at the man who told the others what to do, he said, "I am Aton, the son of Nempie. I will kill Nempie. I will kill him and then I will be the leader of the people." He became angrier as he spoke.

The men around him drew back, and Kez said, "Sooner or later he will learn to speak as we do."

"Nempie," Aton shouted. "I will kill him!"

The men shook their heads and laughed.

Then Kez stepped forward and drove his foot into the captive's chest, knocking him on his back.

"I will kill you, too," Aton roared.

Kez laughed at the man's shouts.

Aton fell silent in the red glow of the fire. Shouting would not help him do what he must do.

"Take those tusks from his arms," Kez ordered.

A man cut Aton's hands free and pinioned his arms. Another tried to take the tusks from his right arm.

Aton struggled, managed to free his left arm, and landed a crashing blow on the head of the man who attempted removing the tusks of Pula, the black boar.

"Hold that man!" Kez yelled. To help bring the captive under control he kicked him in the face. A torrent of blood gushed from Aton's nose with his free hand, he broke the hold of the man pinioning his other hand. With two hands free he grabbed hold of Kez's foot and, twisting it, brought him down.

They rolled over each other several times, and Aton forced them closer and closer to the fire while he tried to wrest the strange looking knife from the leader of these men.

"Pull him off me," Kez shouted.

Several pairs of hands tried to grab hold of Aton, but he was slippery with sweat and was very strong —too strong to hold in the ordinary way.

"Put a noose around him," one of the men shouted.

Aton felt something drop over his head and cut into his neck. The coil around his neck tightened, forcing him to his knees and wrenching him off his opponent. He fought for breath. Suddenly it seemed as if his eyes were going to jump from his skull.

Someone came behind Aton and threw him face forward. His hands were grabbed and tied again. Then the coil around his neck was loosened.

Aton gasped for air. His throat ached and the back of his neck was sore.

"The only way you are going to get those tusks, Kez," Bal said, "is to hack off his arms. If we find other slaves one more or less is not going to matter."

Kez, still breathing hard, looked down at the captive. "You are probably right," he answered, "and I just might do that, but that would be wasting a good slave."

"Should I tell you something?" Bal said, moving closer to Kez. "That man will never be a good slave. You would be wise to hack his arms off and let him go."

"I have seen his kind before," Kez answered. "They either become good slaves or they die."

"Good or bad," Bal said, "they die."

Kez drove his foot into Aton's stomach several times, forcing him to vomit out all he had eaten and drunk. He told his men to keep the noose around the neck, saying, "It will help him remember not to try and fight us any more." Then he moved to where his sleeping skin was and stretched out on it.

Kez admired the man's courage. Whatever those tusks meant to the man, he was ready to die to stop anyone's taking them.

Kez closed his eyes, and before he was taken by the river of sleep he found himself remembering a story he had heard when he was in his father's camp. It concerned a black boar whose tusks were thrice circled and as sharply pointed as any spear.

Aton was awake before the first light. As he listened to the snorts and movements of the small herd of animals, he saw the dark form of one of the camp's guards pass close to the red glow of the fire. Soon the sounds of day and the men around him stole into his consciousness.

"This is your doing, Nempie," Aton whispered, feeling the bite of the cords binding his hands and feet. "This is your doing, Nempie, and when we fight I will kill you slowly, very slowly."

A guard from the far side of the camp suddenly shouted. His words were picked up and repeated by the other guards around the camp.

Aton saw light beginning to show over the mountains. He understood that the guards roused the men when the first light filled the sky.

The men woke quickly and went to the small herd of animals that stood nearby.

Aton saw that the forelegs of each were bound, even though the men brought them water and seemed to caress each of them as if they were women. The animals responded to the men by softly snorting or by pushing their muzzles closely to the men, sometimes against their chests or faces.

As soon as the men were finished with the animals they gathered around the fire to eat and drink. They spoke softly and sometimes laughed. The leader did not talk much and when he did he gestured toward the north where the sun never traveled. Another man gestured in the opposite direction.

Suddenly the leader stood up and spoke.

Several of the men left the fire and came toward Aton. They lifted him to his feet and dragged him to the fire. His body was stained with blood and vomit. From the expressions of the men who held him, Aton knew he stank. When they reached the fire they dropped him near it.

"One man hold the noose," Kez said. "Now cut his hands free and give him something to eat."

Aton was handed a piece of dark, hard food. He sniffed. It was meat.

Kez laughed and said, "He is used to bloodier food than that."

Aton bit into the meat. Though it was stringy and strange tasting, he ate it. He was given a white and sour drink that he did not like. He spit it out.

All the men laughed.

Aton saw a water skin and pointed to it, calling for water in his own language.

Kez nodded and said, "Give it to him. He will soon learn to drink mare's milk."

Aton drank, and when he thought he might be able to run away he leaped to his feet. Instantly the noose around his neck tightened, and he was jerked down into the dust.

The men around him laughed until water ran from their eyes.

Kez said, wiping his eyes, "Perhaps Bal was right. Perhaps I should hack off your arms and take those tusks for myself." He drew his short sword and moved toward the captive.

Aton, who was allowed to get to his feet, faced the leader of the men.

"He stinks," Kez said, putting the point of his sword at the man's throat.

Aton did not move. His eyes touched those of the man who stood before him. There was neither anger nor hate in them, but there was in the depths of their brownness the faint flicker of laughter.

Kez gave a snort and, putting up his sword, said, "I would rather have him give me those tusks."

"Here," Bal said, "give me the sword and I will do it for you."

"Give you the sword?" Kez questioned.

"Only to hack his arms off."

"And push into my belly," Kez said in a brittle voice.

The men quickly formed a circle around Kez and Bal.

Though Aton did not understand what they said, he understood the anger between them. He knew that the man who came to where the leader of the others stood would have killed him if he were given the long knife.

"I did not mean to offend you, Kez," Bal said.

"Only to kill me, eh, Bal?"

Aton moved his eyes from one to the other.

Bal shook his head.

"You are a good horseman and a good hunter," Kez said. "But you are not good enough." And he plunged the sword into Bal's stomach.

Bal seemed to hang on the blade, almost standing on his toes, until Kez shook his arm and pulled the bloody weapon free.

The man dropped to his knees and blood poured out out of the wound, staining the dusty brown earth red under him.

None of the men in the circle moved or made a sound.

Bal sucked in his breath and in a small, almost whimpering voice said, "Kill me, Kez. Do not let me die slowly."

Pointing the bloody sword at Aton, Kez said, "You would have done no less to him."

"I beg you," Bal pleaded, raising his eyes to the sky. Two vultures flew over him in large circles.

Kez turned away. In a loud voice he ordered his men to mount.

Aton saw something that astonished him even more than the killing of the man. The other men climbed onto the backs of the animals, and the animals carried them.

By the end of the first day Aton learned his first word of the tongue spoken by the men who held him captive. The word was "horse." These were men from the Horse People. The next day Aton learned that Kez was the name of the man who led them and Bal was the man he had killed.

During the day's march Aton went on foot, held by ropes between two riders. One rope circled Aton's waist and was held by the rider in front of him, while the rider following behind held the free end of the noose around his neck. A bough was set across Aton's shoulders and his hands were tied to it. Only his legs were left free.

Kez rode at the head of the column while Aton and those who held him were to the rear of all the riders.

Every day Aton was placed in the care of two men. They were responsible to see that during the day he had enough water.

The riders moved from the coming of dawn until night. They stopped only to rest the horses.

Some of the guards treated Aton better than others, and from them he learned that he was a slave, or that was what he would be when they returned to their camp. He understood that the Horse People, unlike his own, did not kill and eat their captives.

At the end of the day Kez ordered the column to halt and the men began to make camp. They hobbled their horses, brought them water, and caressed them the way they had that first morning after Aton had been captured. Usually they camped where there was grass for their mounts, but if there was none they fed the animals handfuls of dried grass which each of them carried in a large pouch that rested behind them on their mount's back with their sleeping skin.

There was always fresh meat at the fire, and Aton quickly realized his captors were perhaps as skillful as the hunters in Nempie's camp.

Whenever Aton thought about Nempie, he gnashed his teeth and grew hot with anger; to himself he said,

"I will free myself and then I will find Nempie and I will kill him." Each day he spent with the Horse People took him farther and farther away from Nempie's camp and into unfamiliar land.

During the journey the country through which they had passed had changed several times. For a while it had been barren and very rocky. Then it had become hilly and for the past two days it was flat and grassy.

At night Aton's hands were freed, and he rubbed his arms to bring feeling into them. Though the rope was removed from his waist, the noose around his neck was left there.

He was given meat and drink and after a few tries he was able to swallow the white water, which he eventually learned came from a mare.

Many days and many nights passed—so many that the moon was almost gone from the sky. Yet the night before Aton had fought Nempie the moon had been very round and very yellow.

When the eating and drinking was completed Aton was once more bound and left to sleep by the fire. Then, more than during the day, he felt his hate for Nempie. It burned inside him with a peculiar heat of its own. And in the wavering blaze of the fire he would see his father's face. Often Nempie's lips were parted in laughter, mocking laughter. Gathering a mouthful of spittle, Aton spat at Nempie's face to drive it away.

Sometimes when his hate for his father had left him for a while, Aton found his head full of memories of Rika.

He wondered if other men had asked for her or whether Nempie had given her to several of the old men in the camp to be held and used by them for as long as they lived or she lasted.

Most women did not live long if they were used by several men, or if they did, something very strange happened to them. They began to talk to spirits and sooner or later had to be killed for fear that they would bring some disaster to the camp.

Aton did not lust after Rika the way Gens lusted for Bisha. She was there and he used her for the pleasure she gave him. Had she not shared his shelter, he would have found someone else to mount. But there was something about her that, even now, when he was so far away from her, seemed to reach out and softly touch him, filling him more with sorrow than desire.

The moon left the sky and the night was filled with star figures and the night wanderers.

Day followed day and Kez continued to lead his men toward the north over which the circle of the sun never traveled.

Aton discovered the difference between his tongue and that of the Horse People was in the way they spoke and not in the words they spoke, though they had words for things he could not recognize. Once able to sound the words as they did he found he could speak to them. One night, when he was brought to the fire after a day's march, Aton slowly told Kez, "I am Aton, son of Nempie."

A sullen light leaped into Kez's eyes, and with a nod he said, "If you had spoken sooner I would have had you tell me where to find Nempie's camp and then you would have had many of your people with you—perhaps even Nempie."

"As slaves?" Aton questioned, still speaking slowly.

"Yes," Kez answered harshly. "As slaves!"

After that Kez always spoke with Aton for a while each night, asking many things about Nempie and his people.

"I will not tell you what you want to know," Aton answered when Kez questioned him about the land where Nempie's people hunted.

"And what is it that I want to know?"

"Where Nempie's camp is."

Kez's brow furrowed and, glaring at Aton, he said,

"I could make you tell me, not only where it is, but also how to get there."

Aton remained silent.

The men around the fire sucked in their breath and waited for Kez to order Aton's torture.

"Then will you tell me," Kez said in a low growl, "how you came by those tusks?"

"I took them from Pula, the black boar," Aton answered, crossing his arms and touching each of the tusks with his fingers.

"A black boar, you say?" Kez questioned, again recalling the story he had heard in Aga's camp about a black boar whose tusks were thrice-circled and spearpointed.

Aton nodded.

"And will you tell me how?"

"Should I tell you, Kez, what you already know?"

Furious, Kez leaped to his feet and struck Aton with his fist, knocking him senseless.

One day, when the sun was still high, Kez halted the column. The men made camp and from the way they tended their weapons Aton knew they were preparing for a raid.

At the fire that night Kez said to Aton, "Tomorrow we will raid a camp for more slaves. The camp is over that way," and he gestured to his left. "You will see how we fight."

"I would fight with your men," Aton offered.

Kez laughed and said, "I am sure you would, but though some of us will have to die tomorrow, I would prefer your not killing any. No, Aton, we are all safer with you watching and not fighting with us."

The men laughed and agreed with their leader.

"Tomorrow," Kez told Aton, "I will bring companions for you. Perhaps even let you use one of the women we take. How would that suit you?"

"Better than most of what has happened to me," Aton answered.

Kez slapped his thigh and laughed; Aton did not laugh.

Even before nightfall the sky became dull gray. Coming from the place where the sun fell into the pit that lay beyond the great desert there was more fire than usual in the sky.

To Kez it was a good omen for the following day's raid and he said to his men, "We will take many slaves." Thrusting his sword at the red sky, he added, "And those who come against us will stain the earth with their blood, even as the sky now runs with blood."

Aton did not see the same omen as Kez. He and all of the people of Nempie's camp would have been frightened by a sky filled with such fire. Nempie would have Tesu look at the future in the lives of a bull, and if he found nothing to explain the fire in the sky Nempie would have had him look at the entrails of a cow to see if something in the past had caused the sky to burn so.

That Kez saw the blood in the sky of those people his men would kill in the raid and that he saw fire confused Aton, especially since they were looking at the same piece of sky.

Was it blood or was it fire?

The question held sleep from Aton.

If he saw it as fire and Kez saw it as blood, would a man from another people see it as something else?

Aton shrugged and looked toward the wavering flames of the fire. They were what they were. No one ever said they were something else—or did they?

Aton shook his head. He wanted to deny the possibility that what were flames to him might be something else to another people and he wanted to drive such thoughts from his head lest they stay with him until the coming of the first light and rob him of sleep.

Often Aton had heard about spirits who, having entered a man's head, would fill it with all kinds of foolishness. He gathered a mouthful of spit and spat into the fire. It struck an ash-covered faggot and with a sizzling sound vanished, taking with it his thoughts.

Later his eyes closed and his spirit journeyed back to where he slew Pula, the black boar. Soon he saw the grove of willows that grew some distance up from the bank of the river.

And suddenly, even as it had already happened, it was happening again: *Pula snorted and came walking out of the willows.*

Pula was darker than the darkness sourrounding him and so large that his back touched the sky.

Aton sucked in his breath and drew his bow.

Pula stopped, pawed the earth and, with a snort said, "Know, Aton, that blood is blood and fire is fire. Kez nor those like him can change what is."

"And what is?" Aton asked, lowering his bow.

"Only that which must be. What must be you will find. You have already begun to seek it out. Now we must do what we previously have done."

Aton raised his bow, drew it and as Pula, the black boar, charged down on him he loosed an arrow. As he already had done, Aton slew Pula, taking from the beast his thrice-circled, spear-pointed tusks. Now all those who saw them on his arms would know that he, Aton, was a man amongst men, a man better than all the others. . . .

The cries of the guards awakened Aton as the first light showed above the mountains out of whose depths it would soon climb. The nearby fire was low and the men of the camp went to tend their horses before they gathered to eat and drink.

"Today," Kez said to Aton, "you will ride a horse. Once we break camp we must move swiftly; to have you walk will slow us down."

"Will I be able to ride with my hands bound like

this?" Aton asked, swinging the bough that lay across his shoulders.

Kez stroked his beard and then he ordered Aton's hands to be bound in front of him. "Your feet will be tied together under the horse's belly and the horse will be hobbled on the top of a hill overlooking the camp. You will have a good view of how my men fight."

"I have seen men fight before," Aton answered.

"I was sure you had," Kez answered with a chuckle, "but today you will see something you have never seen." With a wave of his hand that ended the conversation, he immediately ordered his men to mount their horses.

Aton was set on the back of a light brown stallion and tied as Kez said he would be. Once again he was placed between two guard riders.

The sun was almost at its highest place in the sky when Kez halted the column and ordered Aton's guard to take him to the top of the hill on the left. The guards hobbled Aton's mount and, leaping on the backs of their own, rode back to the column at a trot.

The camp that Kez and his men would soon attack stood on flat open ground below the hill. Its people lived in skin shelters. Small animals, goats, and sheep, grazed on the grass near the camp.

Aton turned toward the column. Kez had rearranged his riders in a long line. Each man rode next to another, and Kez was some distance in front of them.

The horses moved at a walk until they topped a slight rise. Kez held up his long metal knife and his riders began to trot. Swirls of brown dust came to life and died between the hooves of the horses.

Suddenly Kez cried, "Ayah!" and began to gallop.

The riders picked up the blood cry, and with their spears in their hands, charged down on the camp.

From the crest of the hill, Aton watched Kez and his men sweep toward the camp. Their shrill cries rose above the beat of the horses' hooves and mingled with the shouts and screams coming from the camp.

Aton's heart began to pound. He was covered with sweat!

The men in the camp ran to fend off the attack while the women and children fled. In the bright sunlight Aton saw the flash of Kez's metal sword. Almost at once several riders on either end of the line swung off to circle the camp.

Suddenly a flight of arrows like birds of death flew at Kez and his men. A few tumbled from their mounts and bounced on the ground before lying still.

The cries of the attackers became more shrill.

Another flight of arrows were loosed.

Two horses stumbled and several more men dropped to the ground.

Aton moved his shoulders and sucked in his breath. Never before had he seen an attack without having been in it. The excitement of Kez's charge made him struggle against the bonds that held him securely to the horse's back and brought the blood cry of his people to his lips.

Kez's men were met with another flight of arrows and more of them fell. The camp's defenders broke and ran!

The riders went after them, spearing them as they fled. Some were caught on the heads of spears and, screaming, were tossed high in the air. Others were ridden down, trampled under the hooves of the horses.

The drumming of the galloping horses was gone now, but the air was filled with the screams of the dying.

The attackers swept through the camp, wheeled around, and sought other men to kill. Those who were left could not fight any more and dropped their weapons to show they were defeated. Prodded by the spear points of Kez's men, they were gathered into the center of the camp.

The riders who had been sent around the camp were joined by others, and all of them rode through the grass to flush out the women and children. Those who ran were either speared or trampled to death.

The raid was soon over, and vultures circled the camp. In the hot afternoon the smell of blood was heavy in the air.

The old men and women, who survived the onslaught, were separated from the other people and amid more screaming and shrieking were speared to death where they stood. Babies were torn from their mother's arms, tossed in the air, caught on the heads of spears, and thrown on top of the bodies of the old men and woman. Then the children too young to survive a march were killed. Finally any man or woman whose wounds were more serious than cuts were also put to death.

When the killing was over Aton watched Kez fire the shelters in the camp. The black smoke rose; the many columns looked like newly grown trees. Nempie would have burned everything, too.

Kez sent some of his riders out to gather up their own dead. These were placed in shallow graves overlaid with large rocks to prevent the vultures and other carrion eaters from getting at the bodies.

All of the men who were taken prisoner and were well enough to survive the march back to the camp of the Horse People were bound with ropes around their necks and waists. Their hands were tied behind their backs.

Kez and his men fell on the women, raping them on the ground between the burning shelters and the mounds of dead.

The women did not scream loud enough for Aton to hear them, but he did see what was being done to them. He had done this many times. It was the right of the men who won to use the women.

The smoke trees began to dissolve, and all that was

left of the camp were the charred remains of the shelters and the bodies of the dead.

Many of the women were too torn and bleeding to be worth anything after the men were finished. They were stabbed to death and thrown on the other bodies. The other women were bound in the manner of the men.

Kez mounted his horse and ordered his men to theirs. The two lines of captives, flanked by riders, walked slowly away from the place they had lived. None turned back to look at the bodies. The vultures were beginning to tear at those bodies on top of the heap.

Aton did not know when his sense of excitement had vanished, but the blood cry had left his lips and he had lost the need to struggle against the bonds that held him.

Kez and his men had fought well. Their horses had given them enormous strength. What he had seen he would always remember. Kez was as good a leader as Nempie.

Aton looked up at the pall of gray smoke that hung over the camp and that same grayness seemed also to be inside of him.

Was it there because he could not do any of the killing? Or was it there because he had seen the killing in a way and from a place that he never had before?

The killing was as necessary to the Horse People as it was to Nempie's people or any other people whose men need women, or more land in which to hunt, or slaves.

Aton shook his head and spat.

What other way was there but to kill and take from those whom you kill the things you want?

The lines of captives were just below the hill and Kez, waving his long metal knife at Aton, shouted up, "See how many companions I bring you, Aton. See the women. I will keep my word to you. You will have one to give you pleasure. It was a good raid, Aton, with a good catch."

Aton straightened up and, pulling back his shoulders, called out, "I saw it all, Kez. I saw it all."

9

THEIR DUST-COVERED BODIES were streaked with sweat, stained with blood, and smelled of the women they had raped. Kez and his men halted long enough for two of the riders to trot up the hill and fetch Aton.

"You sit astride the horse well," Kez laughed. His eyes were wide and filled with the brightness that comes from killing, from the excitement and danger of it. "Were you one of us," he said, "I do not doubt you would be one of the best, possibly good enough to take this from me." And he waved his sword, which now was spotted like a leopard's skin with the dark stains of dried blood.

"Not yet, Kez," Aton answered with a smile, and his eyes flicked over the two lines of captives.

Kez put the point of the sword against Aton's chest and in a hard voice he said, "Not yet, eh? Not ever! The man who holds this sword in his hand is the leader of my people. My people, Aton. The Horse People."

Kez put up his sword and with a sudden laugh told

Aton, "But you are young. You have not yet begun to be a slave. You will learn that to be a slave is to be nothing. You will learn that as all the others before you have."

Aton was taken off the horse and bound in with the other captives; unlike them, his hands remained tied to the piece of wood that lay across his shoulders.

Kez and his men moved more rapidly than they had before the raid. Whenever any of the prisoners slipped or failed to keep pace, a rider trotted up beside the man or woman and either struck the captive with a rod or jabbed him with the point of a spear until blood flowed.

Even for Aton the pace was difficult to maintain, especially since Kez did not stop to give his captives water, and the sun was bright and hot. The men to whom he was bound were silent. Sometimes a whimper came from one of the women in the line.

Aton looked at the woman next to him. There was no expression on her face. The top part of her covering was torn. From the darkness around her nipples he knew that she had probably dropped several children. She could have been as old as Rika. The insides of her thighs were stained with blood, a sign that she had been used very hard by many men.

The grass that had covered much of the land near the camp that Kez and his men had raided thinned out considerably as they journeyed. The earth soon became hard and so rocky that many of the captives bruised the soles of their feet as they were forced to maintain the swift stride of the march.

The sun was low in the sky, hanging over the western desert before it dropped into the pit. And already the creatures of night were busy weaving the cloak of darkness.

Aton, who thought that the Horse People, like his own, knew the danger of traveling at night, called to one of the riders and asked, "When do we make camp?

The creatures of the night——"

Silenced by a blow across his face, Aton struggled to free his hands.

"The night means nothing to us, slave," the rider laughed. "We ride until Kez orders us to halt."

Aton shook his head.

"And what does that mean?"

"The spirits come with the night," Aton said. "Tell Kez the creatures of the night weave the darkness and the darkness belongs to the spirits."

The guard laughed and shouted to his companions about what Aton had said. All the guards laughed.

Kez rode back to Aton. He, too, was laughing and he said, "I thought better of you than to be a man afraid of the darkness. The darkness is a friend. It conceals what the day reveals. The least of my men, nay, even the boys in my camp, know that the darkness is sometimes a better friend than the daylight."

Aton looked up at Kez. Though there was laughter in the man's eyes, Aton also saw the open expression of truth on the man's face.

Kez wheeled his mount around and rode back to the front of the column.

Aton watched the night come and cover the land.

The march continued. No torch was lit. Except for the quick padding of feet and the movement of the guards as they rode up and down the length of the lines there was no sound. The spirits of the night did not shriek, did not wail, did not make a sound.

The sky was filled with star figures and when the moon came up it was no more than a thin white curve, like a bow well bent. But in its pale light Aton could see that the aspect of the land was becoming hilly and from the star around which the sky turns he knew they had changed their line of march from north to midway between north and west. Almost as soon as he realized this the guards began to shout, calling to the captives to quicken their pace until both lines were moving at a trot.

"There will be food and water ahead," the guards told the weary lines of men and women. "Faster! Faster! Faster!"

The woman beside Aton lost her footing and, with a breathless cry, fell.

Aton grabbed hold of her arm and pulled her along with him.

"I can not keep pace," she told him. "I do not have the strength."

Her speech was slurred more than that of the Horse People but the words were the same.

Aton held on.

"What is happening here?" a guard questioned.

"The woman stumbled," Aton said.

"Let her go!"

The woman tried to pull away and stand, but she could not put any weight on her left foot without uttering a cry of pain. She stumbled.

Another rider came up beside Aton. "You are slowing the others," he said.

"The woman," the first rider said, "can not keep up."

"Take her out," the other man said. "Anyone who can not keep up with the march——"

"I will carry her," Aton offered.

The guards laughed, and the one closest to Aton said, "First you are afraid of the spirits and now you want to carry one of the women. Truly all people other than those of Kez's camp are worth nothing. Take the woman out."

Quickly the woman was cut away from the others.

Aton tried to move between her and the guard, but he caused his mount to rear up and it forced him back.

"Now move!" the second rider ordered, and he struck Aton on the back with a rod.

The woman vanished into the darkness. A short

while later a long drawn-out scream followed the two lines of captives.

Aton glanced over his shoulders. Whoever she was, she did remind him of Rika. Perhaps that was why he had offered to carry her? And he wondered whether he would ever have offered to carry Rika? He never had that kind of feeling inside of him for her. Nempie had given her to him. She was skilled in the ways of giving him pleasure. Yet of all the people whose presence often filled his head Rika was the one he would have enjoyed seeing the most. And he would see her again, when he returned to his people and killed Nempie. He faced forward again and let himself think of how slowly he would kill his father.

"That was a kind thing to offer," the man behind Aton said.

Aton turned his head and looked questioningly at him.

"To carry the woman," the man told him.

Aton looked away and continued to move at a trot. He did not understand what the man had said. He had never before heard the word *kind*; he had never even heard that word from any of Kez's men and they had many words that were new to him.

When the moon was midway in her journey across the night sky, Kez ordered a halt to the march. His men immediately hobbled their mounts, fed them, and brought water from a nearby water hole. When they had watered the horses they led the captives to the water hole and let them drink. They then built a huge fire over which chunks of several freshly-killed deer, wild pigs, and lizards were roasted and thrown to the captives, who willingly ate whatever they caught.

Aton gorged himself on two bloody pieces of deer liver and part of a wild pig's stomach before his hunger was satisfied. The captives were set apart from Kez and his men. Except for the sounds they made while eating, they kept silent.

Kez and his men talked about the raid, the killing they had done, and the women they had despoiled. They laughed and praised each other for their skill in killing or their ability to mount a woman, put their fluid into her, find another, do the same to her, find still another, and have fluid for her, too.

Aton had often heard such talk around the fire in Nempie's camp after a raid. Most men, he had learned, often boasted of more than they could do with the women they took. This he discovered from the women themselves when he mounted them. Some men changed one into two and two into three whenever they spoke about the women they raped, just as some men found it necessary to kill more men with words than they actually had in conflict.

Kez's men fought well, though he did not think highly of the men who defended the camp. The men in Nempie's camp would never have broken and ran. They would have never thrown down their weapons and allowed themselves to be taken prisoner.

Aton heard his name mentioned by the guard who had taken the woman from the line. Laughter followed as the sound of his name moved through the wavering flame of the fire again. He strained to hear more but could not.

Kez suddenly stood up and, followed by his men, came to where the captives were. "Which of you," he asked, "was the leader of these people?"

No one spoke.

Kez repeated the question but he spoke his words very slowly, slurring them as Aton had heard the woman do.

"I am their leader," the man behind Aton said. "I am Besop."

"And your sons, if you have any?"

Besop pointed to three, calling them in turn by name. "Nork, Barrada, and Entu."

Kez nodded and motioned to his men. Immediately

Besop's three sons were cut from the line and brought to where Kez stood.

"And your women," Kez asked. "Where are they?"

"The oldest was killed in the raid; one was taken from the line before you made camp."

"The others. No," Kez said, "the youngest, where is she?"

"Over there," Besop said, pointing to a woman of not more than sixteen summers, whose eyes were wide with fright and whose long black hair touched the nipples of her breasts. "Her name is Linet."

"Bring her here," Kez ordered. When she stood before him, he said, "Know Besop, that here your line ends. There will be no children dropped by Linet and none from the loins of your sons."

Besop moaned.

"Geld his sons," Kez ordered.

The sons were immediately thrown to the ground by Kez's men. Amid agonizing screams the bloody work was done, and the wound seared with a glowing faggot.

"Kill me!" Besop shouted.

But Kez said, "No, Besop, no. You will make a fine slave." Turning to Linet, whose wide eyes were filled with even more terror than they held before, he reached up, brushed her hair away from her breasts, ran his hands over them until the nipples budded and then ordered his men to remove the rest of her covering.

Light from the blazing fire played over Linet's nakedness. Desire awakened in captor and captive alike.

"Aton," Kez called, "I will be true to my word. She will be yours before I give her to my men."

Besop lunged at Kez but was knocked down by one of his men.

"Aton," Kez said, "she will be yours."

"And I will gladly have her," Aton said, his lust aroused by the sight of Linet's nakedness.

"But if I give her to you, Aton, what will you give me?" Kez asked.

Aton suddenly understood Kez's purpose and said, in a voice strange even to his ears, "You can not have what you want, Kez. The tusks of Pula, the black boar, are mine to wear because I slew him. To wear them, I must be slain."

Kez rushed at Aton and lifted his sword but Aton grabbed hold of his arm and stayed its movement.

"You will be treated like the rest of the slaves," Kez said. "You will be treated worse. I can wait for you to die, Aton; I can wait because it will not be long."

"Then wait, Kez," Aton answered, in that strange rumbling voice. With a push he released him.

In a rage Kez turned on Linet and with a swift stroke of his sword gutted her. Screaming, she dropped to the ground. Aton lifted her bloody naked body in his arms and held her to him. She died very slowly, and when her spirit finally separated from her body she cried out, "Aton. Aton. Aton. . . ." The sound of his name filled the darkness of the night.

There was enmity between Kez and Aton now. Kez grew angry at the sight of Aton. In the days that followed he frequently ordered him beaten or withheld water from him when the long day's march was ended.

Aton endured. He did not cry out under the blows delivered by Kez or the riders, nor did he beg for water, as some man might. Through the tempest of Kez's wrath, his step did not falter; he kept pace with those to whom he was bound.

Aton's strength was a source of wonder to everyone. Kez's men whispered about it to each other, but always out of earshot of their leader. The captives spoke about it in low tones when they huddled together at night. And Kez thought about it, wondering, even as all the others did, if Aton's strength came from the thrice-circled tusks of Pula, the black boar?

Through the days of beatings and the nights without water, Aton seldom spoke and then it was only to Besop, who said to him the night after Linet died, "My people too know of Pula, the black boar."

Aton nodded and, looking across the fire to where Kez sat, he answered, "And so does the leader of the Horse People."

"How can you be sure?"

"I am sure," Aton replied and, closing his eyes, said, "I have done what no other man could and I will yet do what no man has done."

"We are slaves," Besop sighed. "We are like the dust that blows across the land."

Aton remained silent. He was not dust. He was the man who slew Pula, the black boar. He was, by his mother's own words, *a man amongst men*. He knew that a man like Besop would not understand these things.

The next night it was Aton who spoke first, and he asked Besop to explain the meaning of the world *kind*.

"It is when you do something for someone else," Besop said, "as you did for my woman when you offered to carry her and when you held Linet in your arms before she died."

"I offered to carry your woman," Aton told him, "because she reminded me of Rika, the woman who shared my shelter in Nempie's camp."

"Then what was your reason for gathering Linet in your arms?"

Aton pulled on his beard. He had often wondered why he had done it.

"Surely you did not want to use her——"

"Yes, I did. When Kez offered her to me I did want to mount her."

"And after she was gutted?"

Aton shook his head.

"Then there must be another answer for what you did."

Aton stared into the flames. In their changing light

he saw it all happen again. As the vision of it was in his eyes, the words spoken between him and Kez were in his ears, especially his voice, the sound of which was strange to him.

"How did you know," Besop questioned, "that Kez would not kill you?"

"Because he had already killed Linet." Suddenly he realized that she had died in his place.

"Then that is why you took her into your arms," Besop said.

"But I did not know that until I told it to you."

"You knew it then, Aton," Besop assured. "You knew it then."

Night after night Aton and Besop spoke; each learned from the other. Aton discovered that Besop's people were very different from the Horse People and from Nempie's people. They did not eat their captives, nor did they make slaves of them. Though they hunted, they raised goats and sheep for meat.

"You see," Besop explained, "we were herders of sheep and goats more than hunters."

"Perhaps if you had remained hunters," Aton suggested, "you might have beaten off Kez and his men."

"The man on the horse always has the advantage," Besop replied.

Aton shrugged.

Many of Besop's people died on the march. Those who fell were cut free from the rest of the line and were left to die or were speared by the riders.

One morning as the shouts of the guards wakened the camp with the coming of the first light, Besop said, "Last night I was visited by the spirit of Nayil. She was the woman you offered to carry."

Aton nodded but his eyes, as they always did when he awoke, moved over the landscape, beyond the limits of the camp, which lay in a shallow depression part of the way up the slope of a hill. He saw several figures on a high distant ridge. At first he thought he was looking at large upright boulders, the kind that men in Nempie's camp had once told him had been put on the land by giants. Aton knew they were men on horses when he saw them move swiftly along the ridge.

"She said," Besop told him, "that I walk with one whose spirit had left his body and then returned to it. It that true, Aton? Were you put down under?"

"No, I was left for dead," he said, watching the distant riders.

"In a raid?"

"By my father Nempie. But who told Nayil about me?"

"Your mother," Besop answered.

Aton nodded. Gesturing toward the ridge where the riders were, he said, "We are being followed."

Besop looked at him questioningly.

"By other mounted men," he said, and, looking toward Kez, Aton wondered if he knew.

"What will happen to us?" Besop asked.

With a shrug Aton answered, "No matter who will win, we will still lose."

Besop's hands trembled, but he said nothing.

Through the day Aton scanned the distant ridges. Occasionally he caught sight of the riders and told Besop where to look for them. Whoever they were, they did not attack. By the following morning they did not show themselves.

Besop was relieved that the strangers had decided against a fight. "More of my people would have died," he said.

"Have you ever seen mounted men fight each other?" Aton asked.

"When I was very young. Then horses and men are slaughtered. Nothing is spared and the horses, like their riders, are eager for the fight."

"I saw that when Kez led his men against your camp," Aton told him.

"Then you saw how poorly we fought?"

"As you said, the mounted man always has the advantage."

Besop nodded.

At the end of that day's march Kez came toward Aton, who braced himself for the blows that he was sure would come. But Kez did not raise his hand. He said, "We were followed for the better part of two days."

Aton nodded.

"I thought you might have seen them," Kez said. There was laughter in his eyes. "And what would you have done if they had attacked us?"

"Probably, like yourself, died, but I would have died bound. You would have died while trying to kill."

"The end would have been the same," Kez said.

Aton shrugged.

"How could it have been otherwise?"

Suddenly Besop said, "He is not like the rest of us."

Kez's brow furrowed, and his eyes darted back and forth between the two captives. Finally they came to rest on Besop. Kez asked, "Tell me why he is not like the rest of us?"

"He has already said too much," Aton said. "Say no more, Besop!"

"Then *you* tell me," Kez said, his eyes flicking to Aton. His face was flushed with anger.

Aton remained mute.

"I will have an answer out of you," Kez shouted, "or I will have your tongue cut out."

"Then know this, Kez," Aton said, suddenly realizing he could summon that strange dark voice. "Then know this, Kez, I am *a man amongst men*."

Kez drew back. His jaw went slack. His eyes were wide with surprise. Then he started to laugh.

Aton's voice rose above the sound of Kez's laughter and said, "It is much easier to laugh, Kez, than die."

"Aton," Kez screamed. "Aton, I will kill you!" And he knocked him senseless but could not drive his sword into Aton, though he held it above the man's heart.

The sudden reach of an enormous hand plucked Aton from the depths of the darkness into which Kez had hurled him.

Water splashed on Aton's face.

He shook his head.

More water poured down on him, making him snort to clear his nostrils. The taste of blood was in his mouth, and he spat. His eyelids fluttered open and though his vision was still blurred, he saw Kez looking down at him.

"Get him on his feet," the leader of the Horse People ordered.

"I can stand," Aton said, spitting more blood from his mouth. Slowly he pulled himself up into a sitting position. Dropping on his hands and knees he managed to gain his feet. He swayed, not sure that he would be able to hold himself erect.

"Even you, *a man amongst men*," the leader of the Horse People said, "must learn what all other men already know when they become slaves."

Though Aton's stance faltered he stood. The fire behind Kez burned brightly, as if it had been recently fed.

"What do you see?" Kez asked.

"What should I see?" Aton responded.

Kez struck him across the face and said, "Tell me what you see."

The blow staggered Aton but he did not fall. "I see you and the fire," he told him. Then he saw something else, off to his left. He squinted in an effort to clear his still blurred vision.

"You see something else?"

"Men," Aton said.

"Yes, men," Kez answered, and he motioned them to move closer to him.

Besop was held by two of the riders and his hands were bound to the shaft of a spear that lay across his shoulders.

"Watch closely, Aton," Kez said.

Suddenly thrown to the ground, Besop cried out.

Three more of Kez's men came to him. One of them held a spear tied into a notched sapling. Another held a large rock, the kind an arrow maker would use to pound large pieces of flint into smaller ones. The other two men grabbed Besop's legs and spread them.

Besop shouted and fought to free himself.

The men who held his legs pulled them up, rolling him up on his back.

Then the man with the spear stepped close to him and jammed the head into the man's bunghole.

Aton staggered back as Besop's shriek of agony rose above the roar of the fire. Writhing, the stricken man struggled against those who held him; their strength prevailed.

Blood gushed from the forced entry.

Aton winced with pain. His own bowels suddenly contracted as if the head of the spear had been thrust into his body.

From Besop's people came a moan like the wailing of the wind.

The man who held the rock smashed it against the end of the spear shaft, driving it deeper into Besop, who cried out to be killed. Again the man hammered on the shaft.

And Besop screamed, "Be kind and kill me, Kez. Be kind!"

There was no kindness in Kez. The man with the rock continued to smite the end of the spear shaft.

"Aton," Besop shouted. "Aton help me die. Help me, Aton!"

"Help him," Kez said, gesturing to Aton. "Help him."

Aton's bowels emptied themselves.

"He can not help you, Besop," Kez mocked. "He has befouled himself."

The spear was well into Besop, and the ground where he lay was wet with his blood.

"Enough," Kez called to the man who held the spear. "Now plant him, as though he grew from the earth."

Two of the men quickly dug a hole and then all three lifted Besop and set the end of the spear shaft into the earth as though it were the trunk of a sapling.

Besop screamed and his blood-splashed legs flailed the air while the exposed length of the shaft became quickly reddened.

"Now, *man amongst men*," Kez said derisively, "Besop is your lesson." Turning away, he went to his sleeping skin on the far side of the fire.

Aton sat down in his own filth. Bound as he was, he could do nothing for Besop. He had killed many men, but he had never done to any of them what Kez had ordered done to Besop. He did not understand it. Even the man he had brought to Nempie's camp he had killed before the women could force him to give them his fluid.

Besop shouted, wept, screamed, and laughed. He called to Nayil and to Linet. He cried to each of his sons. He was never quiet throughout the long night.

Before the first light came he shouted, "Aton . . . Aton . . . Aton, the sword must be yours. The metal sword must be yours. Take it, Aton, and with it you take all of Kez's strength."

Kez ran from the place where he slept, and before he reached Besop he hurled his spear at him. Through the darkness it thudded into the man's chest.

Besop screamed once and then fell silent. His spirit had finally separated from his body.

The first light came, but the guards did not have to call the camp to wakefulness. When the day's march began Besop's body was left where Kez had ordered it planted. The vultures and jackals tore at it before the columns of captives gained the upper ridge of the long slope.

Part III

THE MARCH

10

THE CAMP of the Horse People was many days' journey from the place where Besop had been impaled. During the long march Aton spoke to no one.

Of all the deaths Aton had seen, Besop's clung to him with the sickness of the yellow juice that oozed from the trunks of the big trees close to Nempie's camp. No matter how often he spat over his shoulder, he could not clear his head of the view of the man's writhing on the spear hammered into his body. He could not stop Besop's last words from sounding over and over in his skull: *"Aton . . . Aton . . . Aton, the sword must be yours. Take it, Aton, and with it you take all of Kez's strength."*

Aton understood the meaning of Besop's cry.

Kez's sword was where the spirit of the man's power dwelled. Aton had seen him wield it when he and his men had attacked Besop's camp. It sundered into many pieces any of the stone killing knives it struck, even as the maker of the stone weapon would have had he struck a wrong blow with his shaping rock. The killing knives of Nempie's camp, though they were better made than those that Besop's men had used, would have splintered too, had they been struck by Kez's weapon.

All of Kez's power did not lay in his sword; Aton understood that, too. He knew that some of it also lived in the horse Kez rode and in the man's heart, where the strength and courage of every man lived.

Though the days he had known Besop were few, Aton felt his loss greatly. At night he often sat close to the fire and, gazing into the flames, his head filled with thoughts about the man. Aton was greatly puzzled by what Besop had told him about his dreams. That he, Aton, had been down below to the place of the dead and had returned was of no great significance to him; to Besop it had been.

Many hunters in Nempie's camp had had similar experiences, and he had heard it told by some of the men that when Tesu had been much younger and stronger, he too had gone below to the place of the dead and had returned. He had made the journey to speak with the spirits of people who had died but who had not let go their hold on the place of the living.

Aton wondered if, by making the journey from the place of the dead back to the land of the living, he had gained, even as Pula, the black boar's, tusks had given him, something that other men lacked?

That possibility often caused him to lie awake and watch the night sky pass before his eyes.

Pula's tusks were visible. People could see and touch them. Those who saw them knew that he was a mighty hunter, for only one of great skill could have taken the thrice-circled tusks.

But what sign did he have to show that he had been down under and had returned?

Who would believe that he had seen his mother's

spirit play a game of stones with the spirit of the man whose heart he had eaten?

And why had his mother said to Nempie, when she had dropped him, *"I have brought forth a man amongst men, a man better than all others"*?

To none of these questions could he find an answer. Aton was sure that if he could, he would find the way of freeing himself, returning to Nempie and taking his revenge on his father. That possibility was enough to keep him searching the night sky and all its images for answer.

Though Kez no longer spoke with Aton after the day's march, he was sorely troubled by him. Aton seemed to be wherever his eyes were and when he slipped into the waters of sleep that bathe all men, Kez was afflicted by him.

At night Aton often stood on a dark shore while he floated by in the river of sleep that carried him until the coming of the first light. On some nights Kez looked at Aton through the wavering light of the fire and saw him, though bound to the other captives, sitting separate from them, almost as though he was alone. To see him that way always filled Kez with uneasiness, filling his own head with Besop's words and making him curious about what Besop might have said if Aton had not stopped him.

One afternoon when the sun was in the far part of the sky, over the great desert that lay to the west, Kez called a halt to the day's march. "Tomorrow," he told his men, "we will raid another camp." And he gestured in the direction where it lay. "But now we will rest and prepare ourselves for the coming fight. The people of this camp will not be as easy to capture as those we have taken."

The men laughed and agreed that Besop's people were no match for them.

"This will be our last raid before we go back to our own camp," Kez said.

His riders shouted their approval and immediately began feeding and watering their mounts.

Later, when darkness had almost settled over the land, Kez saw Aton sitting as he had sat so many nights past on the other side of the fire in a kind of isolated splendor though he was bound to other captives. The thrice-circled tusks of Pula, the black boar, glowed white in the light of the fire.

Kez shook his head and turned away; calling his men together, he discussed the next day's raid. With a pointed stick, he drew lines in the dusty earth to indicate the place where the camp was and how they would attack it.

He answered all the questions of his men. Some of what he said brought laughter from his riders, while other things were accepted with silent nods. He told them, "The women of this camp fight as well as the men. If you rape one, be sure that her hands are bound or that she has been knocked senseless, or she might gouge your eyes out or try to rip your manhood from you."

Some of the men who had been with Kez when he had raided this camp vouched for the truth of his words.

"If you beat a woman, she will still keep her thighs shut," said one of those who had had experience with the women of the camp. "You must do what Kez has told you to, or you will lose more than the woman's slit is worth."

"What about later," one of the younger riders asked, "after they are captives for a while?"

"They are not like other women," the older man said. "They do not let a man mount them without a struggle."

"Not even their own men?"

The question made the other riders laugh, and Kez said, "You will have to ask them yourself."

That brought more guffaws from the men. A few more ribald comments were made by various men and there was a great deal of laughter. With a wave of his hand Kez indicated that his talk with them was over.

The men left. Some caressed their mounts; others began to tend their weapons. Kez slowly turned around and in the darkness his eyes found Aton. Almost as slowly as he had turned, he stood up, walked around the fire and approached Aton.

Throughout his conversation with his men Kez believed that Aton was looking at him. He could feel the weight on his back of the man's gray eyes. He had been able to tell his men what they had to know for the next day's raid but his own thoughts were about what Besop would have said before Aton had stopped him. Now he had to know!

Kez stood over Aton, but Aton did not move or look up.

"You have not had much to say recently," Kez said.

Aton raised his eyes. Kez was dark against the red blaze of the fire.

"Surely you must have something to say," Kez commented.

"All that had to be said has already been said."

"Besop was going to say something before you stopped him."

Aton nodded.

"Do you know——"

"Yes, I know."

"Since you know," Kez said, "tell me."

"Is that what brings you to me?" Aton asked.

"Tell me!" Kez exclaimed angrily.

Aton nodded. Gaining his feet, he summoned that strange deep voice to say, "I have been to where all men go but from where few return."

Kez stepped back.

"You know then where I have been?" Aton asked.

111

Kez's eyes went to slits. "No man," he said in a low harsh voice, "has ever returned from there."

"I have."

"You would have me believe——"

"I do not care what you believe," Aton told him. "You asked what Besop would have told you before I stopped him. That was what he would have told you, Kez."

"How did he know?"

With a brusque movement of his hand Aton set his question aside and said, "Besop was a man, even as you are, Kez, but I am *a man amongst men*."

With a howl of rage Kez drove his fist into Aton's belly, doubling him up, and then smashed him in the jaw with his knee. Aton dropped to the ground. Blood filled his mouth and dripped from his nose.

"Tomorrow," Kez said, looking down at him, "we will see if you can make the same journey again."

With the coming of first light the shouts of the guards sounded over the camp.

On waking, Kez's men went to feed and water their horses. Then they returned to the fire to eat and drink themselves. When they finished Kez told his men, "Today we will not ride alone. Today we will have with us he who claims to be *a man amongst men*." He ordered Aton to be taken from the line of captives and brought before him. Kez said mockingly, "Since your spirit has already made the journey, Aton, and knows the way back, it should have no difficulty finding your body should the two become separated again."

"It would be easier to kill me here and now."

"That is not my pleasure," Kez answered sharply. "It was you who claimed to have done what few men have ever done."

"I have been there, Kez," Aton said stubbornly.

"Then you will make the journey again."

"Why?"

"Because," Kez told him, "you are a slave and a slave does what he is told to do."

"And am I to have nothing with which I will be able to defend myself?" Aton asked.

"You will ride unfettered, but should you attempt to escape, one of my men will stop you even if it means starting you on your journey to the land of the dead, where the spirits live."

A black horse was brought for Aton and he mounted it. This was his second experience on the back of such an animal. From watching the way Kez's men rode, he knew that the horse was guided by pulling on the reins to the right, to the left, and that by kicking the animal's flanks with his feet it would begin to run.

When Kez and his men were mounted, Kez raised his metal sword and called to his men to follow him. The sun had already climbed out of the dark insides of the mountains that lay to the east.

The riders moved in two columns. Aton rode in the middle of one of them. The riders did not speak and, except for the sounds of the horses, the land over which they traveled was very still.

There were low, brown hills to the right. To the left was a heavily wooded area, but where they rode the grass was parched.

As the sun rose higher the sky became intensely blue. The horses continually switched their tails to brush away the hordes of flies that plagued them in the heat.

Now and then Aton looked toward the woods but they were always too far away from where the columns were for him to attempt an escape. Aton was sure that some arrow or spear would bring him down and, though he had been down under once, he did not know if he could escape from there again. He could not be sure his mother would be able to help him as she had before.

Kez swung the columns off toward the hills, and the

men began to heft their spears. They spoke in low voices now, boasting of the captives they would take or the women they would rape.

In the past, when Aton had been part of Nempie's raiding parties, he had said many of the same things that Kez's men now said. But as he listened to them, their words sounded like those of children. He did not know why this was so but he knew it was. Perhaps they were frightened?

The riders crested a small hill. The jesting and boasting ceased. The men's chests began to heave. Aton wondered if he would ever again see the sun rise above the mountains.

Below them lay the camp. Though it was larger than either Nempie's or Besop's, its shelters were no different from any Aton had seen before. They were no more than boughs set in a circle, bent over, lashed together, and covered with skins instead of a matting of rushes as those of his father's camp. In the center of the camp were two huge stones on trunks of trees that faced each other. Even from where Aton stood, he could see that one looked like a man with his organ erect; the other was a woman with large breasts and her thighs spread wide.

Kez ordered some of his riders to leave the main column and attack the camp from its flanks. Then he called to Aton, telling him as he rode up, "I want you to ride close to me. I want to see, with my own eyes, what happens to you."

As they waited for the other riders to gain their positions, the horses snorted and nervously pawed the ground in anticipation of the attack. The riders patted the necks of their mounts and, bending low over them, spoke in caressing tones in order to steady them. Aton's animal neighed softly.

"You seem to have a way with your mount," Kez said.

Aton shrugged and, scanning the camp, told Kez, "They know we are here."

Kez nodded and said, "They have known for several days that we were coming. These people are hunters, even as you yourself once were." There was an unmistakable note of respect in his voice.

"Then you will not take many captives," Aton said.

"What we take," Kez replied, "will be enough."

Neither one of them spoke as the other riders moved on to the flanks of the camp.

"Soon," Kez said, preparing to lift his sword.

Aton sucked in his breath. Never before had he gone into a fight completely unarmed. He glanced up at the blue sky. Already the dark wings of the vultures cast shadows over the camp. The possibility that he might die made his heart race and took the wetness from his lips and throat.

Suddenly Kez shouted, "Ayah! Ayah! Ayah!" And wildly waving his sword above his head, he charged down the slope toward the camp.

Aton's mount raced forward, too.

The hillside trembled from the pounding hoofs; the stillness was slashed over and over again by the cries of Kez's men.

Caught up in the thundering charge, Aton shouted the blood cry of his people.

But even as they raced toward the camp, a flight of arrows met them. Screaming in agony, several riders pitched from their horses.

The air thickened with arrows. They hissed, passed Aton, and found another target or dropped into the earth.

Kez and his men rushed down at the camp.

The storm of arrows lessened.

The attackers breached the first line of men, spearing them as they entered the camp. Immediately arrows flew from the sides.

Then the women came at them, seeming to leap up

from the ground. They fought with the ferocity of the men. Some grabbed hold of a spear's shaft and, dragging the rider from his horse, managed to drive the man's own weapon into him. Others hurled themselves on a man to thrust a knife in his back or stomach. They fought bare-breasted, and many of them were so smeared with fresh blood that their nipples glistened red.

The air filled with the screams of the wounded and the dying. Even the horses added their high-pitched neighing to the tumult as some took an arrow or the thrust of a spear. And some riders made their mounts rear up on their hind legs and with their front ones flailing, smash the heads of those who tried to unhorse them.

Kez's men made it through the camp, wheeled around, and were met with another shower of arrows. Those from the flanks were already firing the shelters. The stink of burning skin filled the air. Many more of Kez's men fell.

Aton's blood pounded in his ears. Weaponless, he smashed his fist into the faces and bodies of those who rushed at him.

The riders began to drive some of the people before them. Whenever they had three or four they dropped ropes over them.

The men of the camp reformed and, hemming Kez and his men into a small area of the camp, fought to recapture their own people.

Kez and several of his best riders drove the attackers back. His sword cut through anything it struck. Stone killing knives splintered on it. Spear shafts were severed by a single stroke, and it chopped its way through the arms and heads of those men who came within its reach.

Close to Kez's side, Aton rode with the attackers. And though arrows were loosed at him, not one found its mark. Spears flew harmlessly past him. He did not question why he was not struck down but he soon realized he would not be.

Kez saw Aton and marveled that no weapon touched him. As he realized Aton had not been scratched, he found it necessary for him and his men to fight their way out of the camp.

When they were finally free of it they took with them several men and women.

The camp defenders ran after Kez and his riders, forcing them to charge over and over again. Until the sun hung low over the pit at the edge of the great desert to the west, they fought a running battle with the defenders of the camp.

Kez lost more of his men. Those left were so filled with lust for blood that they killed the wounded captives, spearing them over and over again. When they finished with the killing, they fell upon the remaining women. Often two men used one woman, one entering her slit, the other her bunghole. Some of the women screamed until their voices gave out, while others bled so much they would have to be abandoned and left to die.

Aton watched what was happening and when most of the men were with the women, he grabbed a spear and, wheeling his mount around, galloped toward the oncoming night.

"Stop him!" Kez shouted.

Immediately several of the men tossed the women from them and, leaping on to their mounts, galloped after Aton.

Kez, wet with sweat and stained with blood, joined the chase.

Aton rode his mount as hard as he could. To him it seemed as if the animal's hoofs never touched the ground, but he heard the sound of their pounding on the hard earth above the booming of his own heart. His mount was wet with sweat and foam flecked from his mouth. Aton felt its great body heave for air even as he himself swallowed great draughts of it.

"I want him alive," Kez shouted. "I want Aton alive!"

Aton raced on, hoping that he would vanish into the oncoming darkness. But his pursuers were close behind.

He glanced over his shoulder.

One was almost beside him.

Aton let his mount slow somewhat. When the rider was almost abreast of him, he drove the spear into him.

The rider screamed and dropped from his horse.

The second rider did not make the same mistake. He hung back, and when Kez came up he threw a rope to him and the two of them raced forward, each holding an end of the rope. They swept down on Aton and, using the rope, stretched it between them and tumbled him from his horse. With a few quick loops of the rope around his body, they bound him and Kez dragged Aton back.

11

TORN FROM HIS MOUNT, Aton tumbled into the on-coming darkness where a roaring wind smashed him against the earth over and over again.

He struggled to grab hold of a rock, a blade of grass, a handful of dust, but everything was ripped from his grasp, even the light from his eyes. Whirling out of the darkness into which Aton plunged came Pula, the black boar; the mocking face of Nempie; the image of Gens in his death throes; the soft warmth of Rika's nearness; and the cries of Besop. His legs flailed the air and blood stained the ground under him. Images of the women he had mounted, the faces of the men he had killed—all that had been his life—rose up out of the darkness. In the blackness of his head they were strangely luminous. All the parts of his life whirled around like wind-gusted dried leaves.

In the roaring sound of the wind Aton heard his own muted scream of agony. Never before had he endured such pain. It streaked through him, tore savagely at his limbs and crashed down on his head with the roar of thunder. It splashed the insides of his skull against white-hot stone.

Again and again Pula, the black boar, rose before Aton. Only when his pain became exquisite pleasure could the two speak.

Pula said, "You will know more than this, Aton, before you become what you must become."

"End my pain, Pula!" he cried out.

"The stone gives you shape," Pula answered, and he whirled away into the blackness.

Aton followed after him until he was once again standing in the rushes that grew along the river bank not far from the grove of willows. Aton sucked in his breath, knowing that what had happened would again happen. Snorting Pula walked slowly out of the grove.

He was immense. His back touched the sky and he was blacker than the darkness of night.

Aton drew his bow.

Pula stopped, pawed the earth, and said "Know, Aton, that when you slew me, you gave me life. I was here for you to slay as you were here to slay me."

"I do not understand," Aton told him.

"We must do, Aton, what we have done before."

Aton drew his bow and as Pula, the black boar, charged down on him he loosed an arrow. Aton slew Pula, taking from him his thrice-circled, spear-pointed tusks to wear on his arms for all to know that he was the slayer of Pula, the black boar.

Suddenly the darkness was filled with stinging cold.

The roaring of the wind ceased altogether, leaving behind it only the murmuring of many voices.

Another flood of stinging coldness splashed over him!

Aton opened his eyes.

There were many strange faces peering down at him. Above them the night sky was spread out.

He tried to move, but the pain forced a groan from his lips and blurred his vision.

A man said, "Give him water."

Aton felt the end of a water skin pushed into his mouth. He drank and then began to cough. Pain tore at him, but he turned his head away, letting the water run over him. He held the cry of agony deep in his throat.

"He wears thrice-circled tusks on his arms," a woman said.

"Pula," Aton gasped, "I took them from Pula, the black boar."

The woman gathered him into her arms.

"I will become what I must become," Aton said, feeling the softness of the woman's bare breasts against his face. "I am a man amongst men. I have been shaped by pain. Shaped by pain."

"He raves," the man said.

"Yes," the woman answered, "he raves."

Most of the night was gone before Kez brought his new captives to where Besop's people had been staked down the previous afternoon.

The few men left to guard the prisoners had spent their energies raping the women. When Kez entered the camp he found his men asleep.

"Bring those men here," Kez shouted angrily as he dismounted. For his men to have enjoyed themselves with the women did not bother him, but he was angry that they had left the camp unguarded. No matter what the circumstances, his men always had to be ready to fight and die. They knew this.

His riders brought the men before Kez. All were young and for some this had been their first raid.

They had fought well against Besop's people, but they were not hard to fight. They were more like women than men.

As Kez looked at the men, his eyes moved from them to where Aton sat. Though bruised and battered, the man had been able to keep pace with the other captives. More remarkable, he had not been killed. The arrows and the spears loosed at him had found other marks or had been carried away by a sudden wind. In the rage of the battle Aton had fought; using only his hands and feet, he had fought bravely. His attempt to escape had been as daring as any Kez had seen.

Kez sighed wearily. Sooner or later he would have to kill Aton, and he reluctantly admitted to himself that Bal had probably spoken wisely when he had said, "That man will never be a good slave."

But Kez had seen the hardest of men gentled by the whip. They had been wild horses when they had been taken but like such animals they, too, had been broken.

He moved his eyes back to the men standing before him and said, "I would kill you if that would teach you anything. But the killing ends this life and it is here that you must be taught a lesson that you will never forget. These prisoners," he said gesturing toward the captives, "were given into your care, but you did not care for them. You cared only for your own pleasure."

The men dropped to their knees and pleaded to Kez to forgive them.

"I would geld you as I did Besop's sons," Kez told them, "but that would make women out of you that only a few men could find pleasure with. No, I want you to be able to mount a woman still. I want you to remember what you did for the rest of your lives. You will be slaves. Slaves until your spirit separates from your body. Tie them into the column with the other captives," Kez said, and then added, "to be sure they will never forget why they were made slaves, I will burn out the right eye of each of them."

The men screamed and tried to break away from those who held them. But Kez took a smoldering piece of wood from the fire and, moving from man to man, plunged the burning tip into the right eye of each of the men.

The screams of the afflicted cut through the night. Soon their shrieking was like the wailing of the wind.

The men were soon tied into the columns with the other slaves. The one called Tumi was placed in front of Aton, who was not fully aware of what had happened.

As soon as Kez's men were finished with their mounts, they gathered close to the fire, where Kez sat and broodingly looked at the flames. This past raid had claimed more men than he had thought it would. And he had not taken many prisoners.

He drank some warm mare's milk, and while chewing on a piece of dried beef, he found himself again looking at Aton. He grudgingly admired the man and wished that some of his own men would be like him.

One by one the riders drifted away from the fire and went to their sleeping skins, leaving Kez alone. Though he was very tired, he was reluctant to leave the warmth of the fire. Drawing up his legs, he placed his arms around his knees and then rested his head on them.

Kez closed his eyes but he did not sleep. When he returned to his camp he would have to contend with the anger of the fathers of the men he had enslaved. Some would accept what he had done, knowing that if he had acted any other way the strength of the people would have been lessened. Others would hate him but would keep silent. And one or two might attempt to wrest his sword from him. These he must kill. Kez shrugged. He had killed so many that to kill one, two, or even three more meant no more to him than swatting flies.

Kez shifted his weight and, opening his eyes, looked at the fire. It was lower than it had been, but it was still warm enough for him to want to remain near it.

The low moans of the blinded men drifted over the camp. He had given them their lives, though he did not expect them to live very long as slaves.

Again Kez lowered his head to his knees. Soon the

waters of sleep began to rise around him, and with a sigh he whispered, "Though you claim to be *a man amongst men*, Aton, I am Kez, the leader of the Horse People." Then he slept until the coming of the first light, when the shouts of the guards wakened the camp.

Because the sky was covered with heavy gray clouds, Kez, and those with him, did not see the sun make its way out of the insides of the mountains that lay far to the east. Though the grayness of the predawn light grew brighter, it nonetheless remained gray.

Kez sniffed the air. It had the smell of rain in it. He ate hurriedly and urged his men to do the same.

Each of the captives was given a piece of dried meat and told that there would be nothing more until their next camp was made.

Before the march began, Kez rode up and down the length of the two columns of captives and, stopping in front of Aton, shouted for all to hear, "Anyone who cannot keep the pace today or any other day will be killed." And he looked questioningly at Aton. Pointing his sword at him, Kez said, "I do not mean to be slowed by this one either." Then he galloped to his place in front of the columns.

Kez quickened the pace until the captives were forced to trot. Before long Besop's three sons were cut from the line and killed. Then a woman stumbled and turned her ankle. She was taken by two guards, raped, and speared.

The land became hilly and the valleys between the hills were long and narrow. The steep slopes were difficult for the horses to climb with riders on them.

For the captives each slope was more formidable than the one before. Exhausted from their running, they were driven up the slopes with whips. Each back was bloodied by the lash. Each was blinded by his own sweat and each was tormented by hordes of flies with bloated green bodies. None faltered and Kez knew he had the best of the captives. The weaker ones had died off or been killed. Only the strong had managed to survive the rigors of the march.

The sting of the whip on Aton's back and the great draughts of air that he was forced to suck in drove the dark mists from his head.

The sky was very dark and the air heavy with the smell of rain. Aware now of the cut of the land, Aton quickly realized that Kez was afraid of being caught in a flash flood and was trying to outrun the oncoming storm to gain the safety of high ground.

Knowing that all of the captives would die if a sudden torrent of water rushed down on them, Aton shouted, "Come. Come. It is not for Kez that we must run but for ourselves." His voice boomed out above the whine of the whip and cries of its victims. "Faster," he called out. "Faster. Move faster!"

Tumi shouted back at him, "It is better to be dead than a slave. Better to be dead."

"It is better to live," Aton panted, catching a glimpse of the burned-out eye socket.

"Not for me," Tumi cried out. "Not for me."

"You are one," Aton told him, dimly remembering what had happened the previous evening, "but there are many here. Many who do not want to go below."

That Aton's voice could make the captives move faster than the whips of his men enraged Kez, and he shouted for his men to use their whips more harshly.

The threatening storm did not come. A sudden change in the wind, like a great unseen hand, held it off and turned it away.

When they finally reached high ground and Kez ordered a halt, it was night and the black sky was filled with star figures.

Aton dropped to the ground and tried in vain to raise some spittle in his throat. He stretched out on the ground and looked at the man in front of him. He was young and his beard was the color of dark honey.

"How are you called?" Aton asked, unable to remember the man's name.

"Tumi," the man gasped. "I am Tumi, son of Isso, the seer."

Aton nodded but could not speak again.

Soon a guard handed Aton a water bag. He drank greedily; the water slaked his thirst. A piece of bloody meat was thrown to him. He grabbed it from the air and tore into it with the ferocity of a beast devouring its kill.

When his hunger was satiated Aton said to Tumi, "Perhaps your father can help you——"

The man shook his head. "There is bad feeling between him and Kez," Tumi explained.

Aton did not press him any further but Tumi said, "One day I was to be a seer but now I will be nothing. I will be a slave until I die." His voice became choked. He was still young enough for tears to flow from the one eye Kez had left him.

Aton turned away and looked at the bare-breasted woman beside him.

"I did not think you would survive," she said, "until I heard you call out to us to move faster."

He looked at her questioningly.

"I am called Sinti," she said. "The man behind you is called Likia."

Aton glanced over his shoulder.

The man nodded. He was lean, muscular, and his beard was grizzled.

Aton moved his eyes back to the woman. Her hair was long and black. Her breasts were full and high. They were tipped with small budding nipples. Dried blood stains covered her. Like all of the women, she had been raped by Kez's men. Because she reminded him of Bisha, he suddenly found himself thinking of Gens.

Shaking his head, Aton spat over his shoulder to

drive the thoughts away. Gens had been a fool to have thought he could outsmart Nempie.

"And now where are you?" she asked with a smile.

"Back," he answered. "Back to where I watched a fool die."

She reached out and, touching his arm, said, "I am happy that you live, Aton."

"How do you know what I am called?"

"You told me," she answered, "when I held you in my arms."

"It was a kindness," Aton said.

"And what is that?" Sinti asked.

"There is no other way to call," Aton responded with a shrug.

"Then it has a name?"

"Yes."

Sinti laughed softly.

Aton laughed, too, because he liked the sound of her laughter and the way her bare breasts moved when she laughed. The fire had burned low. Only the guards were about when Aton reached for her. And though he could not mount her, she held his hand between her thighs, hard against the lips of her moist womanhood.

Kez slowed the pace of the march. His captives were too exhausted to continue the way they had when the smell of rain had been heavy in the air.

Now the sky was bright blue, with puffs of white clouds like sheep. The face of the land changed from the wrinkled skin of an old man to grass-covered open country where herds of animals grazed within spear-hurling distance of the moving column of captives.

With the coming of the sun each morning Aton saw the mountains to the east, out of whose belly the sun was born, lessen in size until in the distance they were no more than a gray smudge. He often wondered if he would be able to find his way back to Nempie's camp when he escaped. It would not be easy, but he would

127

go back and kill his father. He would become the leader of his people, Aton's people. Because of his hate for Nempie he would endure whatever happened to him. That hate was a source of strength hidden from the eyes of other men. Even Sinti, whose hand had made the fluid spurt from his organ, could not see it.

And though Sinti knew that he was not one of Besop's people, Aton did not speak of Nempie until one night when she asked him how Kez had captured him.

Aton did not answer immediately. He stared into the flames of the fire and in them he again saw his fight with Nempie.

"My father," he said, "left me for dead."

"Were you wounded?" she asked.

His eyes went to slits and, turning to her, he said, "We fought, Sinti. We fought because Nempie——"

"Nempie?"

And Likia asked, "You are his son?"

"I am his sworn enemy," Aton said," his voice hardening with anger. "I will kill him. Then the people will be known as Aton's people, even as they were known as Nempie's people." And he pounded his fist against the ground, breaking the slender backs of the grass blades that took his punishment.

"Your mother," Sinti questioned. "How was she called?"

"I do not know. Her spirit separated from her body shortly after she dropped me."

"And was she of your people?" Likia asked.

Aton faced him.

The man strained toward him, eager to know more.

"I was told she was taken in a raid," Aton said. "She fought beside——" He stopped. Suddenly he realized the meaning of his words.

"She was my daughter," Likia told him.

"Her name," whispered Sinti, "was Atin."

"Was it she who named me Aton?"

128

"Had she been a boy," Likia said, "she would have had your name."

"Then we are of the same blood?" Aton questioned, looking at Likia.

The man nodded.

Aton looked questioningly at Sinti. For a man to mount a woman with the same blood as his own was against the way his people lived.

"No," she answered. "My father is Arak and my mother was Lana, before one of Kez's men killed her."

And Likia said, "It is not the way of our people for the men to take women with the same blood as their own. It is a taboo."

"Taboo?"

"Something that must not be done because of the terrible results that would come to pass."

Aton nodded, and in a low voice he asked Likia to tell him something about his mother.

"She was gifted with the powers of divination," he said, "and when she was told that Nempie was close to our camp she foretold that she would be taken by him. She said she had seen it all come to pass in a dream."

"And did she say," Aton questioned, "that she saw anything else?"

"Only that from her would come a beginning," Likia told him. "But every woman has that power within her."

Aton remained silent. For fear that they would come to the same end as Besop, he said nothing about how he had met the spirit of his mother or even that she had told Nempie, *"I have brought forth a man amongst men, a man better than all others."* He turned toward the wavering light of the fire. That he had come to know about his mother in such a strange way made it seem that Kez had been guided to the camp of his mother's people for only that purpose, especially when Aton realized that Kez had lost many riders taking so few slaves. And Aton also thought about Nempie.

There must have been something very different in his relationship with Atin that he had allowed her to name him in a manner different from his father's relationship with anyone.

"Nempie," Likia said softly, "was not much older than you, Aton, when he and his men raided our camp. He was stronger than any man I had ever seen, so strong that with his bare hands he tore away the manhood of our people."

Frowning, Aton looked at him.

"It is the organ of the man and that of the woman," Likia explained, "that my people give homage to. Nothing can happen unless one is sheathed with the other. The slit of a woman is more than a place of pleasure for a man. It is the place from which new life emerges."

Aton shrugged and said, "I do not know about such things. My people do not think that way. We are hunters."

"As we are," Likia said. "But long ago we learned where the source of all strength lies."

"In the slit of a woman?" Aton questioned, hardly able to keep the sound of derision out of his voice.

"There and in the organ of the man."

Aton snorted disdainfully and turning back to look at the fire, said, "Perhaps what you say, Likia, is true for all other men, but my strength flows from a different source." And crossing his arms, Aton touched the thrice-circled, spear-pointed tusks that ringed his bare arms. "From these," he told his mother's father, "which I took from Pula, the black boar. And from my hate for Nempie do I gain my strength."

"And nothing else?" Likia questioned.

"It is better that you do not know," Aton responded.

Likia nodded and said, "I hope your strength, wherever it comes from, will sustain you in the days ahead."

"I will go back and kill Nempie," Aton answered.

"And that is all you want?"

"For me," Aton said, "that will be enough."

During the day, Tumi was taunted and beaten by the other riders until, amid the laughter of his former friends, he cried out in agonized frustration, shouting to be left alone. At night, curled up like a small boy, he whimpered himself to sleep.

Occasionally Tumi spoke to Aton. Whether it was on the march or at the fire, his voice was always a whisper, with which he bemoaned his lost place or exalted his father's.

Aton listened. At first he found himself disliking Tumi's complaining, but then he came to realize that Tumi was abused more than the other men who had been punished in the same manner.

Aton said nothing about his discovery to Tumi. Instead he thought about it and when he could not reach some understanding as to why Tumi should be treated one way while the men who were punished with him should be treated a different way, he was puzzled. The source of the difference, he was sure, lay with Kez, as did everything else that happened with the riders and the captives.

One night, after Tumi had fallen asleep, Aton mentioned his discovery to Likia.

"And why should that be?" Likia questioned.

Aton gestured across the low-burning fire to where Kez lay stretched out on his sleeping skin, but he did not speak.

"But why?" Likia asked.

Aton shook his head. For him to speak for a man like Kez would be as foolish as trying to stay the wind by holding up his hand. Many of the things Kez did enabled him to hold sway over his men. Other things he did gave him pleasure, though not in the way a man takes pleasure from a woman.

"Perhaps it is because Tumi calls it down on himself?" Likia suggested.

Aton shrugged.

"The stronger always abuse the weaker," Likia said, "and Tumi is by far the weakest of all Kez had punished."

"I do not know," Aton replied, "if that is answer enough for the way he has been treated."

The two men remained silent.

Eventually Aton drew away from Likia and moved as close as his bonds would permit to Sinti, whose body strained toward him. Though she made the fluid spurt from his organ he could not easily find sleep.

Aton watched the star figures move across the black sky and he listened to the breathing of those bound close to him. Then his eyelids became heavy, closed, and sleep took him.

The next day, before the sun was halfway through its journey, they came to a river and, fording it, enjoyed the touch of the cold, clear water against their bodies. They were like children and, forgetting their bonds, laughingly splashed one another. Even Kez laughed with delight.

Suddenly amid the boisterous play Likia screamed.

Aton whirled around.

A green snake had struck at Likia and was already making its way toward another captive.

Kez and his men shouted and used their whips on the captives.

The roiled water turned the serpent from its path and it came toward Aton. Its green, sinuous length flashed in the bright sunlight.

Despite the shouts and the whips, the captives seemed suddenly turned to stone. They could not move.

Kez and his men stopped and fell silent.

Likia was staggering. More than once he lost his footing and his head went below the surface of the water, only to suddenly bob up.

Aton and the snake dueled. The snake lunged at

Aton but he always managed to avoid its thrust. They circled each other. The snake could have satisfied its rage on others but Aton would not let it. As soon as it turned, he grabbed at it and, taking hold of its flashing green body, whipped it back toward himself.

Likia slipped under the water and did not come up.

The snake circled around Aton and suddenly made a lunge at him. But Aton avoided the serpent's attack and as the green body flashed by, he grabbed hold of it.

Holding the writhing thing above his head, Aton shouted, "Kez, use your sword. Cut it in two."

With a cry on his lips, the leader of the Horse People galloped forward and bringing his sword, stopped its movement before the blade touched the convulsed body of the snake.

"He is yours, Aton," Kez laughed. "He is yours." Then he ordered Likia to be cut from the line and the march resumed.

The snake struggled for its freedom but Aton held fast and slowly tightened his grip on the snake's twitching body.

The riders stayed far away from Aton, afraid that he might suddenly hurl the serpent at them; the captives, too, tried to keep some distance between themselves and him.

Aton's arms became weary and pain filled. They became numb, and it seemed as though his fingers would singly open of their own accord. Nevertheless he held fast.

"Aton," Kez called mockingly, "you are surely *a man amongst men.*"

And Aton, his voice dark with anger, answered, "Each of us, Kez, is what he is. *I am a beginning, even as I am a man amongst men.*"

In a fury Kez galloped back to where Aton was; raising his sword, with a tremendous stroke he drove it down. "Die now!" he shouted. "Die now, Aton!"

"No!" Sinti screamed. "No!"

Aton hurled the convulsed body of the snake at the sword and stayed its downward thrust.

The blade struck the twisting, muscular body, shivered in Kez's hand, and then sundered the serpent in two.

Aton lowered his arms. Looking at the enraged Kez, he remained silent, but Kez's eyes went to slits and gazed at Sinti.

That night after the long day's march Tumi asked in a whisper, "Why did you do it?"

Ever since it had happened, Aton had asked himself the same question

"No man who can flee," Tumi said, "chooses to stay and fight with a green one."

"The choice was his," Aton answered. "I only turned to frighten him away."

Tumi shook his head.

Later, after Tumi had been taken by sleep, Aton moved close to Sinti. He said, "I could do nothing to stop Likia's spirit from leaving his body. I would have had him live and tell me more about my mother."

"At least," she whispered, touching Aton's bearded face, "he is no longer a slave."

"I would have set him free," he said tightly. "He was my mother's father. I would not have left him a slave."

"But you are——"

"I will take Kez's sword, Sinti," he told her. "I will take it and gain his power."

"He will kill you, as he wanted to today."

"I will take his sword."

For awhile they were busy with each other's bodies and when it was over Sinti asked, "What did you mean when you said you are *a man amongst men?*"

"It is what I am," he answered.

"I would have you only as a woman can have a man," she told him passionately. "I would take you into my body before the leader of my people and say

134

those words that combine the spirit of the man with that of the woman. I would do that for you, Aton."

"In Kez's camp," he said, "I will mount you as a man mounts a woman."

"Yes," she sighed. "Yes, it must come to that."

The next morning before the day's march, Kez came up to Tumi, looked at him, and, without a word, walked away.

That day the riders beat Tumi more than before.

"Kez wants me to die," Tumi whispered to Aton as they sat before the fire. "He does not want me to reach the camp alive."

"But why would he want to kill you?"

"My father was against the raid," Tumi explained. "He foretold the death of many riders, some even by name. He warned Kez that he would not take many prisoners, but Kez laughed and said that he was not reading the signs correctly."

Aton nodded and wondered if Tumi's father had also foreseen his son's downfall. If he had he would have tried to persuade Kez not to go on the raid.

"There was bad feeling between them before," Tumi said. "But now it comes to Kez wanting me dead."

"But why?"

"To strike at my father," Tumi wept. "To bring his line to an end. I am his only son. His only child."

Aton understood. Nempie would have done the same thing and so would he.

"If this had not happened to me," Tumi complained, "I would have become a seer but now I will die. I will be beaten until I falter, and then I will be killed."

Aton remained silent.

With tears streaming out of his eye Tumi looked at Aton and whispered, "Kez is afraid of you. Yes, he is afraid of you. He was warned about you, Aton. He was warned, but he only laughed."

"Warned about me?" Aton asked, moving closer to the weeping man.

"I do not know any more. But it has something to do with those tusks on your arms. It was all foreseen."

"What else was foreseen?"

"Ask my father," Tumi said. "Ask Isso and he will tell you."

Aton looked toward Kez.

And Tumi whispered, "Ask him not to leave me for the vultures?"

Aton nodded.

Tumi drew away and lay down. Curling up, he sobbed until sleep came to him.

By the following afternoon the land changed again, becoming bare and rocky. The two columns of captives threaded their way through narrow, sun-scorched canyons whose many-hued walls rose high above them. The signs of game became few and water was rationed at the end of the march.

With the coming of darkness, it grew cold; but there was not enough wood to keep the fire going all night. By the first light the captives were shivering and numb.

"I will not last much longer," Tumi said. "Last night I saw myself dead."

Aton silently chewed a piece of dried meat.

The march began when the sun touched the top of the canyon and shortly the cold left them. It felt as if they walked through fire. The stone of the canyon was hot. Often the ground ahead looked as if it had turned to brown water.

One of the guards rose up beside Tumi and called to him. When he looked up the guard struck him across the face. The blow knocked Tumi to his knees.

"On your feet!" the guard shouted.

Aton moved forward and, reaching down, started to lift Tumi, but the guard crowded his mount close to Aton and forced him away. "On his own!" he shouted.

Kez came.

"He cannot keep the pace," the guard said, pointing to Tumi.

"Cut him out," Kez ordered.

"No, Kez," Tumi cried. "No, Kez, I can get to my feet." And he did, but the guard knocked him down again.

"Cut him out," Kez told the guard again. He wheeled around and began to trot to his place at the head of the columns. When he heard Aton call to him, he turned again and rode back.

"Do not leave him for the vultures," Aton said.

"They would not want him," Kez responded, looking at Tumi, who was being dragged away by the guard.

Even as Aton repeated what he had said, Tumi's death scream echoed and re-echoed through the canyon.

"Leave him," Kez shouted to his men as he galloped back to his place in front of the columns.

12

Numb with cold, Aton stared at the band of night sky that lay across the narrow opening at the top of the canyon. Few of the star figures were visible, but from the peculiar light up where the walls were chiseled out, Aton saw shadows and guessed that the moon was full and bright.

Since he had fought with Nempie, many full moons had come and gone. Perhaps as many fingers as he had on one hand?

The distance he had come was so great that the mountains were no longer even the gray smudge that stood in the east between the earth and sky. They were gone. He and all the captives traveled in a strange land.

Shaking his head, Aton stretched out and closed his eyes, hoping for sleep to quickly take him.

Sinti called softly to him.

He moved closer to her.

"What did you mean," she asked, "when you told Kez that you were *a beginning?*"

"I do not know. But my mother said that she would bring forth *a beginning*. When I spoke to Kez the words came the way I said them."

"To say that you are *a man amongst men,* that you are *a beginning*," Sinti said, "must make you the enemy of all men, especially those like Kez."

"I am not the enemy of all men," Aton answered.

"But by saying those things," she countered, "you make yourself different from all men."

"No man but me, Sinti, could have taken the tusks of Pula, the black boar. I do not understand why I should have been the one, but I was."

"And to what purpose?" she questioned. "To become a slave in Kez's camp?"

"I do not think so," he answered. "I do not think so."

"Kez hates you," Sinti told him. "It glows like fire in his eyes whenever he looks at you."

"Fear and hate," Aton whispered even lower, "often go hand in hand."

"What is it that you want, Aton?"

"I want his sword."

Sinti started to speak again but Aton reached under her covering for the tuft of hair, where her thighs began.

Opening herself to him, she said, "I do not understand your purpose, but if I could I would change it. I would make you more my slave than Kez's. I would —" Her words were lost in a low moan.

As she gave him pleasure Aton growled low in his throat, "I will be no one's slave. I am *a man amongst men, a beginning*."

"Yes," Sinti whispered. "Yes!"

Aton looked closely at her. In the glow of the meager fire he saw tears glisten on her cheeks. Brushing them away he said softly, "I do not understand all of the things that have happened to me."

"And you are not afraid of what lies ahead?"

"No," he answered. "I must do what I was chosen to do, Sinti."

"And are you certain that you were chosen?"

"I am certain," he said, knowing that blindly he had come to understanding.

"And tell me, Aton, what were you chosen to do?"

"I cannot answer that," he said. "I can only tell you that I was chosen."

"Perhaps to die before you live?" she suggested.

"I have already died so that I could live." And before she could further question him, he said, "Do not ask any more, but know that I have been to the world below and have come back. Now sleep. Sleep."

"Does Kez know?" she asked.

"Yes."

"You have said more than enough to make him hate you."

"Sleep now," he urged her.

"Aton, I am afraid," she said.

He reached out and slowly stroked her until sleep took her, then he looked up at the night sky and let his spirit wander to the top of the canyon where the moonlight was bright.

13

THE LAST DAY in the canyon was the worst. The captives were not given any water, and the air was so hot that it became painful for them to breathe. Kez did not slow his pace.

He shouted, "Soon we will be out of this place." And he ordered his men to use their whips to make sure that none of the captives slowed the march.

In the late afternoon a sudden breeze moved over the two lines of prisoners. They looked at each other and without speaking they began to run toward it. As they ran, the breeze became stronger and stronger.

Each one took great gulps of the cool air. They ran until finally they gained the opening to the canyon where they stopped, too exhausted to continue.

Far before them the land sloped down to a long, open expanse of grassland where herds of horses grazed. Off to the right lay the glistening band of a river and up on the bank, beneath towering rock cliffs, lay Kez's camp, the home of the Horse People.

Aton could see the smoke from many cooking fires. The camp was so large that he could not reckon its size.

"We will be there before nightfall," Kez said, ordering them to head directly for the river.

Aton saw that the camp was well protected. Already there were several riders coming toward them from the camp. To the left, where the land was very flat and seemed to be the place on which the sky rested, riders guarded the camp.

Kez dropped back along the columns until he was abreast of Aton. Then he said, pointing with his sword toward his camp, "There you will learn to be a proper slave."

Aton said nothing.

Kez pointed back from the direction from which they had just come and said, "That way lies death, Aton. You will never find your way out of there. Even some of my men lose their way in those narrow canyons. And from there," he explained, pointing his sword at the cliffs above the camp, "you could not escape. Others have tried and have fallen to their deaths or made excellent targets for my bowmen. Out that way, where the earth and sky come together, my riders would stop you."

Aton remained silent.

"And what is your answer to what I have told you?" Kez asked.

Aton made a sweeping gesture with his hand and said, "Then I must stay until I leave."

Kez made his mount rear and, forcing Aton back, roared with laughter. As soon as he wheeled away from Aton the roar of laughter died in his throat. If Aton was the stranger of prophesy, he would have expected him to come in some way other than as a slave; he would have expected him to be a leader of a people like himself; he would have expected him to be worthy of killing, of proving to his people that he would be their leader until someone took the sword from him.

Glancing back at Aton, Kez chuckled to himself. Strong as Aton was, he was, regardless of his strange claims to be *a man amongst men*, to be *a beginning*, or to have made the journey to and from the world below, no more than the other captives—and they were all slaves.

Kez took his place at the head of the columns and, at a walk, led them down to the river.

The western sky, where the great desert lay, began to bleed when the first shadows of twilight came over the land, bathing it in blood.

Aton remembered this was a good omen to Kez. As he moved with the other captives to the bank of the river, he wondered how many more strange notions he would come to know in the days ahead.

And would they be any stranger than those of his own people, whose fear of spirits prevented them from moving at night without a lighted torch?

He glanced at Sinti, whose people seemed to think that the source of all power lived in the organ of a man and the slit of a woman. Yet that foolishness did not prevent them from being great hunters. They fought well enough to beat off Kez's attack and follow him for a distance.

Since he told Sinti that he had been chosen, Aton found himself wondering who chose him?

His mother?

From what she had said to Likia and Nempie, it would have seemed so.

But why would she have been the one woman to bring forth a son who would be *a man amongst men, a beginning*?

And who had chosen her?

Surely not Nempie. Had he known, when she spoke

them, the true meaning of her words, he would not have hesitated to kill her child.

Aton shook his head. And as he stepped into the cold river, quit thinking about who had chosen him.

When he reached the opposite bank he lifted his eyes to scan the high rock cliffs above the camp of the Horse People.

Much of the face was gouged, as if a huge claw had been scraped against it. There were enough ledges and crevices to make climbing easy, though as Kez had told him, the top of the cliffs were very high.

As Aton moved his eyes across the face of the wall again he suddenly realized that some of the ledges had been cut out of the rock, while others were part of it. Those cut out were straighter than the others and along each of them were one or more cave openings.

He knew that some people lived in caves. When Aton was a boy, Nempie had taken all his people to a place several days' journey from the river. After a bloody fight with the people who lived in the caves, Nempie told his people that they would live in them until the sun came back again and the days grew warmer.

All but the captives had fled from their cave dwellings. The women captives were given to the men who had asked for them, although Nempie had no liking for women who had lived in the caves.

Aton's eyes went from the caves to the campsite. Was it possible that the Horse People once had lived in caves?

He looked at the nearby riders. They rode as if they were one with their mounts. He was sure that they were not cave people. His eyes moved back to the caves.

As Aton looked at the caves, the riders who had left the camp were thundering down on the columns of captives. Their shouting brought a response from Kez's riders, some of whom galloped toward the oncoming riders only to be called back by Kez, who ordered the columns halted.

As the men from the camp drew closer, they slowed their pace from a gallop to a trot and then a walk. They spoke with Kez, and he gestured back to the men and women he had captured. Then the men rode along the lines of prisoners.

To Aton they were not much different from the other riders, although they were older. All of them were lean and muscular and where there was no hair on their face, the skin was nut-brown.

When the men came to Aton, they stopped. One called to Kez, "Where did you take him?"

Kez said, "I found him. He is Aton, son of Nempie."

"He is a slave," the man said.

"That is what he must learn," Kez responded. "He claims to be *a man amongst men, a beginning.* But Grug will change his mind."

The man pointed to Pula's thrice-curved, spear-pointed tusks and asked, "Why was he allowed to keep them?"

"Because," Aton answered, "I took them from Pula, the black boar, when I slew him."

The man looked questioningly at Kez. Suddenly his foot shot out, but Aton saw it coming and, grabbing hold of it, pulled the man from his horse and sent him crashing down on the ground with such force that he struggled to regain his breath.

The other riders laughed as they crowded Aton back with their horses.

Kez waited until the fallen man was on his feet before he said, "So now you see something of the trouble I had, Arri. Like a wild horse, he needs breaking."

Arri remounted and, looking over the captives, sullenly commented, "For so few, Kez, many men have not returned."

"No one knows," Kez said looking straight at him, "who rides today and who will ride again. The men of the first camp we raided did not fight back. At the next camp both men and women fought."

Arri's brown eyes flicked over Aton again and he asked, "And this one here, did he fight you?"

"Many times."

"And you did not kill him?"

"It would be foolish to lose a good slave."

"He will not be a good slave, Kez. You are mistaken if you think you can tame him."

"Then say it is my pleasure that he lives," Kez said. "I will yet have him give me his tusks. I could take them, I know. But I would have him beg me to take them."

Suddenly Aton realized that Kez was different from Arri, and so were those who had come with him from the camp. Kez was more like Nempie than he was like Arri.

Aton looked at the riders who had been with Kez. Even the oldest was not yet old enough for the difference between him and Kez to be recognized. But now that Kez was in the company of men his own age or older, Aton knew that Kez's father could not have come from the camp of the Horse People. It was unlikely his mother had come from them. Kez must have come from another people. He must have been driven out of his father's camp.

More riders were coming from the camp.

"It is Isso," Arri said, "and several of his kinsmen. Where is Tumi?"

Kez did not answer and slowly eased his mount around to face Isso.

Isso came up at a gallop and abruptly reined in. He was a thin man, with a small head and very bright rat-like eyes that quickly scanned the faces of the men who had been on the raid.

"Tumi is dead," Kez told him.

Isso sucked in his breath. It made a whistling sound when he released it.

"He was asleep——"

"And for that he is dead!" Isso exclaimed shrilly.

"He was asleep, Isso, when he should have been awake guarding the camp," Kez explained, uttering each word slowly. "For that I enslaved him and burned out his right eye."

From Isso came a wordless scream of agony.

"And back there," Kez said, still speaking very slowly, "back there in those scorching canyons, he could not keep pace with the others. On my word he was killed."

One of Isso's kinsmen raised his spear and thrust it at Kez.

But Kez saw the movement and understood the man's intentions. His sword flashed through the air, covered the spear shaft, and with a forward thrust dug deep into the man's chest.

The wounded man's eyes went wide and his mouth fell open. Blood spurted out of it. Without a whimper he slid off the horse as Kez shook his sword free. The dead man dropped to the ground with a thud. Kez said to Isso, "Many men were lost. All fought bravely. There were others to whom I gave the same punishment. They are bound in with the captives. They did not slow the march. But Tumi——"

"He was my son," Isso shouted. "He was my only son!"

"And that one there," Kez said, pointing to the body, "is your kinsman. Had I not killed him, he would have killed me. Your son, Isso, was left for the vultures——"

Isso shouted, "It is not yet over between us, Kez. I will heap suffering on you as you have on me."

The others slung the body of their kinsman over the back of the horse, and Isso turned and galloped back toward the camp.

Arri motioned the men to return and said to Kez, "Isso will cause you more trouble than ever."

"If it is too much," Kez answered, "then I will kill him."

Arri nodded and rode after those who had been with him."

Kez turned and glared angrily at Aton. "Fool, do you think Arri or any of the Horse People know about Pula, the black boar? And if they knew, do you think they would care?"

"But you know, Kez, you know about Pula. You know because——"

Kez reared his horse. It flailed the air with its forelegs.

Falling back, Aton shouted, "You are not one of them, Kez. You are not one of them. You, like all the captives you brought here, are in a strange land."

"I am their leader!" Kez shouted, forcing his horse to follow Aton.

Aton leaped up and, grabbing hold of the rearing animal's muzzle, steadied him. "I have learned much about horses since I have been with you," Aton said.

"But not that you are a slave," Kez responded, easing his mount back.

"I am like you, Kez," Aton said.

Kez looked at him questioningly.

"I, too, am a leader of people."

"These here?" Kez pointed to the other captives. "Besop's men would not be worth much in a fight, and there are not many from the other camp——"

"A people," Aton told him.

"The slaves already here?"

"A people," Aton said again.

"I should have killed you, Aton, when I found you," Kez said, shaking his head. "I have heeded Bal's advice, but know this, Aton: I will not put one mistake on top of another. You will, as I told Arri, yet beg me to take the tusks of Pula, the black boar, from you. And when you do, it will be my pleasure to take them or refuse, to let you live or to kill you."

"You should have killed me," Aton answered, looking straight up at the leader of the Horse People.

Kez nodded, turned his mount away, and gave the order for the columns to move again.

Part IV

A SLAVE

14

THE DOGS BARKED at the captives and snapped at their legs as they followed Kez and his riders into the camp, which was even larger than Aton had suspected when he viewed it from a distance.

There were many, many round shelters. They were larger than those in Nempie's camp or any of the camps Aton had seen. They were covered with horsehide; each one had its own fire pit.

The people stopped whatever they were doing and moved along with the captives to the center of the camp, around which, and illuminated by the light from torches, were several posts, each topped with the skull of a horse.

The faces and bodies of the people were touched by the wavering light, where they stood beyond the circle of posts. They were silent.

Kez raised his sword. Freshly stained with the blood of Isso's kinsman, the blade's burnished sheen had dulled to a dark reddish hue. As he rode around the circle, touching each of the skulls with his sword, Kez shouted, "These I have brought you, Earth Shaker. These men and women are slaves to you. They will do what must be done to keep your anger from us."

The people chorused, "To keep your anger from us."

Kez made the journey around the circle of skulls again and repeated the words.

The people responded, "To keep your anger from us."

Again Kez rode from skull to skull and repeated what he had said.

Again the people cried out, "To keep your anger from us."

Kez reined in and dismounted.

Arri entered the circle and in a strong voice he said, "You, Kez, and those who rode with you have done well."

The riders dismounted.

And Kez said, "The raid is over. We have returned to camp. The captives are now slaves."

The people beyond the circle began to shout and stamp their feet. A wooden drum boomed.

The families of the riders came into the circle and grouped around them. Several women came to Kez.

Suddenly above the tumult of rejoicing came the shrill cry of Isso, wailing for his dead son.

"Tonight," Kez told the captives, "your bonds will be cut and you will be taken to the other slaves." Then he called out, "Grug, come forward and take them."

A large man came into the circle. He was taller than anyone else and at least as broad as Kez. More remarkable than his size was the dried-grass color of his beard and hair.

"Tomorrow," Kez told Grug, "I will talk to you about them. Tonight feed them well, but do not beat them."

Grug laughed and said, "It is better to beat them

soon or they might think that they were something other than slaves."

Without answering Kez turned his attention to the women who had come to him.

Greg ordered the slaves to follow him. They moved through all the Kez's camp and around the bend of the river, where there was another long row of posts set into the soft earth. They, too, were torch-lit. Each was topped by a human skull. There were many skulls, some not yet picked clean by the crows, who would have come to them after the vultures.

Grug gestured toward the skulls and said, "It takes many days for a man or a woman to die on the stake. And after the vultures and the dogs have their way with the body all that is left is the head. Those heads belonged to slaves who were caught trying to escape, or who refused to work, or became to sick to live."

Not far from the row of skulls they came to the place where the other slaves were kept. It was a large area near the river. There were a few trees on one side upon the slope near the base of the cliff, but the soil was rocky. There were crude shelters, similar to those in Nempie's camp, scattered around.

None of the slaves already there stirred or bothered to look at those who had come to join them.

Grug cut the ropes binding the new captives and, pointing to a large fire pit where part of the carcass lay, asked, "Which one of you will cut the meat for the others?"

No one answered.

He repeated his question and added, "I will not do it, and none of the other slaves will do it."

Then a man said, "Let Aton do it."

"Yes," another agreed. "Let Aton do it."

The two voices became three, then the three swelled into many, with Sinti joining hers with the others for Aton to cut the meat.

"Aton," Grug questioned. "Which of you is Aton?"

"I am," Aton answered.

Grug nodded, and going to where the slave stood, drove his fist into the man's stomach without even looking at him.

Aton doubled up with pain. His vision blurred but he understood what Grug had done.

"Know by what you have just seen," Grug told them, "that you have nothing—not even one to cut your meat—unless I do it for you, or tell someone else to do it."

"I will cut their meat," Aton said, straightening up.

Grug whirled around ready to strike again.

But Aton caught Grug's fist in its flight and said, his voice rumbling with dark fury, "I will cut the meat!"

Almost at once the newcomers were surrounded by other slaves. Never had they seen anyone dare oppose Grug.

Grug struggled to free his hand.

"I will cut the meat!" Aton repeated, tightening his hold.

Grug nodded.

"Tell them!" Aton said.

Writhing with pain, Grug haltingly told them, "Aton will cut the meat."

Aton cut the meat and fed those who had made the long trek with him. Then he took Sinti by the hand and led her from the fire to a place where the trees grew on the slope beneath the rock face of the high cliffs. There on a bed of grass he removed her covering and mounted her.

She wrapped her naked thighs around him and, drawing his head down to her bare breasts, whispered, "This I would have done before the elders of my people, Aton, and before the great figures in the camp."

"The ways of your people," Aton told her, "are strange to me."

Sinti laughed and, arching her naked body against his, asked, "Is this strange to you?"

"I have not been with a woman———"

Sinti screamed.

Before Aton could move several pairs of hands tore him from Sinti's body. He fought to be free but ropes were quickly thrown over him and drawn tight. Breathing hard, but bound too securely to struggle any more, Aton saw Grug. Then his eyes went to Sinti. Naked, she was also bound.

Grug said, "You will die, Aton, for what you have done. A slave who opposes his master dies. Tomorrow when Kez comes, you will die, and when the dogs and vultures finish with your body I will take your head and mount it before my shelter."

"What will happen to the woman?" Aton asked.

"Kez will say," Grug answered.

Aton and Sinti were dragged from the slope of the hill back down to where the slaves were. When they came close to the shelters, Grug shouted, "Come see Aton. Everyone come and see Aton. See what happens to a slave when he opposes his master—and I am your master."

All the slaves came forth to watch.

When Grug reached his shelter he looked down at Aton and mockingly jeered, "Where is your strength now, Aton? I was told by others who came with you that you held the green death in your hands for most of the day. I was told that you fought with many of the riders and once even stayed Kez's hand when he tried to strike you with his sword. These things I was told and some even said that you have claimed to be *a man amongst men, a beginning*."

Aton said nothing.

"Tomorrow," Grug said, "when the spear is hammered into your body you will whimper and cry like a babe who has lost its mother's teat."

Aton remained silent.

With a snort of disdain Grug raised his whip and beat Aton until his chest and arms were red with blood. "Let no one bring him water," Grug warned the other slaves, "unless he is anxious to know my whip. Now go back to your shelters and think about what you have seen and what you will see tomorrow, when Kez orders the spear to be hammered into Aton's body." Then he went into his shelter.

Aton's body twitched. His throat and lips were dry, and though he heard Sinti whimpering, he could do nothing to assuage her fear. He looked up at the star figures but they quickly blurred.

The night became colder and Aton could not stop himself from trembling. Occasionally when he was able to forget that he was in pain or that he was cold, he thought about his coming death.

Would he, as Grug had said, cry out like a child?

Would he scream as Besop had screamed when Kez's men had planted him in the earth?

Aton shook his head and, closing his eyes, hoped that sleep would take him. The sound of Sinti's whimpering held sleep away from him.

Could he have gathered enough spittle in his mouth to wet his throat and speak, he would have told her that, if he could have, he would have taken her as his woman to live in his shelter. He would have said those words to please her.

Sleep finally did come and he let its black waters take him. Out of the luminous blackness came the spirit of his mother. She stood above him and, silently shaking her head, floated away. Besop came, too, writhing in agony at the end of the spear. When it seemed that Pula, the black boar, might emerge from the luminous darkness, the shouts of the guards drove sleep from Aton. He opened his eyes as the first light spread over the camp.

The fire was built up and Grug left his shelter to cut the meat for the slaves. "I would feed you, too, Aton,"

Grug called, "but it would only be a waste of good meat."

"Feed the woman!" Aton forced himself to shout.

Grug cut a piece of meat, picked up a small round object that was on a stone on the fire, and came to where Sinti was. He took the rope off her and gave her the meat; handing her the other object, he said, "It is slave food. The women make it from the grain."

Sinti moved her eyes to Aton.

He nodded.

She quickly devoured the meat but hesitated eating the other food.

Grug took it from her and said, "You will learn to eat it. Every slave does." And he returned to the fire. Sinti stayed close to Aton. "What will you do?" she asked in a whisper.

"Nothing," he answered.

Sinti stood up. Naked, she walked to Grug and, kneeling down in front of him, asked to be allowed to give Aton water.

"In exchange for what?" he asked, looking at the dark thatch of her womanhood.

"Whatever you want of me," she told him, spreading her bare thighs to arouse him.

"Give him water," Grug said.

"And slave food," Sinti added.

He looked at her questioningly.

"The women of my people are skilled in the ways of giving a man pleasure."

Grug nodded and said, "Bring him water and slave food."

Sinti took a gourd of water and a piece of slave food from one of the rocks in the fire and brought them to Aton. Then she lifted his head, gave him drink, and broke off pieces of slave food from the larger loaf.

Aton chewed on it and managed to swallow it, but to him the water was more vital than the slave food.

"You will be his woman," he said.

She did not answer.

And Aton told her, "I would have had you for my own woman."

"Though he uses me, Aton," she said, looking at Grug, "he will not ever know me."

As the memory of her body under his came like a sudden bloom into his skull, Aton turned his face from hers. His throat tightened and a mist came before his eyes.

As she reached out to touch him, Kez and several other riders came around the bend of the river. She drew back. Wide-eyed with fright Sinti ran to Grug. But he was already on his feet, coming toward her.

She threw herself on him and pleaded to him not to ask Kez for Aton's death.

"You have already spoken for all that you can give me," he said, pulling her off him.

"There are things that I can do for you that no woman has ever done for you," Sinti cried.

"You will do them," Grug answered, "no matter what happens to Aton." And he left the woman on her knees while he went to greet Kez.

The leader of the Horse People brought his mount to a halt. Looking down at Aton, he laughed and said, "I must assume that you and Grug have disagreed."

Grug quickly explained what had happened between the two.

Kez frowned.

"I took him while he was mounting that woman there," Grug said, pointing to Sinti, who was still on her knees.

Kez recognized Sinti and said, "On the march they were at each other, her hand drawing the liquid from his organ and his hand between her thighs, making her moan with pleasure."

"I ask for his death," Grug said.

Kez squinted down at the overseer, who was, after all, a slave himself, though because of his size and strength was used to subdue the other slaves. "And how would that help him to become a proper slave?" Kez asked.

"You yourself said," Grug reminded him, "that the punishment for opposing me is death."

"Yes," Kez agreed. "I did. But Aton is not like other men. He needs something more than his own death to make him understand that he is nothing more than a slave."

"No, Kez," Aton said.

Kez looked at him and, nodding, said, "I told you what would happen, but I did not think it would happen so soon."

"No, Kez!" Aton shouted.

Kez motioned toward Sinti.

He ordered her to be brought to him.

She leaped to her feet and tried to run but two of the horsemen with Kez rode after her and quickly dropped ropes over her.

"But why should she suffer for him?" Grug asked.

"Because it will make him suffer."

Aton strained against the bonds holding him. "Kez, she is guilty of nothing," he yelled.

The two riders brought Sinti back. Quickly thrown to the ground, her hands were pinned down by two slaves and her thighs were held wide by two other slaves.

One of the riders took his spear, and, by tying it to the bough of a slender sapling, lengthened its shaft.

"Kez," Aton shouted, "do not do it!"

"And why should I not do it?"

"Kez," Aton screamed. "I will give you what you want. I will give you the thrice-curved tusks of Pula, the black boar."

"I do not want them."

"Take them, Kez," Aton pleaded. "Take them but do not kill her."

"Oh, Aton," Sinti wailed. "Aton, oh Aton, do not give him your power!"

"Take them," Aton cried. "I beg you, Kez, take them. But do not hurt her."

"Are you begging me, Aton?" Kez asked.

"Yes. I beg you."

"Cut his bonds," Kez ordered. "Now, Aton, crawl on your knees to where I am."

Aton crawled.

"Now beg."

Aton begged.

"Give me the tusks," Kez told him.

Aton slipped the tusk off his left arm and handed it to Kez, who immediately put it on his own arm. Then Aton handed him the tusk from his other arm and Kez adorned his right arm with it.

"The power that these give to you, Aton," Kez told him, "is now mine."

"Let Sinti go," Aton said. "Let her go!"

"Release her," Kez ordered.

Aton turned and began to run toward her. But even as he ran a spear outdistanced him and, striking Sinti in the right breast, tumbled her backward. Aton stopped and, wheeling around, charged at Kez, only to be driven back by Kez's rearing mount.

Aton dropped to the ground and tears streamed from his eyes.

After Kez and his men rode off, Aton went to Sinti's still warm body and pulled the spear from it. He shook his head and lifted her into his arms. The slaves who had gathered to watch opened a way from him as he slowly walked toward the slope of the hill where he had taken Sinti the night before.

When he reached the place he set her body down and looked up into the blue sky. The black winged vultures already flew in slow circles over the slope.

Aton lowered his eyes and scooped out the earth

with his bare hands. He worked until the sun was low in the western sky. His hands bled but he did not stop until the opening was deep enough and long enough to hold Sinti's body. Then he set it down into the depression and covered it with earth. On top of the earth he placed many large rocks.

"Seek my mother," Aton said when he finished, "and tell her what has happened to her son. Tell her, Sinti, of all the woes that have befallen her son. Tell her that Kez now has my power. Tell her that I am not *a man amongst men*. I am not *a beginning*. I am as Besop had said—nothing more than dust. Tell her all that, Sinti."

Aton stood up, uttered a deep sigh, and slowly returned to the camp. None of the slaves looked at him, and he went directly to the fire, where Grug was cutting meat.

Aton waited but Grug did not offer him any meat. And when Aton asked for his food Grug answered, "To eat you must beg."

And Aton begged.

Grug threw him a piece of bloody meat and a loaf of slave food.

When he had finished eating Aton moved away from the fire. He found an abandoned shelter close to the slope below the face of the cliffs. He stretched out, looking at the sky through the opening in the roof. He wondered what a seer might see of his future in the stars?

"I must even beg for my food," he whispered and, turning on his side, he hoped that sleep would come to him soon.

The wind came up and he listened to it moan as it blew against the face of the rock cliff.

The waters of sleep began to swirl around Aton. He could still hear the moan of the wind but now there was a different sound to it, a voice that called to him by name over and over again.

Aton rose up and, leaving his shelter, went to Sinti. She waited for him.

"Oh Aton," she said, "I now know what your purpose is."

"Tell me."

"Find it, Aton, and you will know. Find it, Aton, and you will know."

"I have given away my power."

"What was yours, Aton," she told him, "will always be yours. You are *a man amongst men, a beginning. . . .*"

When he awoke at the coming of the first light, Aton was in his shelter, but he remembered what Sinti's spirit had told him.

15

As THE GRAY of first light rapidly brightened, Aton moved down from his shelter to the fire, where Grug was cutting meat and apportioning loaves of slave food.

Before Grug could speak Aton said, "I will have what is mine to have."

Grug looked up at Aton.

"If it must be now," Aton told him, "I am ready."

Grug hesitated.

Aton said, "I have already made my choice."

"I will cut meat for you," Grug told him.

Aton nodded. When Grug handed him the meat and slave food he devoured them rapidly. Then he looked up at Grug and said, "You choose wisely."

Grug did not anwer but, using his whip on all of the slaves, he drove them from the fire and into the fields where they toiled until the sun was low in the western sky.

In the following days Aton soon realized the men of

the Horse People did nothing other than hunt and ride. And the women of these people were always in their shelters to give the men pleasure.

The slaves did everything. They broke the soil, used planting sticks to make holes for the seeds, and cut the grain when it became ripe. They moved rocks, scraped horse skins, and carried water from the river to the shelters of their masters.

Even amongst themselves, the slaves were separated from each other by the kind of work they did. The lowliest were, like Aton, field workers. The most important were those who tamed the wild horses. Over all of them was Grug, the overseer.

The women slaves were often used by the men of the Horse People, especially the younger ones, who had not yet taken a woman into their shelter. The women died sooner than the men.

Some of the men soon became too weak to work. These Grug had impaled and when nothing more than their heads were left he mounted it on a post until, from the efforts of the vultures and the crows, it too became a skull.

At night, when the slaves returned from their labor, many were too exhausted to eat and crawled away to their shelters to sleep, often to die.

Aton survived. The heat, the thirst, the sting of Grug's whip meant nothing to him. Patiently he waited for the day when he would wrest Kez's sword from him and regain the tusks of Pula, the black boar.

There were also nights when everyone sat at the fire and listened to the slave, Dahsan, tell stories. Even Grug listened to the man who, when he spoke, could change his voice to make it sound like that of a woman, a child, or an old man.

Dahsan, Aton was told by another slave, came from a people who lived at the end of the river, where the land stopped and as far as a man could see there was water, even to the place where the sky touched earth.

Dahsan's people took their food from the water the way other peoples took it from the animals in the forest or on the plains.

Though Dahsan was a small, frail man with graying hair, he often worked in the fields beside Aton. When they rested in the blaze of the afternoon's heat, waiting for the women to bring the water bags to them, Dahsan always told a story that made Aton laugh.

After awhile they became friends, sharing not only their toil but also their meat and slave food. Dahsan seldom spoke about his life before he was taken into slavery, and when he did, it was always with a wave of his hand as if to dismiss what he was going to say before he said it. He was openly curious about Aton and Nempie's people. Aton told Dahsan about the fight between him and Nempie, and how someday he would go back to the camp beside the river, kill Nempie, and claim the people for his own.

"That is why," Aton told him, "I am *a man amongst men, a beginning*. That is my purpose."

But Dahsan laughed at these words and, slapping his thigh, shook his head and said, "There must be more to your purpose than that, Aton."

"That is enough for me," Aton responded.

"For you, perhaps. But there are others to satisfy."

"Who are they?"

"You know them better than I do," Dahsan replied.

Aton shook his head.

"You do," Dahsan answered. "You do."

Then one day while they waited for water, Aton looked toward the slope where he had put Sinti under the earth. His mound of earth and rock was clearly visible.

"You could not have stopped her death," Dahsan said in a low voice.

Aton moved his eyes from the distant mound to the face of his friend.

"Death," Dahsan said, "no matter how and when it comes, is no more than the dark side of Yahweh, as night is to day."

"I do not understand," Aton told his friend.

"All that we see, all that we are, belong to Him."

The woman came with the water, and after they drank they worked without speaking. Whenever Aton thought about what Dahsan had said he smiled. And when they left the field at the end of the day Aton would have asked his friend to tell him more about Yahweh, but Grug came to him and said, pointing to the camp where the Horse People lived, "Isso is waiting for you at the river."

Aton looked at him questioningly.

"I do not know what he wants," the overseer said. "But it is unwise to keep him waiting."

Aton nodded and walked toward the river.

"Run!" Grug shouted. "Run!"

Aton continued to walk, and when he reached the river he saw Isso standing in the shadow of a large rock.

"I was told," Isso said, "that you and my son were bound together in the line of march."

"Yes."

"I was also told that you tried to help my son."

Aton nodded.

"What were my son's last words?" Isso asked, leaning on a staff of wood.

Aton told him.

Isso sucked in his breath. His green eyes blazed with fury and he said, "But Kez left him for the vultures."

Aton nodded.

"I foresaw it all, Aton," Isso said in a quavering "Did Tumi tell you anything else?"

"To ask you what was foreseen."

voice. "Even to your coming." He pointed to the sky, where the star figures were beginning to show themselves. "There is where I saw it."

"And what do you see now, Isso?" Aton questioned.

Isso crossed his lips with his thin finger and whispered, "You are a beginning, Aton, you are a beginning." And he silently drifted away into the oncoming twilight.

Aton returned to the slaves. When he came to the fire he took his share of meat and slave food.

"What did Isso want?" Grug asked.

"Only to speak," Aton answered, thinking of Isso's words.

"Why to you?"

"Ask him," Aton responded with a shrug.

Grug leaped to his feet and, raising his whip, sent it hissing at Aton. "I asked you," he shouted. "And by the Earth Shaker himself, you will answer me."

Aton rolled away. But the hiss of the whip followed. Then suddenly he reached out and, catching hold of the rope, tore it from Grug's hand. He sprang to his feet.

Grug shouted for a club. A slave tossed him one and he drew closer and closer to Aton.

Suddenly Dahsan shouted, "Here, Aton!" and threw a stout stave to him.

Grug rushed at Dahsan. And before the story teller could run, Grug smashed his club over the man's head, dropping him to the ground.

With a low growl, Aton sprang at Grug, laying the stave across his back.

Grug fell to his knees, and as Aton came close, he rammed his club into Aton's stomach, sending him tumbling backward. Scrambling to his feet, Grug leaped on top of Aton and began to pound his head against the ground.

Aton struggled to break Grug's hold, but the man's hands were like the jaws of a ferocious animal. Aton sought Grug's eye and, jamming his finger into it, pulled it from its place.

Grug screamed with pain and let go of Aton's head.

Aton threw Grug off him. Leaping to his feet, he took up the club and brought it down again and again on Grug's head until nothing more than bloody pulp remained.

Breathing hard, he went to Dahsan.

"I go to where you have already been," his friend gasped, "but I shall not return. Forever I will dwell in the house of Set, the dark side of Yahweh. Aton, I am not afraid!" And then Dahsan's head lolled off to one side.

Announcing that Aton had killed Grug, one of the horse tamers ran from the place of the slaves to the camp of the Horse People.

Kez ran from his shelter. The slave saw him, dropped to his knees, and in a breathless voice told him, "They fought. Grug killed Dahsan, the story teller, and Aton killed Grug. He beat his head in."

As the slave spoke, the men of the Horse People gathered around him and Kez. Some had their spears and some only carried torches, whose wavering light cast a reddish hue over those nearby.

"I came here to warn you," the slave said, looking up at the leader of the Horse People.

"And did you or any of the others try to stop Aton?" Kez asked angrily. He had had his fill of Aton; he should have killed him.

The slave remained mute.

Kez nodded and then, thrusting his sword into the man's neck, shouted, "Then die, slave, as so many of the others will before this night is over."

The slave screamed and managed to pull away from the point of Kez's sword. A fountain of blood gushed from the wound and cascaded down his bare chest. "I came to warn——" he began and toppled forward as blood poured from his body.

"To the slaves," Kez shouted. "Burn all their shelters. Kill those who stand in your way. The women are yours. But do not kill Aton. I want him alive. I want him alive."

Brandishing his sword, Kez turned and ran to where the slaves were. Screaming their terrible blood cry, his men came after him. Soon blooms of fire burst forth in the darkness. Many of the slaves tried to run but were speared in their flight. Others were too frightened to move and let themselves be herded by Kez's men to the brained corpse of Grug. Even these were jabbed with spears until not one escaped a wound.

"I want Aton!" Kez shouted above the roar of the many fires and the screams of the women. "I want Aton!" But he could not find him among those slaves that his men had gathered near the fire. "You there," he said, pointing with his blood-stained sword at one of the slaves. "Come here."

The slave hesitated.

"Come here!" Kez screamed.

The slave came to him.

Kez struck off his right arm.

The man shrieked.

Kez hacked off his left arm and shouted, "I will do that to all of you, unless I am told where Aton is."

Someone called out, "He is on the slope, below the high cliff."

Kez looked at the bleeding slave and with a nod plunged his sword into the man's heart, killing him instantly. Then he turned and, gesturing to several of his men to follow, went for Aton.

Kez found him digging in the earth. Near him was the body of Dahsan, the story teller.

"Take him," Kez shouted, motioning his men forward.

Aton whirled around and, knowing that he could not fight all of them, let himself be taken.

"You will die," Kez told him. "I will have it done slowly."

Aton was dragged down to where the other slaves

were. There Kez ordered his men to make a cross-tree from the trunks of two saplings bound together at their centers. To this, with arms outstretched and legs spread wide, Aton was bound.

"I will let you watch what the vultures and the dogs do to Dahsan's body," Kez told him, "so that you will know what they will do to yours." He commanded several of the slaves to carry Aton to the slope of the hill, where they set him down against the face of the high cliffs. Then Kez said to everyone on the slope with him, "He who gives Aton food or water will be placed beside him, to die like him." Then turning to Aton, he informed him that he would come at the end of each day.

"And so will I!" Isso said, suddenly pressing forward from the throng.

"And I will, too!" Arri called out, also coming forward.

Kez was too surprised to speak.

"If he survives three days," Isso said, "he will live."

"He dies!" Kez roared.

"By your own hand, Kez," Isso told him. "You must kill him if he lives past three days and three nights."

"Long before you came to our people," Arri said, "that had been the way we followed."

"I never remember having heard that before," Kez responded.

"It was," Isso told him.

"It was," Arri echoed.

Kez shook his head. For him to have killed Isso would not have caused trouble, but killing Arri would arouse the ire of the people. Arri was almost as powerful as he was himself. As his power came from his sword, Arri's came from the horses. Of all the men in the camp, he was the only one who could show other men how to tame horses. And he was the one who sacrificed to the Earth Shaker.

"As you say," Kez said, "if Aton survives three days

and three nights, he lives." He purposely paused before adding, "Unless I kill him with my own hand."

Isso moved and passed Kez to stand in front of Aton. Crossing his lips with his finger, he said in a voice loud enough for only Aton to hear, "If you survive, Aton, Kez will not kill you."

Aton nodded and, looking down at all those who stood on the slope, he told them in his dark rumbling voice, *"I am a man amongst men. I am a beginning."*

The night passed slowly for Aton. From his strange perch he looked down on the glowing embers of the slaves' shelters, or up at the star figures that moved in measured paces across the vastness of the sky. Now and then the darkness was shredded by the piercing shrieks of a woman in the hands of Kez's men, or the breeze made a sighing sound as it tried to free itself from the limbs of the trees.

Once he looked down at Dahsan's body and said aloud, "We are closer than I had ever thought we would be and might be closer still if my spirit should separate from my body."

Aton shook his head and, closing his eyes, began to feel the gnawing pain devouring his shoulders. In an effort to ward it off he pulled his shoulders back and strained his muscles attempting to lift himself on his own hands. The exertion made him sweat. When he succeeded in moving himself the weight of his own body forced him to relinquish his small success. It became an effort to ease himself down since a sudden drop ended with a breathtaking wrenching pain.

The first light was heralded by the calls of guards about the camp. As the darkness thinned to gray the smoke from the smoldering shelters combined with the mist laying over the river. Soon the sun came up, its light first spreading over the far side of the river and then moving along the length of the valley as it rose fully above the rock cliffs.

Dogs from the Horse People's camp were loosed. Finding the scent of those who had been killed the previous night, they went in search of the bodies. Soon they discovered Dahsan's corpse. Several came at once. One was black, another was brown, and the third was gray. They bounded up the slope with their red tongues hanging out and their sharp white teeth flashing in the sun. They tore at Dahsan's body, mouthing chunks of his body until their muzzles and chests were red with blood. Other dogs came to devour Dahsan's body and soon their muzzles and chests, too, dripped blood.

The dogs tore into his entrails and pulled them over the ground. They stripped most of the flesh from the body. A few tried to leap up and sink their teeth into Aton's feet, but his shouts drove them away.

Before the sun had gone half its journey across the sky the remains of Dahsan began to stink. As the dogs, heavy with the man's flesh, moved off to sleep, the vultures fluttered down. Some immediately stuck their beaks into Dahsan's eyes, others peeled the flesh from his bones. More and more floated down until the upper part of the slope was covered with them and the air was filled with their sound. By late afternoon they had devoured the stench of rotting meat.

After the vultures moved away, the crows came, noisily telling each other of the meat they had found. Aton neither saw nor heard them. The blazing sun had made him cry out, "Give me water and I will give you Sinti's body, too. It lies there where I put it. Give me water!"

And when it seemed as if a fire raged in his skull, Kez came, called to him, and said, "Only Dahsan's bones remain. Here, look at his skull."

The skull was thrust in front of Aton's eyes; he turned his head away.

"Tomorrow," Kez told him, "I will come again."

Kez laughed. "I do not think he will last the three days, Isso. I do not think he will last."

Night came and Aton shivered from the cold touch of darkness. His body was numb but sometimes a sudden spasm of pain ran through him and he moaned in agony.

Another day came but Aton remained wrapped in night until the sun touched him. He opened his eyes and wept dry tears. The sun scorched him and dissolved everything into a red orb that hung somewhere deep in his skull. With each beat of his heart waves of pain surged through him.

When the sun was low Kez came and mocked him.

Aton listened and, shaking his head, croaked, "I am *a man amongst men, Kez. I am a beginning!*" And then darkness crashed over him. He fell into nothingness until the next day's sun returned and pulled him back to where he hung from the cross-tree.

As night fell over the land a sudden thunderstorm swept off the great plain. The clouds grew to mountains. From peak to peak long jagged streaks of lightning played. Rain fell over the land.

The water gushed over Aton and, like some withered tree drenched by the same rain, he felt the throb of life in him. He lifted his face and, opening his mouth, let the water find its way into his throat.

The storm moved up the valley. Lightning still jumped between the clouds; the boom of the thunder echoed up and down the valley even when the sky cleared overhead and the star figures became visible.

Aton closed his eyes and, though the glowing red orb was gone from his skull, he was wracked with fever and consumed with pain. He moaned and writhed on his cross-tree. Often he shouted his defiance at Nempie or called for his mother to end his ordeal. And finally when he could no longer stand it he opened his eyes and tried to pull himself free, only to scream in agony. He screamed until the blackness turned red and his voice gave out. His screams softened to a moan. When reduced to silence he looked down at Dahsan's bones.

In the darkness they glowed white.

One by one each of Dahsan's bones came together and, rising to its feet, the skeleton said, "You were chosen Aton, you were made *a man amongst men to be a beginning.* Yahweh gives and takes all, even that which Set takes to the Underworld is given by Yahweh. His is all!"

"Pula!" Aton shouted. "Pula, the black boar!"

The bones of Dahsan swayed to and fro. Raising their skeletal arm they said, "Call Him what you will. He is what He is and you are a part of Him, even as I am, though I will dwell in the dark house of Set forever."

"Pula!" Aton cried. "Pula, the black boar!"

"And in the end, Aton," the spirit of Dahsan said, "you will be the beginning."

"Pula," Aton screamed, "I want only to die!"

The bones dropped to the earth in a heap. Out of the darkness came blacker darkness that enfolded around Aton and blotted out the sky and the star figures in it.

And then what had already happened began to happen again: *Pula the black boar snorted and came walking out of the willow grove.*

Pula was darker than the darkness surrounding him and so large that his back touched the sky.

Aton sucked in his breath and drew his bow.

Pula stopped, pawed the earth, and with a snort said, "My tusks are His sign."

Aton raised his bow, drew it and as Pula the black boar charged down on him, he loosed an arrow. As he already had done, he slew Pula, taking from the beast his thrice-circled, spear-pointed tusks. Now all those who saw them on his arms would know that he, Aton, was a man amongst men, a beginning. . . .

"Tusks," Aton yelled. "Pula's tusks. They are mine, mine. A sign for all to see. A sign."

Neither day nor night existed for Aton. Often he saw himself, held in huge hands as he had once held the convulsed body of the snake. When this vision came, he waited for someone to come and end his agony with a stroke of the sword. By the end of the third day he hung limply from his fetters. All his strength was gone and from his cracked, dried lips came a sigh.

Below Aton, but unseen by him, Kez, Isso, and Arri watched him.

"He lives," Isso said, noting the movement of Aton's lips.

"It is now your choice, Kez," Arri told the leader of the Horse People, "whether he shall continue to live or whether—"

Kez moved away from his two companions. Raising his sword, he thrust it into Aton. "He is yours now, Isso." He pulled the bloody blade free. "Do with him what you like," he said as he rushed down the hill.

Together Isso and Arri cut Aton down.

"Will he live?" Arri asked.

Isso shrugged and said, "I will use all my skill to make him live."

"To your shelter or mine?"

"To yours," Isso said. "Kez fears you more than he does me."

16

ATON WAS SET DOWN close to the small fire in Arri's shelter. Isso stripped him of his skins and, taking a burning faggot from the fire, held it close to the slave's wound.

"It is not deep," he said, looking over his shoulder at Arri, who stood in the company of his women and children. "Kez was in too much of a hurry to—"

"Will he live?" Arri asked, anxiously.

"His youth and strength are in his favor," Isso answered. Turning away from Arri, he brought the fire-tipped faggot down to the wound.

Aton groaned and brought his legs up.

The stink of burning flesh quickly filled the confines of the shelter. Arri's women made soft gasping sounds while his children stayed close to the women. Eliti, the youngest of Arri's women, whispered, "Is he the slave who held the green death in his hands?"

"The same," Arri answered, watching Isso, who now washed all of Aton's body with hyssop.

"I must have some marjoram," Isso said.

"I will fetch it for you," Eliti told him.

"Ask Nanda for it," Isso said.

Eliti left the shelter and went on her errand.

And then Isso asked for some grain fermented water. Another of Arri's women brought him a small cruseful. Lifting Aton's head, he forced him to drink.

Aton coughed and moaned but swallowed some of the grain water.

"He must be fed only the marrow of bones for the next few days," Isso said.

"I will see to it," Arri answered.

Eliti returned and handed the marjoram to Isso. She looked down at Aton and saw his lean, hard body. That he was exceptionally strong was evidenced by the many stories she had heard about him—not only that he had held the great death in his hands for most of a day, or that he had killed Grug by knocking his brains out, but that he had said, even as Kez had him mounted on the cross-tree, that he was *a man amongst men, a beginning.* Never had she ever heard of any man who claimed that. To her he looked no different from any other man; even his organ was the same as Arri's.

Isso passed the marjoram under Aton's nose.

Aton jerked his head away.

The sudden movement brought a soft, sudden eruption of laughter from the children.

But Isso's equally sudden demand for silence abruptly stifled any sounds. Again he passed the herb under the slave's nose.

"His eyelids flutter," Isso said and, setting down the marjoram, he lifted the man's head in order to give him more grain water to drink.

Aton's vision was blurred. When he felt the cruse against his mouth he turned away. Whoever held it forced him to drink. Swallowing the liquid was painful but he managed to get some of it down; it was strangely warming to his insides.

Isso lowered his head and, again turning to Arri, said, "If there is a woman whose breasts are filled with milk he should also have that."

"I will suckle him," Eliti responded. "I have not yet finished weaning my baby, Tilo. There is enough milk for both."

"He must be kept warm," Isso said.

Another woman brought forth a horsehide and Isso placed it over the slave. Standing, he told Arri, "It would be wise to keep watch over him and should he become hot with fever, he must immediately be given a potion of rue and grain water. In the morning I will come and give him some fresh stallion blood to drink."

"Each of the women will watch over him," Arri answered.

Isso nodded and motioned Arri to follow him from the shelter.

Outside Isso said to Arri, "Let us walk to the river."

The two men did not speak until the sound of the flowing water was louder than their whispered conversation.

"He will be like a child for many days," Isso said. "Possibly for as long as the coming and going of a full moon."

"Are you sure—"

"He is the son of Nempie," Isso told him. "And Kez himself has often boasted that only someone from his own blood line could ever take the sword from him. It was all foretold. Aton is the stranger."

"But Kez must also know who he is," Arri said.

Isso nodded.

"Then why has he been unable to kill him?"

"He almost did."

"But you yourself said the wound was not deep," Arri responded.

"There are many influences on a man's life," Isso said. "Even I cannot know all of them. Kez and Aton are bound together, that I do know. And if Kez had truly wanted to kill him he would have thrust straight and deep into his bowels or his heart. But something caused him to strike off to the side and weaken his thrust. You were there. You saw it too."

Arri nodded.

"When he is strong enough," Isso said, "I will have him pass between the bare thighs of my woman and make him my son."

"He will still be a slave," Arri commented.

"Will you show him how to tame horses?" Isso asked.

"I will if that is what you want."

"It is."

"And what of Kez," Arri questioned. "What will he do when you take a slave of your son?"

"Mock me," Isso answered, "as he has mocked me in the past. But his praise would only anger me. All that I want from him is his death, and that he will not give me."

Arri chuckled.

"But some way I will goad them into a fight," Isso said. "Perhaps each will kill the other and then one of our men would wield the sword."

"Is that your hope?" Arri asked, somewhat surprised by Isso's revelation.

"My hope is," Isso answered, "for my people."

"And what if Aton should live?"

"He is young enough to need our help. He knows nothing of our ways. He would have much to learn."

"And you think he will let us teach him?" Arri asked.

"He will be my son," Isso said with a shrug.

"And what if Kez should kill him?"

"It has not been foretold that way," Isso said.

"But should it happen?"

"Then we will say that Kez is truly worthy of being our leader," Isso told him.

Again Arri chuckled.

The two men turned and left the river. They parted at the entrance to Arri's shelter without speaking again.

Arri entered the shelter. The fire was low. Except for Eliti, who held Aton's head to her breast, the other women and children were asleep.

"Does he take the milk?" Arri asked, standing over her.

"Yes. He sucks strongly," she answered, looking up at him.

"He is a man." Arri said, "not a small boy not yet weaned."

She moved Aton from one breast to the other.

"Do not let him have so much," Arri cautioned, "that there is not enough for your son."

"There is enough for both," she answered, lifting her hand and moving it through Aton's hair.

Watching her suckle Aton aroused Arri and he said, "Enough. He has had enough. Come lie with me."

Eliti set Aton's head down on the ground and went to Arri filled with an excitement she had never felt before.

In darkness Isso began to ascend the narrow ledges on the face of the rock cliffs above the camp. Many of the ledges were natural, some formed within Isso's memory when the Earth Shaker in his fury had smashed whole sections of the cliffs to dust. Other ledges had been hacked out of the living rock by countless slaves.

Though Isso knew his way, he moved cautiously, lest he lose his footing and plunge into the darkness of the valley below, where each shelter of the camp was marked by the red glow of night fires.

Sometimes he paused and looked up at the night sky. He saw that the star figures were dimmed by a thin white crescent moon. This was auspicious since the moon so closely resembled a bent bow. He would nock the arrow to it and aim it at Kez.

The thought of Kez made him gnash his teeth in anger, made his hands tremble, and tears flow from his eyes for his dead son Tumi. Wiping his eyes with the back of his hand, he continued his slow climb up the face of the cliff.

Isso moved along the ledges, where the entrances to the various caves looked like yawning mouths. Kez feared what was in those caverns and kept away from them except on the days when the black and white stallions were sacrificed to the Earth Shaker. That only happened on the night that was longer than all other nights and then again on the night that was shorter than all other nights.

Isso continued to climb, wedging himself into the great lateral cracks in order to gain the higher reaches of the cliff. Where he went only the ledges made by the Earth Shaker remained. Often Isso was forced to stop and regain his breath. Finally he reached his goal, a small opening that lay a short distance from the top of the cliff.

He stooped very low to enter the cave, where the darkness seemed heavier than the night outside. Unlike some caves lower on the face of the cliff, this one smelled of water. In its depths water trickled down the rocks and formed a small pool.

Several bats whirred in the air nearby. To keep them at a distance, Isso flailed his arms. He squatted down and, taking his fire tool, quickly set ablaze a nest of tinder.

When the tiny flames leaped up from the glowing embers, the lizards and rats scurried away, and the bats kept to the deep recesses of the cave.

Isso nursed the fire until the blaze was strong enough to be fed with more than twigs, though it was not yet ready to be given small faggots, all of which he had brought there earlier. The cave had nothing in it that could burn.

When the fire became more vigorous, Isso gave it

more wood to devour. Its wavering light grew brighter, revealing, close by, several small cruses and sticks whose ends had been frayed.

Isso nodded with satisfaction. For the past three nights, since Aton had been placed on the cross-tree by Kez, he had made the perilous climb up to the cave, bringing with him what he needed. Now that Aton had survived the sword wound, Isso would enlist the help of the Earth Shaker to let Aton live and avenge Tumi's death.

The fire burned brightly now, and the cave was warm enough to make Isso sweat. He started another fire against the side wall, which was flatter and smoother than the other.

The wall grew warm and then hot. Isso stamped out the fire and, dipping his hand into one of the cruses, quickly spread a white ground of crushed chalk and water over the surface of the rock. The heat of the fire dried the area quickly. Picking up one of the frayed sticks he dipped it into a pot of red dye and slowly made the figure of a man, while incanting, *"This is Kez, the leader of our people. This is Kez all covered with blood. Covered with the blood of Tumi my son, who would have served you as I have served you, oh Shaker of the Earth. . . ."*

Isso dipped into another cruse and drew a blue figure of a man and incanted, *"This is Tumi, whose spirit weeps in my ear because he was left to the vultures and the jackals. He cries to be left at rest but will not rest until Kez is dead, until Kez's spirit is separated from his body. . . ."*

Isso then dipped his stick into a third cruse filled with yellow ochre taken from the river bank and mixed with water. He drew a third picture of a man and incanted, *"This is Aton, a slave taken by Kez. He was the one to help Tumi and now I ask you to help him, oh Shaker of the Earth, help him live so that he may bring down Kez, separate his spirit from his body, and bring rest to my son, Tumi, who weeps in my ear at night. . . ."*

Isso then drew other figures. With each he incanted its relationship to the others. Arri was there, Grug, whom Aton had slain, and Isso's woman, with her thighs spread wide, to bear Aton.

"It is to you, oh Shaker of Earth, that I must turn," Isso wailed. *"To you to give Aton the strength to wrest Kez's sword from him. To you whose strength moves the earth and everything on it, allow Aton to borrow some small part of your power to bring Kez to his end and rest to my son. . . ."*

Isso set down his stick and looked at his work. The story was there, even to how Kez had blinded Tumi and then had him killed. It was there for the Earth Shaker to see and understand the grief of a father for his dead son.

Issa sat down and looked at the images he had painted. Then he stood up and going to the picture of Aton, placed a bow and arrow in his hands, with the arrow aimed directly at Kez.

As he crawled out of the cave the first light was already coming up over the rock cliffs and the guards were shouting to each other.

Isso glanced back at the cave. The remnants of the fire glowed red in its black interior.

Aton healed slowly. For days and nights his body was so wracked with pain that nothing else mattered. His memories of the past and his dim perceptions of Arri's shelter were destroyed by the agony he endured.

Isso's potions made him sleep. Though his spirit looked for Pula, the black boar, he could not be found; nor could he find the spirits of anyone he knew. The spirits of Besop, Sinti, and Dahsan eluded him.

Sometimes he opened his eyes, either when his head was held to enable him to be fed the marrow of bones recently made hot, or when he was cradled in Eliti's arms and suckled at her breasts. With her firm nipple between his lips and her warm milk flowing into his mouth, Aton was often aware of his nearness to a woman and even that he was at her breast.

The stronger this awareness became, the more Rika fluttered through the mist of pain that swirled through his skull. One day, when he was at Eliti's breast, his eyes fully opened and he found himself looking at a young woman with long black hair, very pale skin, and eyes the color of hazel nuts. It was the strange expression on her face that held his interest. There he saw deep satisfaction and desire mingled with the other.

Slowly he lifted his hand to the other breast.

Eliti looked down at him and in a whisper said, "If it is known that you are well enough to touch my other breast, both will be denied you."

He let his hand fall back to his side and asked, "Who are you?"

She gave him her name and added, "I am the youngest of Arri's women."

"How long have I . . . ?"

"Sucked at my teats?"

"Yes."

"Since the night Arri and Isso brought you here."

"And how long ago was that?"

"More than the passing of a full moon."

Aton nodded. All those days and nights were lost to him.

"You will still need more days of rest and food before you are strong enough to go out again."

Aton raised himself on his elbows and looked around. The shelter was empty. "This is Arri's shelter?" he asked.

"Yes."

He reached for her breast again and she leaned slightly forward to allow him to put it into his mouth. But as he began to suck it, his organ hardened.

"You are stronger than you think," she chided.

"That is only show," he said, taking her breast from his mouth. "I do not think I could mount a woman now."

She laughed and moved away from him.

He tried to follow her but the exertion made his breath come hard and brought flashes of pain to his body that blurred his vision. Exhausted, he dropped back on his pallet.

Aton's strength soon grew and he was able to hobble around, close to Arri's shelter, with the aid of a staff. He ate with the others of Arri's family and no longer had any need to be suckled by Eliti.

Almost every day Isso came to see him. Aton said, "I owe my life to you and to Arri."

"I would make you my son," Isso told him.

Aton laughed and said, "It is not something that you with all your power can do, Isso. I am the son of Nempie and was dropped by Atin."

They went almost as far as the river, since going the full distance was still beyond Aton's strength, before Isso said, "If you pass between the bare thighs of my woman you will be born again and be my son."

Aton stopped and putting his full weight on the wooden staff, said, "No man, Isso, is born again."

"It is a way to provide those who have no children with an heir."

"And would I still be a slave?"

"Yes, even as Tumi would have been."

"And my name——"

"It would remain the same," Isso told him.

"Then to what purpose?" But almost as soon as he had asked the question Aton knew the answer. "That way you undo what Kez has done."

Isso nodded.

"And I incur an even greater wrath than I had before against me?"

"Are you afraid of Kez now?"

"Not now, not then, and not in the future."

They began to walk toward Arri's shelter again. Isso said, "I have made it possible for you to fight him and win."

Aton shook his head. "I have heard those words before, Isso," he told the seer.

"My brother Gens said words similar to the ones you just spoke. Now his bones lay scattered in a camp that once stood in a long narrow valley. I myself will choose when to fight Kez. Now I would lose, even if I passed between the bare thighs of your woman to be reborn again as your son."

Isso did not answer. There was something very different about Aton, though he could not immediately understand what it was.

When they reached Arri's shelter Aton said, "Because you did not let me die on the cross-tree I will do what you ask and pass between your woman's thighs to become your son."

Isso smiled and said, "As soon as you are stronger I will make a big feast and let the whole camp come and witness your birth."

"If that is what would please you," Aton said, "then do it."

"It would please me greatly," Isso responded. He turned to go, but Aton reached out and taking hold of the seer's arm stayed his movement.

"Why this hate between you and Kez?" Aton asked.

Isso cast his deep-set eyes about and leaning close to Aton he said, "Kez is not one of us."

Aton nodded.

Isso wondered if Aton knew that he was a blood relation to Kez? But from the way the man was looking at him he guessed that Aton did not know and that all he wanted was an answer to his question.

"Kez came here," Isso said, "when my brother Caddi was leader of the Horse People. He came through those canyons there. No one knows how he found his way. He came with his metal sword and as is the custom challenged Caddi to a fight. Caddi knew that he could not win that fight if Kez fought him with his metal sword and so he refused to give Kez battle. Then Kez enraged the people by telling them that Caddi was a woman, was less than a woman, even less than a slave. The people became angry with my brother and tore him to pieces."

"And you saw," Aton asked, "that Kez came through those canyons?"

"He is really the only one here who can go through them. All of the other men become lost. It is easy to die in those canyons."

"I have seen many die in them," Aton said with a sigh. "Even your son, Isso, died in them."

"There are many here in the camp," Isso said in a choked voice, "who would like to see Kez dead."

"I will not do your killing, Isso, or theirs," Aton said. "But when I must, I will do my own killing. That is the way it must be."

Isso nodded. As he looked at Aton in the bright sunlight the man seemed to lift himself on his staff until he stood tall and straight, and said, "You are not the man who Kez had set on the cross-tree."

Aton shrugged and answered, *"I am a man amongst men, a beginning."*

"I have heard that is what you claim."

"It is what I am, as you are what you are and Kez is what he is."

Isso shook his head and admitted that he did not understand.

"Nor do I," Aton told him.

"Then why do you speak the words about yourself that will enrage those who hear them?"

"Because," Aton said, "they must be said."

Again Isso told him that he did not understand.

Aton nodded and said, "If I could tell you what it all means, Isso, I would, but I know no more than what I have said."

Then they parted. Isso went to his shelter and Aton entered Arri's, which was empty. He lay down on his sleeping skin and, closing his eyes, slipped into sleep.

Soon, however, he was awakened by someone close to him. He opened his eyes and saw Eliti.

Silently she offered him her breast.

He took it greedily and wordlessly moved his hand under her covering to where her slit was already wet with anticipation.

"Are you ready to mount a woman?" she giggled.

Aton stripped away her cover and removed his own. Eliti splayed her naked thighs for him and he entered her.

Aton moved until Eliti moaned low in her throat and wrapped her naked legs around his back.

Together they thrashed around on the sleeping skin until he felt her body tense, then shudder under him. Then his own pleasure gushed out of his organ. Naked, they rolled away from each other.

"Arri is too old to make me feel like that," Eliti said later.

Aton did not answer.

"We will be together again," Eliti said.

"And if we are caught?" Aton questioned.

"We would be stoned to death," Eliti answered, "and left for the dogs and the vultures."

"Then we must be sure," Aton said, "not to be caught."

Eliti laughed and fondled his organ again, making it hard enough to slide once more into her slit.

Isso was true to his word. When Aton was strong enough to move about with the aid of a staff he let it be known throughout the camp that on the first night of the next new moon his woman Nanda would open her bare thighs to let Aton pass through them. Before the ceremony Aton learned from Arri that he would show him how to tame horses so that he might have a better place when he returned to the slaves.

"That is Isso's wish," Arri told him.

"And who now holds Grug's whip?" Aton asked.

"Porip," Arri answered. As if he could tell what Aton's next question would be, he said, "He is not a slave. He is one of us. I do not think he will be as hard with you as Grug was. He was with Kez when you were captured."

Aton looked at him questioningly.

"He is in my blood line," Arri said.

Aton would have asked Arri why he had helped Isso save him but one of the riders had beckoned to Arri and he left his side. Aton did not think Arri had given him shelter and let Eliti suckle him without a purpose that went beyond Isso's need to avenge the death of his son Tumi.

From Eliti he gained new knowledge of mounting a woman. She seemed more skilled in the ways of giving a man pleasure than Rika or Sinti had been. Such knowledge did not come from the Horse People. Aton had seen the ways of the men with women and they were direct, with nothing preceding or following the coupling.

When he questioned her about the diverse ways she fondled him or asked him to fondle her she only laughed and told him that she had been taught. She never said who her teacher had been.

In his daily walks through the camp Aton never came upon Kez though he frequently had the feeling that Kez was watching him. The older boys always followed him at a distance. If he suddenly wheeled around they scattered like so many leaves before a gust of wind.

Sometimes he saw one of the riders who drove the columns of captives from where they were taken prisoner to the camp. Between him and those men there was a kind of bond. Though few stopped to speak with him, all acknowledged his presence with a nod or a gesture of the hand.

Captive and captor, Aton soon realized, were always bound together until the latter relinquished his hold on the former.

One afternoon when Aton was at the far end of the encampment, he discovered that the Horse People, unlike the slaves, who used the grain to make food, mixed the grain with water and let it rot until what resulted was what they called grain water, a liquid with a sour smell that was used only on special occasions or given to those whose spirit was about to leave their bodies.

Aton realized that Isso had given him much of it to drink after he had been taken down from the cross-tree more dead than alive. The grain water and the herbs that Isso had put into it had kept him alive. For that he would always feel kindly toward the seer. Aton learned from an old slave whose task it was to fill large earthenware cruses with the liquid, that the grain water was used by the Horse People when the black stallion and white mare were sacrificed to the Earth Shaker.

Aton nodded as though he understood the man and went his way. He knew nothing about the Earth Shaker although he remembered having heard the name before. He thought of questioning Eliti about the Earth Shaker and the sacrificed horses, but dared not lest he bring her to her death as he had brought Linet and Sinti to theirs.

Aton wandered unmolested around the camp of the Horse People. He became so familiar that even the young men, who would soon begin to ride with Kez, stopped following him.

Often he climbed the slope that lay at the far side of the place where the slaves were kept. He went there only duirng the day when the slaves were in the fields or doing other work for their masters.

He would sit on the ground, close to where he had set Sinti down under. Near him were Dahsan's bones picked clean by the dogs, vultures, and crows and bleached white by the sun.

From that vantage point he could see up the broad valley to the canyons out of which Kez had led them, then to the west, where the sky and land would come together and finally to the north, where Dahsan's people lived and the land gave way to water.

Aton could only see where the earth and sky would meet, as it did in the west. Behind him, where the sun was born out of the insides of the distant mountains, were the rock cliffs that rose above the camp like a huge wall.

As he looked at the land he realized that while it provided protection for the camp of the Horse People it also held him and the other slaves prisoner.

The great plains that lay to the west and north would make any man who escaped an easy prey for Kez's dogs and men. To the south were the canyons where lay certain death to anyone who entered them; and behind him were the cliffs, whose heights and narrow ledges would provide poor coverage for any man fleeing from Kez's bowmen. There were the caves, and he would turn to look at them, wondering why the Horse People had bothered to cut ledges into the face of the cliff in order to reach the openings?

The answer to such a question, Aton knew, would come eventually, even as would answers about the Earth Shaker and the horses sacrificed to him.

To ask about the unexplained might arouse Isso's and Arri's anger. That would indeed be foolish for Aton had learned that every people has its own mysteries, as he and Nempie's people had Pula, the black boar.

Aton had strong feelings for Eliti. He was unable to have enough of her, and at night when he would hear Arri with her—for she was his youngest woman—Aton seethed with anger. He knew now what Gens had felt whenever Nempie placed his hand on Bisha. He understood how the slit of a woman could make a man kill his father, brother, or anyone else so that he alone could possess it.

When they were together Aton would do anything to keep her in his embrace. She had taught him to wrap his arms around her and press her naked body against his. She had taken his hand and moved it over the moist warm lips of her slit, spreading them with her fingers, guiding his, and then showing him where to rub her to give her the most pleasure.

Then she bent over him and, placing his organ in her mouth, brought his fluid from him, drinking all of it even as she would take water. Another time she moved him between her splayed thighs, telling him to use his lips and tongue on her sex until she moaned with pleasure.

Her skill to delight him was beyond his reckoning. She was ever present in his head when she was not in his arms.

On those afternoons when the whole camp lay blasted by the heat of the sun, Aton found some hidden place in the high grass on the other side of the river where he and Eliti lay naked in each other's embrace. On other days they made use of Arri's shelter, thrashing with passion in Aton's sleeping-skin.

After they had satisfied their lust for each other they talked about Arri, or his other women, whom Eliti claimed envied her.

Aton listened and told her about his adventures, but never mentioned how he had gone down below and returned or even that he was *a man amongst men, a beginning*. These things were too dangerous for her to know.

Once when they had finished with each other and lay in the high grass looking up at the intensely blue sky that was spotted here and there with white bits of clouds, Eliti said, "I come from a people who live on the far side of the rock cliffs. I was taken in a raid before my woman's blood began to flow. But my people are wise in the ways of pleasure. Kez used me first, and then he gave me to Arri."

Aton beat his clenched fists against the ground. "I want you for my woman," he told her. "I do not want Arri to mount you."

"I can not deny him what is his to take," she said, touching his face with her fingers.

Aton fell on her and buried his face in the soft warm mounds of her breasts.

"Take me with you when you go," she whispered.

He raised his head and looked up at her.

"Take me with you, Aton."

"If I go," he told her, "I will take you with me."

Eliti smiled and said, "You will go Aton. You will go." Then she reached down and caressed him.

Aton did not understand how Eliti knew that he had been thinking about escaping.

Perhaps it came to her while they coupled.

He had often heard men in Nempie's camp say that a woman, though a man mounted her, took from him more than she gave. Perhaps that was the way Eliti discovered what was in his mind.

But she did not know that if he managed to escape he would go back to his own people. He told her that, even as she played her cool hand over him.

"Where you go," she answered, "I will go."

He stopped her hand and, taking it in his own, said, "I go back to kill my father Nempie, and claim his people for my own so that they will be known as Aton's people."

"I will go with you no matter what you will do or where you will go."

Aton looked around him. Above the limit of the high grass were the rock cliffs, where the light from the sun on the face made the openings to the caves even darker. Facing her again he said, "We might hide in the caves——"

"No, Aton," she exclaimed, "not the caves!"

He was about to press his suggestion but her frightened face stopped him.

"To these people," she said in a whisper, "they are sacred."

Aton shook his head and told her, "I do not know what you mean."

"They belong to the Earth Shaker."

"And who is he?"

"He . . . he . . . he lives in those caves," she said.

"Have you ever seen him?"

"No. But he is the one to whom the black stallion and white mare are given on the night that is longer than all others and again on the night that is shorter than all others. Isso knows all of this. He sees it in the stars. He tells us when to sow and when to reap. He can even tell from the number of stars the number of days from one event to another."

"Has he ever seen the Earth Shaker?" Aton asked.

"He is too terrible to look at," she said and then, gesturing toward the rock cliffs rising above the camp on the opposite side of the river, added, "He lives in those caves."

Aton took Eliti in his arms and said, "We will find another way." As he spoke his eyes scanned the caves.

Later that night when Arri took Eliti to him and Aton could not stand to hear either Eliti's moans of delight or Arri's grunts of pleasure, he crawled out of the shelter, stood in the darkness, and looked toward the face of the rock cliffs and the caves.

On the first night of the new moon everyone gathered in the center of the camp, where a huge fire burned. The air was heavy with the smell of roasting meat.

Nanda, Isso's woman, was old. Her long hair was

stringy. She stood naked by the fire. Her tits sagged like the udders of an old mare. She seemed bewildered by what was happening.

Many of the people held torches and walked along with Isso as he led Nanda to where Aton would pass between her naked thighs to be born again as her son.

Aton, too, was naked but his body glistened with oil. The wavering light of the fire played over it, revealing his corded muscles and the scar where Kez had wounded him with his sword.

Somewhere out of sight several hollow logs were thumped and Isso began to chant. "This I do for all to see. This I do for all to know. This I do to beget a son, a son whose son will continue my line, the line of Isso and his father's father. This I do for all to see. This I do for all to know that Aton will be my son."

The onlookers began to shout and stamp their feet to the beat of the drum.

Isso stripped off his covering and, naked, led Nanda around the fire three times. Then he chanted, "This I do to bring forth my new son."

Nanda lay down on the ground near the fire and opened her naked thighs.

Isso mounted her, chanting, "This I do for all to see how I put life into my woman from whence will come my son Aton. This I do for all to see that Aton is my son."

Placing his organ into her slit, Isso moved until Nanda moaned and he gasped as the fluid passed from him into her.

Isso rose from Nanda's thighs and taking her by the hand, led her around the fire many times. At the completion of each circle he shouted, "See how my son grows. See how my son grows inside the belly of my woman."

Aton watched and waited until Isso summoned him. This way was strange to him. In Nempie's camp no man ever took another man's son and claimed him for his own. A man's son was his own or he was someone else's. But no man in Nempie's camp was foolish enough to think that by passing a man between the naked thighs of a woman that man became her son and thus the son of the man to whom she belonged.

When Isso had made nine full circles around the fire the watchers shouted and stamped their feet. Isso ordered the meat cut and the grain water given to all.

The people ate and drank; the drink made them laugh and shout like children. Men and women fell to the ground and satisfied their lusts.

At the height of the frenzy Isso shouted, "Come, Aton, come my son. Nanda is ready to bear you."

Aton came to where Isso stood.

"She is ready," Isso told him.

Nanda spread her legs. She smiled at Aton.

He nodded, dropped to his knees, and crawled between Nanda's naked thighs.

"My son is born," Isso shouted. "I have a son!"

Aton scrambled to his feet and immediately Isso handed him a gourd filled with grain water.

"Drink my son," Isso told him, "and may the Earth Shaker favor you."

Aton drank. The grain water tasted sour, but quickly warmed his insides. He saw Eliti standing off to one side with Arri.

She was drinking and laughing.

Even as Aton looked at her his organ began to swell with lust.

Isso called for meat, handed Aton a piece, and urged him to eat.

Then Nanda put her hands around Aton and called him her son.

But Aton, his head suddenly filling with mists, could only see Eliti.

She had removed her coverings; her naked body moved to the wild beat of the drums.

Staggering toward her, Aton suddenly faced Kez and stopped.

Isso came to Aton's side and said, his words slowed by the mists of the grain water, "I have a new son, Kez, a new son."

"As the other one was a slave," Kez answered, "so is this one."

"He is my son!" Isso exclaimed.

"Then he should be no different from the one I left for the vultures," Kez said, and lifting his sword, drove the point into Aton's right eye.

Aton screamed with pain and dropped to his knees. The gore of the eye ran down his face.

Isso rushed at Kez.

But Kez lowered his sword.

Isso ran into it. He screamed as the blade pierced his stomach.

Kez lifted Isso into the air on the blade of his weapon and then with a swift movement flung him to the ground. Then to Aton, Kez said, "Now you are marked like his son."

To the silent witnesses Kez pointed to the dying Isso and told them, "He took another son to spite me, to continue his line. I am Kez, your leader. None of you will come against me either by guile, as Isso has tried, or with a weapon, as none of you have yet tried. I have made you the most powerful people in the land. All fear you. You are the master of many because I am the master of you."

"Kez," Isso sputtered. "Kez, you are——" Blood poured out of his mouth and he died.

Kez turned, looked at Aton, and said, "It is better, Aton, to have one eye than none."

"Even with one, Kez," Aton answered, "I see more than you do with two. You are blind, Kez."

Kez threw back his head and roared with laughter. Soon almost everyone was laughing at the dead seer and the slave with one eye.

17

ATON RETURNED to the slave quarters and built a shelter for himself below the slope where Dahsan's bleached bones still lay. His wound, though denying him full vision, still permitted him to see the world and all in it as if it lay under a pall of deep twilight. The swift upward movement of Kez's sword had slit his eyelid and brow, marking him for life with a scar so frightening to look at that Eliti ran from him when he approached her in the tall grass where they once had given each other pleasure.

Aton avoided the other slaves and they avoided him. He came to the fire only to be given his share of food by Porip, the new overseer, who was not as ready to use the whip as Grug had been.

During the day Aton went with the other horse tamers, and Arri taught him how to rope and break a wild horse. It did not take long for Aton's skill to surpass that of all the other horse tamers. He soon rode as well as any of the Horse People.

The work, though it was always hard and dangerous, gave Aton a sense of excitement that often made him forget he was a slave. He came to understand why the men who rode with Kez lavished such care and devotion on their mounts.

Aton was eventually allowed to take a horse from the herd, break it, and train it for himself. He chose a fast gray stallion who threw him many times before he could gain control.

"And what will you call him?" Arri asked as he watched Aton walk the animal in a small circle.

"Shadow," Aton answered, patting the lathered neck of the horse.

"It is suitable."

Aton nodded and, turning away, trotted down to the river, where he dismounted and allowed Shadow to drink.

In the passing days Aton began to feel a growing restlessness, almost as if his need to mount a woman would make him seek out one from those who were slaves, or to try again to lay with Eliti. When he did mount one of the women in the camp the uneasy feeling remained with him.

One night when he came to the fire for food, Aton looked at Porip. The overseer was similar to the Horse People. He was lean, muscular, and his legs were bent from having spent so much of his life on the back of a horse.

Suddenly the overseer looked at Aton. Each held the other's eyes. And then Aton said in a voice loud enough for everyone to hear, "I will cut the meat for my people."

The slaves at the fire ceased their eating and looked toward Aton, who stood.

"I will cut the meat for my people," Aton repeated.

"And who are your people?" Porip asked.

"Those who came here with me," Aton told him, wondering if the overseer would challenge him.

But Porip had been warned before by Arri not to anger Aton, lest he arouse the wrath of a powerful man. Suddenly remembering how Aton had held the green death in his hand for most of the day, the overseer said, "It is your right."

Aton took the knife and cut the meat for his fellow slaves. Then he took his share of meat and moved away from the fire to eat alone.

After he had cut the meat the feeling of uneasiness left him and the other slaves no longer avoided him. He took none for a friend.

He climbed the slope up to Sinti's grave and, sitting close by the mound covering her, looked down at Dahsan's bones and remembered what his skull had said about Yahweh. After a while Aton heaved a great sigh, stood up, and walked slowly down the slope to his shelter, still not knowing why Dahsan's skull should have spoken to him about Yahweh.

Determined to know more about Yahweh, Aton asked Arri about him.

Arri did not know about him and said, "It is the Shaker of the Earth to whom we must make sacrifice. He is the one whose anger is too terrible to withstand." He went on to explain how the Earth Shaker can move mountains or change the bed of a river.

"Is he stronger than Yahweh?" Aton asked.

"He is the Shaker of the Earth," Arri answered and rode off.

By asking other slaves Aton discovered that there were several who had heard about Yahweh from Dahsan and they told him about Zell, a slave who knew more than anyone else about Yahweh.

Aton sought out Zell and found him sitting in front of a small shelter near the river.

Zell was thin as a reed and already past his prime. His face was gaunt, his eyes deepset, and his hands long and thin. He did not look up when Aton approached him, but he did say, "I wondered how long it would take you to seek me out." His narrow lips parted in a smile.

Aton squatted down to the small fire and said, "I did not know that I would seek you out."

"I knew," Zell told him. "Dahsan had told me, 'Aton will seek you out Zell. He will come to you and you will serve him as he will serve Yahweh.'"

"And how will you serve me, Zell?" Aton said.

"I will tell your story to your people," the man answered.

"And what will you tell me of Yahweh?"

"Only what Dahsan told me," Zell responded. "He said that you are *a man amongst men, a beginning,* and you will be the voice of Yahweh as I will be your voice."

"I do not need your voice," Aton responded, annoyed at the man's gibberish. "I came only to ask you about Yahweh."

"It is you who must tell me," Zell answered.

"Only a fool would tell another man something he knows nothing about!"

Zell did not answer.

"And that is all Dahsan told you?" Aton questioned.

"If he had said more," Zell answered, "I would tell you."

Aton stood up and started away.

But Zell called him back and asked, "How long will you remain a slave, Aton?"

"Until I can find a way out of here."

"I will come with you," Zell said.

Aton returned to the fire and squatted down.

"There are others who would go with you," Zell told him.

"From here," Aton said, "I go back to kill Nempie my father."

"There are those who would follow you."

"His people would become my people," Aton continued. "It was Nempie whose cunning brought me here."

Zell said nothing.

"That is my purpose," Aton told him. "That is why I am *a man amongst men, a beginning*. I will put an end to Nempie and become the leader of his people."

"And what will you give them?" Zell asked.

"I will take Nempie from them," Aton said. "That is what I will give them."

Zell waved his hand in a broad gesture. "There are things here," he told Aton, "that you could give them. The grain out of which our food is made."

"Slave food!" Aton snorted with disdain.

"Food," Zell replied. "Food that could help them when game is scarce—and you could bring them horses. Horses that would make them strong, as strong as the Horse People, perhaps even stronger?"

"Alone?" Aton questioned.

"That is why you must take others with you," Zell said. "They will take the grain and horses for you. But you must lead them."

Aton remained silent and stared into the glowing embers of the fire. Once he had thought about taking Eliti with him, but that seemed as if it had been part of some dream.

"There are even those among the Horse People," Zell whispered, "who would follow you, Aton, if you took Kez's sword from him."

"And what choice would they have, since he who holds the sword is their leader?"

"It is wiser to start with something than nothing," Zell counseled.

"I am something," Aton responded angrily. "I am *a man amongst men, a beginning*." Scrambling to his feet he hastily left Zell's fire. He would not kill Kez for anyone but himself or for any purpose but his own.

Aton's sleep was restive. His conversation with Zell breathed on the red embers of his hate for Nempie and changed them into a raging fire burning inside him. "All that I have endured," he whispered into the darkness of his shelter, "has come from your hand, Nempie." He sat up and, hugging his knees, found himself thinking about Zell.

Aton did not like the man and wondered why Dahsan had chosen him to speak to? He shrugged and was about to stretch out again when he suddenly realized that Zell, or possibly even Dahsan, had given a great deal of thought to escaping and that grain and horses would be welcomed by his own people. Taking them out of the valley would not be easy. To do it he would have to kill many of Kez's riders. Even if, as Zell said, there would be many willing to follow him, they still would not be enough to fight all of Kez's riders.

Suddenly Aton felt that he could not remain in the confines of the small shelter and, scrambling outside, he looked toward the far end of the valley where the canyons were. "There," he said aloud, "is the way out. There is where I will lead them!" He moved his eyes up to the sky filled with its star figures. Sucking in a great draught of cool night air he said, "I will come, Nempie. I will come to kill you."

As he turned and stooped to enter his shelter a sudden breeze sprang up. Its movement riffled the leaves of a nearby tree and the night was filled with soft laughter.

Aton saw more of Zell and quickly came to realize that the man was going blind. He did not speak of it until Zell himself made mention of it.

"The world and all that is in it," Zell told him one night as they sat together, "is gray. Even the flames are gray though they are lighter than the ground around them."

"It is the way everything appears to me in my right eye," Aton said.

Zell nodded.

"For how long have you been this way?" Aton asked.

"More days than I can reckon," Zell said. "Past many sacrifices of the black stallion and the white mare. Kez took me in a raid on my people, who live beyond the canyons near the mountains to the east, out of whose insides the sun is born each day."

"I know those mountains," Aton told him. "I could see them from my father's camp."

"Tell me about your father."

And Aton told him about Gens, about Pula, the black boar, and about Nempie, his father. "So now you understand," Aton asked when he had finished, "why I must go back and kill my father?"

"Yes," Zell answered.

Another night Aton asked Zell to speak about his people. "I know nothing about you," he said.

"There is really nothing to know," Zell told him. "Before I was taken captive by Kez I was a story-teller to my people. I was called Zell, the story-teller."

Aton laughed and said, "That is what I will call you."

"If that is what pleases you, Aton," Zell responded, "then do it."

"Dahsan was a story-teller, too," Aton commented.

Zell shook his head.

"He was," Aton insisted. "I heard him tell many stories. He could even change his voice to make——"

"Dahsan was more than a story-teller," Zell said, his reedy voice scarcely audible above the hiss and crackle of the fire. "He was a seer, with powers greater than those of Isso. Dahsan foresaw your coming, Aton; he even foresaw your agony on the cross-tree. You were promised, Aton, and he was waiting for you to come."

Though the night was warm, Aton suddenly felt chilled and he whispered, "Are you a seer too, Zell?"

"No," Zell answered, "I am no more than what I

have told you. I am Zell, the story-teller. I am even called upon by Kez to tell him and his women stories. If it were not for my story-telling I would have been dead. Probably Grug would have had me impaled as he had so many others who had become as worthless as myself."

Aton nodded.

And Zell said, "When the day comes, I will lead you to Kez's sword."

"If you are only a story-teller, Zell," Aton asked, "why do I feel as though you are bending me like a bow?"

"Because," Zell answered, looking at Aton with his dull eyes, "we are all bows and arrows to each other. That is the way it was meant to be."

Aton accepted the answer though he did not understand it. And in the days that followed he purposely kept himself away from Zell to think about the story-teller's words, especially those about what Dahsan had foreseen.

If Zell had spoken truthfully then Dahsan had indeed been a great seer, far greater than Tesu, who had read the future in the liver of a cow, or Isso, who had seen it in the star figures of the night sky.

Whether it was the effect of Zell's words, or his own need to escape from the bondage of the Horse People, Aton rode each day farther and farther up the broad valley to the opening of the canyon. It would be the only way out of the valley that would offer him and his followers the possibility of eluding Kez and his riders.

Though he was unable to reach the opening through which Kez had brought him and the other captives, Aton could see there were several fractures large enough to allow a mounted man to pass through. He had no idea where they led.

If they came to an abrupt end some distance from the opening then he and all those with him would be trapped and Kez could kill them at will.

He could not chance that happening and decided to use the same opening to get out as they had used to enter the valley.

At night Aton returned to Zell and told him of his decision, explaining why he had made it.

Zell listened and when Aton was finished, said, "One of the other openings leads to where Arri keeps the herd of black stallions and white mares that he alone tends."

They also spoke about the custom of the Horse People to make sacrifices to the Earth Shaker.

"They say," Zell explained, "that the Shaker of the Earth, as he is called by them, lives in the caves."

"I, too, was told that by Arri's woman Eliti," Aton said.

"Did you mount her?"

Aton nodded and then remembering that the storyteller's almost blind eyes could not have seen his gesture, he answered in a low voice, "Yes." And then he quickly added in a tone of bitterness, "But since Kez slit my lid and brow I am too terrible to look at."

Zell brushed Aton's words aside with a swift movement of his hand and said, "The people fear the Earth Shaker. It is fear, Aton, that makes them sacrifice to him. Fear is even more powerful than Kez's sword. And if men can not see what they fear it makes them even more afraid. I tell you Aton," Zell exclaimed, "there is great wisdom in that and Dahsan knew it. He told me to tell you about it when I thought you were ready to hear it. People fear more those things they can not see than they do the things they see. Remember that, Aton. The Earth Shaker is fear."

"If the Earth Shaker is fear," Aton asked, "what is Yahweh?"

Zell pointed a finger at him and said, "I am waiting for you to tell me, Aton. I am only a story-teller. You are *the man amongst men, a beginning.* I have only been telling you what Dahsan told me."

And once again Aton found it difficult to sleep. Zell's words were like flocks of birds that flew in circles inside his skull. Men feared spirits. They feared pain and they feared death. As Zell had said, they feared most what they could not see, what they themselves could not understand. And no man understood why his life should end in death or why the body should rot and stink after the spirit has been separated from it.

Finally the waters of sleep took Aton and he slept soundly until the guards shouted to one another at the coming of the first light. When he awoke Zell's words were still with him and from them came a feeling of strength, of power such as he had not felt since he had given the thrice-circled tusks of Pula, the black boar, to Kez.

Even his mount, Shadows, sensed Aton's new strength and as soon as Aton was on him he swung around and raced toward the canyon at the far end of the valley.

Aton gave the animal his head, hoping that he would be swift enough to bring him still closer to the opening before he turned round.

Shortly, the drumming sound of his own horse's hoofs was joined by the pounding sounds of other hoofs. Aton glanced over his shoulder.

Two riders were after him at a gallop. One was Arri—he could tell that from the way he rode. The other, he soon realized, was Kez.

Both men shouted to him.

Aton bent low over the neck of his mount. He realized his pursuers probably thought that he was trying to make for the opening of the canyon.

Again he glanced over his shoulder and through the swirling dust could see the flash of Kez's sword in the bright morning sunlight. Knowing that Kez would cut him down without the slightest bit of hesitation, Aton turned his mount and at a slower pace went toward those who had come after him.

Soon Aton slowed his horse to a walk.

Kez raced up to him and reined in sharply, making his mount rear. He was streaked with sweat and held his sword ready to strike. "Where were you going?" he demanded to know.

Arri joined them. He, too, was streaked with sweat.

Aton patted his mount's neck and said, "He ran. It took me awhile to stop him. He——" The breeze had suddenly dropped and flocks of birds suddenly took to the air; even the vultures and crows were flying.

Kez, too, sensed that something was happening.

Aton pointed to the birds and said, "The wind is gone."

And then Arri said in a choked voice, "There is a black edge on the sun. Quick, to the camp. To the camp." He wheeled away and broke into a gallop.

Kez went after him.

And Aton raced after them.

Soon the three of them were galloping back to the camp together. They splashed across the river and, dismounting, joined the others in the camp who were already aware of the blackness spreading over the sun.

"Quickly," Kez ordered, "beat the drums. Everyone beat on something. Make noise. Frighten the demon off."

The drums began to sound and the women and children shook gourds.

The blackness spread over the sun, slowly devouring it.

Many of the women began to scream. Some of the people dropped to their knees and pleaded for their lives.

Kez had his men build a huge fire in the center of the camp, but even its flames could not stop the black demon from swallowing the sun.

As the shadow of night fell over the earth the stars began to show themselves. Some of the old men wailed that death would soon come to all of them, that the Shaker of the Earth would bring them all down.

Aton saw Zell at the other side of the circle and moved to where he stood.

"Are you afraid?" Zell asked in a low voice.

"I have never seen anything like this," Aton answered, looking at the sun, more than half of which was already in the stomach of the blackness.

"It happened once when I was a boy," Zell said. "It will pass."

Aton looked questioningly at him.

"It will pass," Zell assured him and, as if he knew Aton's thoughts, he said, "Remember it. Look how frightened everyone is. Even Kez and Arri are frightened. They fear it!"

"It is surely an omen," Aton commented.

Zell nodded and said, "But who can tell whether it bodes ill or good?"

Aton looked up. Most of the sun was gone and around the edges of the darkness glowed a strange light. And then it was night. The sun had been completely swallowed.

The beating of the drums and the shaking of the gourds stopped. Even the wailing of the women and the old men stopped. A great silence, as deep as the darkness that hid the sun, fell over the land.

No one moved, and as Aton looked up at the black orb of the sun around which flared a peculiar light, he saw the flocks of birds circle around and around, like so many dark specks in a black sky.

Suddenly Kez shouted to his people to help the sun fight the black demon. His voice boomed out in the silence, louder than Aton had ever heard it. And the people responded. They did what he told them to do.

The fire was fed more wood. The drums were pounded until their booming sounded like thunder.

Then very slowly the blackness moved a bit and the people began to shout that the sun was fighting its way out of the demon's stomach. More and more of the sun became visible.

To help the sun escape, Kez told his men to shoot arrows at the blackness.

Half the sun was once again visible. The star figures faded and the darkness that lay over the land lightened to gray. Almost all of the sun was free now, and there was rejoicing in the camp.

"We will sacrifice to the Shaker of the Earth," Arri pronounced, "for giving us back the sun, for helping us to drive off the black demon."

18

WHEN THE SUN RETURNED, the day was as it had been before, though the sun's position had changed. It stood now almost at its highest point. The flocks of birds had settled down and the other animals had also ceased their frightened scurrying.

"We have saved the sun!" Kez shouted to his people.

And his people answered him with the same words.

"It is an omen," Arri said, standing close to Kez, "and we must offer sacrifice to protect ourselves."

Kez turned on him. "Who will say whether it is good or bad?" he demanded.

"Only Isso could have——"

"Isso is dead," Kez growled. "I will hear no more about him."

"And by whose hand?" Arri asked, his brow flushed with anger.

Kez raised his sword and answered, "By this hand, Arri. By this hand because he tried to undo what I had done." Then he remembered that he had chased Aton toward the opening of the canyon and he shouted for him. When Aton came to him, he asked, "Did Isso give you any of his skill to read the signs?"

"I did not need his skill," Aton answered.

"If he could hear that," Kez said, "he would think you an ungrateful son. It was his skill that held your spirit to your body."

"That is not the skill——"

"Tell me," Kez demanded sharply, "whether what we have just seen is a good or bad omen?"

"It is no better or worse, Kez, than I am," Aton responded, giving his voice its deep rumbling tone.

"You are not an omen. You are nothing. You are a slave."

"I am more, Kez, much more, I am *a man amongst men, a beginning.*"

"It is I who wear the black boar's tusks. It was you who gave them to me."

"Even my giving them could not change what was, or what is, or what will be." And pointing to the sun Aton said, "Make sacrifice, Kez, lest the blackness come again."

And then the people shouted, "Make sacrifice, Kez, lest the blackness come again."

"It is not the right time," Kez argued.

But the voice of the people was stronger than his. Slowly he turned to Arri and nodded.

Arri raised his hands high above his head and when the people became silent he said, "Because the darkness that came was unnatural, we will make our sacrifice at night and give the Shaker of the Earh two black stallions."

The people shouted their approval.

And Arri said, "It will be done the first night that the moon is gone from the sky."

The people dispersed and Kez, mounting his horse, rode back across the river to the open grassland where herds of wild horses ran.

That he had been forced to bow to Arri's will rankled him but he was even more angry with Aton since he was the one who had actually told him to make the sacrifice.

He worked his mount into a gallop.

The more he challenged Aton, the more he was challenged by him. With his efforts to kill him, he had not succeeded and even recently he was told that Aton once again cut the meat for those captives who had come to the camp with him.

Had Aton been any man but his brother's son he would have killed him a long time ago, but Kez, though he was now leader of his own people, still remembered the ways of his father's camp. There only Aga and his sons fought for the women and to be the leader of the people. The other men did not fight each other. If one fought another both were stoned to death by all the people.

Kez brought that same custom to the Horse People when he became their leader. He was the only one permitted to take the life of another man. But Aton was not just another man.

He slowed his mount to a walk and patted the animal's steaming flanks. Aton, he had to admit, was no ordinary man. He had seen strong men before, but none were as strong as Aton, none had his ability to live when he should have died.

Kez shook his head and, looking back toward the camp, found himself wondering if all that Aton claimed about himself was true?

Any man could say that he had slain Pula, the black boar, and had taken his tusks. Remembering what Aton had told him about his father, Kez could readily understand Nempie's anger.

And any man could claim that he had been down below and had returned. Who could speak against something like that?

Kez dismounted and let his horse graze while he,

too, chewed on a blade of grass. He was sure that Aton had guessed there was some connection between them. But probably no more than that they came from the same land and that was because he had been foolish enough to show Aton that he had known about Pula, the black boar.

Kez suddenly found himself thinking that he might reveal to Aton their true relationship. Perhaps even as Isso had done, adopt him. And when the time came for him to surrender his leadership he would give the sword to Aton.

These thoughts were worth thinking more about. That way he would turn an enemy into a friend!

Kez leaped back on to his mount and, at a trot, returned to the camp, where already Arri was beginning to prepare for the sacrifice. Kez reined in and watched the slaves at work. That the Shaker of the Earth was a powerful spirit he did not doubt, but that he could be satisfied with the blood and meat of horses always seemed strange to him. He looked up toward the caves.

His brow furrowed and a slight tremor shook him. He hated the caves but, because he was the leader of the Horse People, he had to go whenever a sacrifice was made to the Shaker of the Earth. It was the custom of the people before he came to them. He did not doubt it would remain after he left them. But for anyone to place images on the walls of caves was frightening. There were certain things that were better left undone.

Suddenly he realized that Arri had stopped what he was doing and was looking at him.

Kez let his frown slip away and with a nod walked his horse to where his shelter stood.

The night was filled with star figures. There were torches from the river to the center of the camp, on the posts that formed a circle, and on the edges that led to the caves.

The people waited until Arri was in sight. And when he came across the river leading two black stallions, a low murmur of approval passed over the camp, like the sigh of the wind.

Aton, standing next to Zell, watched what was happening. Arri was bare-chested and his body was streaked with yellow and white clay.

The horses neighed and seemed reluctant to be led into the wavering light of the torches. But Arri spoke to them and they left the river.

"Kez has come," Zell said, gesturing to the part of the circle that opened on to the pathway that led to the river.

"He, too, is marked with yellow and white clay," Aton commented.

"It is their way," Zell commented.

Arri led the stallions slowly up from the river and just before he entered the circle of skulls he cried out, "To you, oh Shaker of the Earth, we bring these gifts. To you we bring the best of what we have."

From the far side of the circle a drum began to sound and then another answered it from a place on the other side of the camp. From the other side of the river a third drum started to throb.

"That is the voice of the Earth Shaker," Zell whispered to Aton.

The drumming soon filled the valley.

And again Arri cried out, "We offer you blood and meat, oh Shaker of the Earth, the blood and meat of two fine horses. We are your people, the Horse People, and all that we have is yours."

Kez moved into the center of the circle as Arri entered it.

A strong breeze caused the flames of the torches to bend. In their light the shadows of the men and animals grew long and thin.

"Drink first, oh Shaker of the Earth," Arri called

out, looking up toward the face of the rock cliffs of the caves.

A child darted into the circle and handed him a clay bowl.

"Drink first," the people shouted.

And Kez, lifting his sword, drew it swiftly against the neck of one of the horses.

The animal whinnied with fright and reared up, but a stream of hot blood gushed into the clay bowl.

A third man came into the circle. He took the bowl from Arri and swiftly poured some of the blood on each of the posted skulls.

"Drink the blood," Arri cried.

The drums began to throb again and the wounded horse, its chest now wet with blood, began to stagger.

Kez went to the animal and, using a knife, quickly cut the skin away, exposing the beast's quivering muscles.

"If he succeeds in flaying the horse before it topples over," Zell said, "it is a very good omen."

Aton shook his head. He had developed a liking for horses. What he watched angered him.

The animal whinnied softly. Its legs began to give way but it fought to keep them.

Kez worked swiftly. He had stripped most of the skin away from the body and was working to remove the part that covered the head when suddenly the horse's forelegs gave way and the animal dropped to the ground.

A sigh of surprise and dismay came from the crowd.

Before Kez had finished, the horse rolled over.

Zell looked at Aton and said, "If the same thing happens to the second horse, the omen will be very bad indeed."

Kez tore the bloody skin from the body and handed it to Arri, who draped it over his shoulders and pulled the top part of it over his eyes. Then Kez severed the head from the animal and impaled it on an empty post.

The smell of blood made the other horse difficult to manage.

Arri could not get him to stand still long enough for Kez to cut his throat.

When the animal did settle down he reared up again as soon as Kez lifted his sword. The movement was so sudden that Kez missed his mark, and the blade opened the animal's chest.

The wounded horse became frantic. It neighed loudly and tried again and again to smash Arri and Kez under its wildly flailing forefeet.

The people began to shout and the sound of the drums throbbed in the night.

"Had I something to kill with," Aton said, remembering how he had killed the stranger he had taken captive to stop the women from abusing him, "I would kill the animal."

"And be killed yourself," Zell told him. "That horse must die by Kez's hand alone. It is their way."

Aton snorted.

Kez suddenly rushed at the horse and drove his sword into the animal's neck. The horse came to an abrupt stop, and when Kez pulled his sword free a fountain of blood poured out.

Arri went through the same ritual with the blood and Kez flayed the animal. But this one, like the first, dropped to the ground before Kez finished taking its skin. And when he finally had it, he draped it over himself as Arri had done with the first skin. Then he cut the head off and impaled it on the second post.

Other men entered the circle and began to cut up the carcasses. The heart of each of the horses was given to Kez, and Arri was given the animal's penis. As others led the way, Kez and Arri began the long climb up the face of the rock cliff to the cave where the Earth Shaker lived.

"And after the Earth Shaker is fed," Aton asked, "then what is done?"

"It happens up there," Zell said. "No slave is allowed up there. Something is done, but only Arri and Kez go into the cave to do it. When Isso was alive he would go too. But everyone else stays along the ledges; you will see them."

"I have seen enough," Aton told him and started to move away.

"Stay," Zell said. "When Kez and Arri return, the rest of the meat is taken and roasted. Everyone eats and grain water is given——"

"Does the Earth Shaker really live in the caves?" Aton asked.

"The Horse People say he does," Zell answered.

"Whatever makes these people strong," he told Zell, "must be up there in the caves."

"You will be killed if you go up there," Zell said.

"Perhaps I will be killed if I do not go up there," Aton responded.

Zell did not answer.

19

SINCE ATON HAD WITNESSED THE SACRIFICE of the two black stallions to the Earth Shaker, the caves tantalized him. They kept sleep from him at night. During the day they often drew his attention. For the time when he would become the leader of a people, as Zell had assured him he would, Aton had to know their secret. He had to see for himself the measure of the Earth Shaker.

Aton remembered that Pula, the black boar, was so huge that his back blotted out the entire sky and all the star figures that were in it.

Was the Earth Shaker that large, or was he just small enough to live in a cave?

Why were the Horse People so frightened of him?

Could he fight the Earth Shaker and win as he had fought the snake of the green death and triumphed over it?

Aton said nothing about his intention to Zell, but he suspected that the story-teller knew what they were, as he seemed to know so many other things, especially what Dahsan had told him about Yahweh.

Aton listened to all he had to say but when Zell spoke about Yahweh as Dahsan's skull had, Aton could only shrug his shoulders and answer, "Who can understand something he can not see?"

"And did you see Pula, the black boar?" Zell would ask.

"I slew him and took his thrice-circled tusks," Aton would answer.

"And do the Horse People see the Earth Shaker?" the story-teller would question.

"They must. Kez and Arri must have seen him or they would not fear him."

Then Zell would say, "Fear, Aton, is the binding that holds the Horse People to the Earth Shaker."

"And what held Yahweh to Dahsan's people?"

"He never told me," Zell would answer. "For him it was enough that there was Yahweh."

Aton would shake his head. He did not understand, and when Zell repeated that Dahsan had foreseen his coming, Aton would tell him, "I was taken captive. I was brought here by Kez. I did not come."

"But for what purpose?"

Aton would feed the fire a few more pieces of dried wood and waited until they burned before he would say, "For the same purpose that I am *a man amongst men, a beginning.*"

"Yes," Zell would answer, "for that purpose."

"We talk, Zell, and when our words cease I am not sure that either of us has heard what the other said."

Zell would laugh and assure Aton that he had listened very carefully and then would say, "There will be many who will follow you when the time comes, Aton."

"You have been busy at that?"

"Yes," Zell would tell him.

"The only way is through the canyons," Aton would say.

"They will follow you when you give the command. But do not keep them waiting too long or they will lose interest. It must be soon, Aton."

There were many similar conversations as the moon passed again through its various phrases, while Aton waited impatiently for the mist of the river to grow dense and spill over the land.

On such a dark night Aton made his way up the slope of Sinti's grave where Dahsan's bones lay. From there he moved along the base of the rock cliffs until he came to the place where he could use the cracks and crevasses to begin his climb.

Hand over hand he crawled up the wet slippery rock. The mist hid his movements from the guards below, but it also prevented him from seeing where his next hold or step was going to be.

He was like a blind man. He felt his way up from one foot-hold to the one above it. Often he was forced to stop his upward movement and walk across the face of the cliff before he could find a suitable way to continue the climb.

His hands and feet soon became cut and bruised. The jagged edges of the rocks tore his bare arms.

Aton gained one ledge and paused to catch his breath. Though he was wet with sweat the cold touch of the river mist made him tremble. Below him lay the camp of the Horse People. Above him rose the rock cliff, hidden from sight by the mist of the river.

He began to climb again and found two ledges, one a short distance above his resting place and another at the end of it. By then he had to move hand over hand, blindly feeling his way from one purchase to the other.

He stretched his arms to their limit and, using his finger to tell him if the outcropping was wide enough to hold him, he proceeded. His hold was so strong that he tore fragments of living rock from the great mass that rose invisibly above him.

Gaining another ledge, he was so anxious to stand without fear of falling that his feet tangled. He lost his footing on the slippery rock and, feeling himself begin to pitch backward, evoked all his strength to hurl himself against the cliff.

He dropped to his knees and struck his forehead against the rock face, opening a large gash that streamed blood.

His chest heaving, Aton remained huddled against the face of the cliff. That he had almost fallen made him more cautious than he had been before.

His pace slowed. As he moved closer and closer to where he was sure the lowest level of caves was, he wondered if the Earth Shaker could hear him.

Suddenly, as if a hand had reached down, the mist was brushed aside. A wind sprang up, blowing from off the open plains that lay beyond the river. The sky filled with stars and as Aton looked up he saw the dark entrance to one of the caves just above him. He reached, put his hands on the ledge, and felt it quiver.

Aton did not move. His heart raced.

The Earth Shaker knew he was there!

The ledge moved under his hands. He looked behind him. Even though there was no moonlight, he could see where one ledge led to the other. The way back to the bottom of the cliff would be easier than the climb up.

The ledge trembled again and from the heights above him pieces of rock were dislodged and went crashing down to the camp below.

The guards began to shout, "He moves! The Shaker of the Earth moves!"

People ran from their shelters with torches in their hands.

The ledge above Aton quivered again. A huge chunk fell away. Without hesitation, Aton turned and began scrambling down the face of the rock cliff. He ran, leaping from ledge to ledge.

To him it seemed as if the entire cliff was beginning to shake.

More rocks jumped away from it and crashed down on the camp below.

The screams of many soon filled the night.

As Aton reached the base of the cliff the earth beneath his feet began to quiver. He ran back to where the slaves were. They too were aroused and milled around with torches in their hands.

Aton went to Zell and asked, "What is happening?"

"It is time, Aton. It is time to take Kez's sword," Zell told him.

Almost as Zell spoke, the top of the rock cliff crumbled and fell into the camp of the Horse People, killing many.

Aton took Zell by the hand and together they ran to Kez's shelter.

Kez stood, holding his sword in one hand and a torch in the other.

Aton ran to one of the Horse People, and with a blow in the face dropped him to the ground. He took the man's spear and, wheeling around, shouted, "Kez, the time is now!"

Kez rushed at him and, heaving the torch, tried to burn Aton's face.

Aton darted off to one side.

"Ayah!" Kez shouted and rushed at his challenger.

Aton feinted to the left with his spear.

Kez raised his sword.

But Aton hefted the weapon from his left to his right hand and hurled it.

The spear whirred through the air.

Kez rushed forward. The spear passed over him and he came bearing down on Aton, who flung himself at Kez's legs, tumbling him to the ground.

The two wrestled, each trying to fling the other from him.

Aton was too close for Kez to use his sword.

Time and time again they rolled over each other, while above them the rock cliff glowed with a crown of flame and the screams of the dying people mingled with the frightened whinnying of the horses.

Aton finally broke Kez's hold on the sword. The weapon dropped to the ground and Aton shouted to all who watched the struggle, "Let no one touch the sword!"

And those who gathered to see which of the two would survive, left the weapon where it fell.

Kez freed himself of Aton's hold and sprang to his feet.

He kicked Aton in the chest and sent him sprawling.

Aton groaned with pain. His breath was gone and he scrambled out of Kez's reach.

Kez went for the sword and rushed at Aton, who gathered earth in his hand and flung it in Kez's face, blinding him.

Aton gained his feet and once again struggled to force Kez to drop the sword. He drove his knee into Kez's groin and tore the sword from his hand. He swung it across Kez's right shoulder.

Kez screamed and fell to his knees.

"Take the tusks," Zell shouted. "Take the tusks. They are yours. They are your sign."

Aton struck at Kez's left shoulder. And then even as the fingers of Kez's dismembered hand still moved, Aton took the tusks from each of the limbs and slipped them on his own arms.

Kez screamed. From where his shoulders had been now gushed two fountains of blood.

"Kill me!" Kez cried. "Kill me!"

Aton lifted the blood-stained sword and shouted, "I am the leader of the people. *I am a man amongst men, a beginning.*"

"You are——" Kez said but to silence him Zell rushed to him and drove his foot against the stricken man's throat. Then, taking a spear, Zell hurled it deep into Kez's heart.

Aton looked around him. The Horse People and the slaves had seen what he had done and were afraid to move. The cliffs above the camp were red with fire and burning rock streamed down its side. The air was filled with the stink of fire.

The earth began to shake again. Several large cracks appeared. The river dropped into one of them and the grassland on the other side of it suddenly rose up and belched flames. Then from the far end of the valley, where the canyons were, mountains came to be where there were none before.

Some of Kez's riders ran toward Aton brandishing their weapons. No spear found its mark.

Amidst the flames and cries of the injured, Aton raised his voice and shouted for all to hear, "I am your leader. *I am a man amongst men, a beginning.* I will lead you out of here."

"How?" many cried. "How will you lead us when the Shaker of the Earth has destroyed us? The rock cliffs burn with his anger. The grass burns with his fury, and he has swallowed the river. How will you lead. . . ?"

Aton glanced at Zell and answered, his voice as thunderous as the crashing mountains, "I will follow Yahweh. You will follow me. And I will follow Him. He will lead us."

The earth trembled and the people ran, scattering in all directions.

"Hear me," Aton shouted above the grinding of the rocks and the roar of the fire. "Hear me and know that I will lead you from here. Gather your belongings. Take the horses and grain, and we will go from this place of death. Slave and freeman are all one. There is no master save whom I serve. I am your master through Him. I am *a man amongst men, a beginning.*"

Amid the death and destruction the people followed Aton's bidding. They gathered before him, even as the rock cliffs spewed forth fountains of hot ash that burnt their clothing and singed their hair.

Aton mounted his horse and, taking the lead, slowly worked his way up the valley to where the dreaded canyons lay.

Zell rode at his side.

In every direction the land was burned beyond using.

"The work of Yahweh," Zell whispered. "Blessed be His name for He has given us our freedom."

Aton gave a snort of disdain and rode on silently. It was he who hacked off Kez's arms to take back Pula's tusks. He was *a man amongst men, a beginning.*

20

ALL THROUGH THAT FIRST NIGHT when the Earth Shaker tumbled the rock cliffs down, caused mountains to swell up where none had been, and loosed fire from the depths of the earth, Aton led his people toward the canyons.

Shouting above the roar, he rode up and down the line of his followers, exhorting them not to falter, to move faster and faster. Many trotted. Many could not keep the pace and fell to the ground weeping with exhaustion, but Aton could not stop. He left them to die.

Several of Kez's bolder riders challenged his authority, but he wasted no words on them and smote them with his sword, leaving their bodies for the wild dogs and vultures.

The darkness of the night was emblazoned with the terrible red glow of fires. Smoke and ash filled the air, blacking out the clear glow of the star figures.

Aton rode beside Zell and said, "I have seen the hot wind of death, and I have endured the long march with

Kez, but never have I witnessed anything like this. It is beyond reckoning."

"It is Yahweh's will," Zell answered.

"The Earth Shaker——"

"All is in Yahweh," Zell said.

Suddenly the earth beneath them trembled.

Zell screamed and his mount reared.

Aton grabbed the horse's bridle and steadied the animal while behind them the earth, like a hideous black mouth, yawned open and devoured many of the people in the column before it closed again.

Aton released Zell's mount, turned and raced back to where the rest of the people stood, too terrified to move. "Hurry," he shouted. "Hurry. The earth could open again."

They did not move and Arri called out, "Where do you lead us, Aton?"

"Through the canyons," Aton answered, pointing to them with the sword.

"We will die."

"You will die if you stay here."

"The Shaker of the Earth has taken many of our people. Perhaps his anger has cooled."

Aton shouted, "Look around you, Arri. The very land burns with fury."

"Then his anger will scorch those of us who are left."

"Not if you follow me," Aton told him. And because he first moved them with it, he shouted, "Follow me and I will lead you to Yahweh. I will lead you to Him."

"It is to the Shaker of the Earth that we must go."

"He is but a part of Yahweh," Aton shouted, repeating Zell's words for his own.

The earth trembled again.

Knowing it had come to a battle between Yahweh and the Shaker of the Earth, Aton roared, "It was I who angered the Shaker of the Earth, Arri. It was I who went up to the caves where he lived and challenged him."

The people moaned and shouted their hate for Aton. Several of Kez's riders wheeled out of the line and with their spears held low prepared to run Aton through.

"And this is what you have brought us to," Arri said, encompassing the ruin around them with a wave of his hand. "This is what your challenge has heaped down upon us."

"No," Aton shouted. "I am *a man amongst men, a beginning.* The words came from Yahweh and I spoke them. Even now it is Yahweh who makes the Shaker of the Earth tremble. And it was He who gave me the strength to kill Kez and take his sword. I am your leader and you will follow me as I follow Yahweh."

The people turned to each other and spoke about what they had just heard.

"There is no time now to talk about Yahweh and His greatness," Aton said. "Now we must get away from here."

The men raised their spears. Aton rode to the head of the column and took the lead.

To most it seemed that the first light of the sun was longer in coming than it had ever been but that was because the sky was filled with clouds of dark ash. When the light came it was gray. Through it Aton could see the mountains that had risen during the night. They were off to the right of the canyon and their slopes were red with flame.

The sun rose higher, and through the grayness was a circle of fire. The trees and grass on either side of the valley were withered from the heat or reduced to glowing embers. Carcasses of many animals and birds were strewn over the land.

Some of the people called to Aton, asking him to halt so that all could rest awhile.

"If we rest," Aton answered, "Yahweh will desert us and we will be sure to die."

The people continued to follow him. He led them into the bed of the river, now baked dry by the heat of the fires all around it. He took them to the opening of the canyon but the space between the two walls was now closed.

For most of the day Aton searched for a way through the rock wall, while some bewailed their fate and others blamed Aton for the terrible disaster.

Then when the red circle of the sun was low in the western sky Aton found a breach in the rock wall large enough to allow a man and a horse to pass through.

"And what will be on the other side?" a man asked.

"A way to the other side," Aton answered.

"And what if the sides of the canyon move together?" another questioned.

And still another shouted, "How will we find our way in the darkness?"

"There is enough light from the fires all around us," Aton answered, "to show us the way." And then, impatient with the fear of the people, he shouted, "Those who follow me will find Yahweh but those who do not will find death." He rode into the opening without looking back.

Frightened by his words, the people followed.

The canyon was very narrow and very dark, though at the top the sky glowed red from the fires. Soon the canyon became narrower, forcing the riders to dismount and lead their horses single file.

Between the walls the air was hot. Every breath of the people filled their chests with fire. They moved silently, their heads bent and their throats parched. Aton told them not to drink until they stopped. But many did not heed his words and satisfied their thirst from the water skins they had taken with them.

The first light seeped into the canyon. The sky was still filled with clouds of dark gray ash. In the distance they could hear the angry rumble of the Shaker of the Earth as he fought Aton's Yahweh.

The canyon became wider and the riders remounted. The red circle of the sun floated over the top of the canyon. The heat brought forth whimpers of anguish from the women and children. Many of the older men dropped from their mounts and were left to die, their bodies leaning against the walls of the canyon.

"Call a halt," Zell croaked, "or we will all perish."

"And what of your Yahweh now?" Aton answered, his own voice raspy with dryness. "Where is he?"

"With you always," Zell said.

Aton snorted and looked back at his ragged column of followers. They lacked his strength to continue.

"They are only men, women, and children," Zell told him, "while you are *a man amongst men, a beginning.*"

Aton nodded and ordered a halt.

The people dropped where they were. Most were too exhausted to care about food but all wanted water. Aton quickly discovered that the greed of some denied water to most of the others.

In the fast fading light of the canyon he climbed up the wall and, looking down at the people, told them what had happened. "None will drink unless all drink. Now the water skins will be guarded by Porip and the men he chooses. Anyone guilty of taking water when the rest of the people have none will suffer death. Those who will come out of the canyon with me will thank Yahweh for the wisdom He has given me."

That night Aton forsook the offer of water and sucked on a small round stone to bring moisture into his mouth. He sat with his back against the wall and his hand around Kez's sword which, like himself, the horses, and everything else, was covered with gray ash. But he did not have to see its burnished surface to know its power. He could feel it in his hand. Let Zell have his Yahweh. He would take the power of the sword and the power of Pula's tusks. With such power he would some day meet his father and kill him. He looked at the followers. Those who survived his journey would stand with him when he returned to his own people and claimed them as his own.

Aton slept little, and as soon as the first gray light showed itself in the canyon he rose and called everyone to wakefulness. Before the day's march he doled out the water.

"There will be no stop," he said as soon as he mounted, "until we find our way out."

"But we thought you knew the way," Eliti shouted at him.

The people echoed her words.

"I only know," he answered, "that we must make our way out of these canyons as quickly as possible or we will die in them."

"But you said," she cried, "that you were following Yahweh."

"Follow me," Aton responded, "follow me and you will follow Him." He turned and began the march.

The second day was worse than the first and the third worse than the second. The days were fused into the nights by the heat of the sun and the numbing cold at night. Wood was scarce and the small fires warmed many people. Food became scarce and the people began to eat the seeds and the grain they had brought with them until Aton put that under his own protection. Horses died, even though they were given more water than the people.

At the end of several days, when Aton sat alone and the rest of the people had gone to sleep, Eliti left Arri's side and came to him.

"I have watched you these many days, Aton," she whispered, "and my body craves yours. I was wrong to look away from you. Now I do not even see the wound." She reached up to touch it with her fingers.

Aton turned his head away.

"You are changed," she told him, letting her hand drop to her lap.

234

"I have always been what I am," he told her.

"No," she said, "I know the man I held in my arms, the man who took milk from my breasts like a child, the man who sheathed his organ in my body. I know him but you are not——"

Aton waved his hand in front of him and said, "These are my people, Eliti, even as you are one of them and I must lead them out of here."

"Will you, Aton?" she asked.

He nodded and said, "I will."

Wordlessly Eliti crawled back to Arri.

Aton led his people out of the canyons to a rich grassland where a river flowed. The men, women, and children ran to the water and flung themselves into it. Aton also drank the cool waters.

That afternoon Aton and some of the riders hunted several large animals. At night he cut the meat for everyone who was strong enough to eat.

When the others had moved to sleep, Aton sat by the fire with Zell. "We will rest here for a few days," he told the story-teller. "The mounts need it as well as the people."

"Then where?" Zell questioned.

Moving his hand toward the south and then to the west, Aton said, "To the land of my father."

"And that is still your purpose?"

"Yes."

"And what of Yahweh's purpose?"

Aton shrugged and said, "I can not answer for it."

"But it was He who helped you bring the people through the canyons."

"I brought them through, Zell," Aton answered. "I remembered the way I came with Kez and I backtracked. It was no easier one way than the other. But it was I, not Yahweh, who led them here."

Zell said nothing.

Aton became uneasy with his silence and angrily told

him, Yahweh is yours. The sword and Pula's tusks are mine."

"But you used Him," Zell said accusingly.

"And will again," Aton responded, "if I can make the people do my bidding by doing it. I give Yahweh to you, Zell. Tell the people anything you want. Tell them what Dahsan told you about Him, but—"

"I will only tell the people," Zell said, "of how you serve Him. When the time comes, Aton, I will tell your story with His as I was meant to do."

"I will not stop you," Aton said. "Now get some rest. Tomorrow brings another day with many things to do."

"Will you sleep?" Zell questioned.

"After I speak with the guards around the camp," Aton said. "We must not allow ourselves to be taken by surprise. The slaves with us have suffered for their freedom and those that were free have also suffered enough to remain free."

Zell's thin lips parted in a smile.

Aton left Zell sitting by the fire. He did not understand why Zell was smiling. Then with a shrug he told himself that he did not care what the story-teller did.

21

ATON RESTED HIS PEOPLE for many days, and when they were ready to move he used riders the way Kez had. Several rode far enough in front of the column to give warning of any danger ahead; some lagged behind for the same purpose, while others guarded the flanks.

Game was plentiful and the water skins were always filled. In the evening when camp was made they looked back from where they had come. It was still covered by a dark gray cloud of ash. Sometimes flames leapt up from the burning land accompanied by the terrible thunder of falling mountains.

Aton continued to press south and west, although he was still a long way from Nempie's camp. Much of what he saw he remembered from the time he had been along the same way with Kez.

When they reached the river where he had fought the green death, Aton told Zell about it. That night in the camp Zell recounted the story of Aton's battle with the snake.

They listened without making a sound and when Zell finished his tale he said, "Know from this and all other things that Yahweh stands with him."

The people agreed with Zell.

They crossed the wrinkled land as quickly as possible, but the journey was difficult. During the day it was unbearably hot and at night the cold quickly numbed their limbs. They slept close to one another very near the fire. One night Eliti came to Aton. She said nothing to him, and lying down next to him, she lifted her covering for him.

He mounted, and with a deep groan of pleasure, satisfied himself.

And Eliti whispered, "Take me from Arri."

Aton shook his head.

"But I am more yours than his," she said. "It is you who gives me pleasure, not him. Take me from him, Aton."

"I will take," he answered, "what you give. But I will not take something that belongs to another man because I am Aton and he is less than I."

Eliti pleaded with him.

And again he said, "No."

Suddenly Eliti began to scream.

The guards rushed into the camp and many of the people grabbed firebrands.

Naked, Eliti shouted that Aton had raped her. That she had left Arri to relieve herself and as she was returning Aton had grabbed her. Her tears glistened in the reddish glow of the torchlight.

Arri came forward. The people became silent.

"Is this too Yahweh's doing?" Arri asked, speaking slowly.

Aton's hold on his sword tightened. He took a deep draught of air. He could have easily cut Arri down the way Kez would have in the same situation. And that would have ended it. But instead he said with a sigh,

"No, Arri, it is my doing. But I did not take her by force. She came to me."

"He lies," Eliti screamed. "He lies. He is nothing more than a slave. He is nothing more than a slave."

Arri stretched forth his hand to Eliti and said, "Come."

She stepped backward and pointing a finger at Aton she shouted, "He mounted me even when he lived in our shelter. I gave him my breasts for their milk but he wanted my slit for pleasure. He deceived you, Arri. He deceived you. Ask him."

Arri looked questioningly at Aton.

"She speaks the truth," Aton said.

The people grumbled loudly and one of the men shouted, "That is not our way. One man can not mount another man's woman. That is not our way."

"Stone them!" someone shouted.

Others took up the same cry.

Then Aton, his voice like the boom of thunder, shouted, "I was not of your people. I was a slave. Your ways were not my ways. I was nothing, even less than a horse."

"But she knew," Arri answered. "Eliti knew."

"She, too, was taken captive," Aton reminded him.

"I took her as my woman."

"No," Aton said. "Kez gave her to you."

Once more the people became silent.

"Neither one of us were of your people," Aton said. "I because I was taken captive and made a slave and Eliti because she came to you the same way and was given to Arri by Kez. She was as much a slave as I. But her work was to give Arri pleasure while mine was to first work in the fields and then to tame horses."

Arri pulled on his beard.

"Let the matter rest," Aton suggested. "And from this time on we will follow the way of your people. Let Eliti go with a man of her own choosing, Arri."

"Do you want her as your woman?" Arri asked.

"No," Aton said, looking at her. "No." And then turning his eyes to Arri he asked, "Do you want her?"

"Yes," the man said. "I want her."

"Will you go with him now?" Aton asked her.

She nodded and said, "I will go with him."

Arri extended his hand and she took it.

"There is still much of the night left," Aton told the people. "Go back to sleep. Tomorrow we have a long hard march. He waited until everyone was settled again before he sat down at his own fire. For awhile he stared at it and thought about what had just happened. That he did not have to kill Arri pleased him immensely. The man had given him food and shelter when he had most needed it. And as for Eliti, Aton could do no more than shrug. There would be other women for him who were just as skilled at giving a man pleasure. He shrugged again and let the waters of sleep take him.

Several times Aton and his people were attacked. Once by his mother's people when they passed near their camp. In that fight many of the riders took arrows but few were killed. When they were struck by other riders many men died and several women were carried off. Aton was splattered with blood before the coming of darkness ended the fight.

After many days on the march Aton brought his people to the place where Besop had been impaled. The spear still stood upright in the ground where it had been planted. Besop's bones lay scattered.

Aton gathered his friend's bones together and put them down under and placed rocks on the mound before he once more took the lead of the column.

Soon the mountains in the east came into view. Aton told the people that they were near their goal.

"Where Yahweh lives?" one of them asked.

Realizing he had made a mistake, Aton answered, "He is everywhere."

They came to the long valley where Nempie had left

Aton for dead, and Aton led his people along the ridges, pointing to where he had fought a long time ago.

When they made camp, Aton told Zell what had happened to him there in the long valley and how he had made the journey to the place where all men go but from where few return.

"Dahsan," Zell said, "called it the House of Set, keeper of the Underworld and all that is in darkness."

"I saw my mother there," Aton said. "She played a game of stones with the stranger whose heart I had eaten. He had won but she warned me in time so that I could flee."

Zell nodded but did not speak again that night.

Within three days Aton was back in the land he had known most of his life. He found Nempie's old camp by the side of the river and let his people use it. Then he began to search for Nempie but there was no sign of him or his people.

"Perhaps," Zell suggested, "they were driven off."

"There were no other people as strong as Nempie's," Aton told him.

"There is always someone stronger," Zell answered.

"No," Aton declared angrily. "Nempie was the———"

"It is foolish to be angry because you can not kill him," Zell said.

"That was my purpose," Aton answered, stirring the fire until sparks flew in every direction. "That was my purpose."

"But you already have a people."

Aton shook his head. "As I became Isso's son," he said, "by passing between the naked thighs of his woman, these people have become mine by living through that night of fire and falling rock. No, Zell, I will look for myself. And when Nempie's people are mine I will bring the two peoples together."

"I will go with you," Zell said.

"No. If something should happen to me, you would die."

"Nothing will happen to you. You are in Yahweh's hands."

Eventually Aton agreed to let Zell accompany him. The next morning he summoned the people and told them that he and Zell would be gone for awhile.

"How long?" Arri asked.

"I do not know," Aton answered. "But I will need several horses and grain. I do not want to come empty-handed to my own people. To you, Arri and Porip, I leave the camp and all those in it."

"Will you bring Yahweh back to us?" one of the men asked.

"He is already here," Aton whispered.

"And will you take Yahweh to your own people?" the same man questioned.

"Yes," Aton said. "I will take Him wherever I go. His power is beyond understanding."

In early morning Aton and Zell left the camp and rode toward the mountains in the east.

When they were a distance from the camp Zell said, "You know that we will never return to them?"

"Yes," Aton answered.

They rode in silence awhile longer and Aton said, "But I did lead them to Yahweh, Zell, did I not?"

"Yes," Zell responded, "as you will lead others, even yourself."

Aton glanced at the story-teller but did not answer.

Part V

ATON, THE LEADER
OF THE PEOPLE

22

ATON AND ZELL ranged far and wide looking for Nempie and his people but in all their wanderings found no sign of them. Occasionally they came upon an abandoned camp. From the way it had been left Aton knew it had belonged to a people other than those of his father. When Nempie left a camp he always burned everything in it.

Many times Aton and Zell were forced to flee and, galloping as fast as they could, put distance between themselves and other hunters. If they had not been well mounted they could not have escaped their pursuers.

Even though they preferred to avoid battle there were times when Aton was forced to cut their way through the hunters who strove to pull him and Zell from the back of their horses.

They were, in its season, scorched by the hot wind that blew across the land from the great desert to the west. When the tops of the mountains turned white they trembled at the harsh touch of the cold wind that came out of the mountains. They endured driving rain and blowing sand but their search revealed nothing.

One night, when they were numb with cold, huddling close to a small fire, Aton said, "We will not find Nempie. We will not find him or his people even if we spend the rest of our lives looking for him."

Zell held his hands toward the fire. Sensing that Aton had more to say, he did not speak.

"I do not understand," Aton said, "how this could have come to pass. Have I come here to sit shivering before a small fire to ask *why?*"

"To fullfill your purpose as Yahweh had intended," Zell said, his breath steaming in the cold air as he spoke.

"My purpose," Aton answered, "was to kill my father and to claim his people for my own."

"That was your purpose?" Zell said.

"All that has happened to me," Aton responded sharply, "has been for that and that alone. I came to kill Nempie and I cannot even find him. I will never find him. And for that, Zell, am I *a man amongst men, a beginning?*" He pounded the fist of his right hand into the palm of his left. "For that did I take the thrice-circled tusks of Pula, the black boar? For that did I make the journey to what you call the House of Set? For that did I hold the green death in my hands? For that did I suffer on the cross-tree? For that did I lead the remnants of the Horse People and their slaves out of the valley of fire and falling rock? For what purpose, Zell, tell me for what purpose did all those things and more happen if it were not to kill Nempie and take his people for my own so that they would be called Aton's people instead of Nempie's people?"

"Perhaps it was not Yahweh's purpose," Zell suggested.

Aton snorted disgustedly.

"Will you return to the camp of——"

"No," Aton said. "They are not my people. I was their slave."

"But you became their leader," Zell countered.

Aton nodded and said, "When I gathered up Besop's bones and put them down under I knew that I would not stay with them. The best that they have—their horses and their grain—I also have." He paused, and then with his brow furrowed, he continued, "And in return for what I took from them I led them to safety and left them Yahweh. I had not thought of it that way until now but that was the way it was. I have no feelings for them, Zell. Perhaps we can find another people whose leader I can challenge."

"My own people live near here. We can find them."

Aton suddenly laughed and he asked, "Would that be Yahweh's purpose, Zell?"

The story-teller shrugged and said, "His purpose was to bring us together through Dahsan. Having done that, He brought us here. I do not know any more than that, Aton. I am not a seer who can see into the future. For me, even the present is all but gone from my eyes. Yet I can see into the past and know that what has happened, happened because of Him, because of Yahweh. My people are not far from here and though I can not give them to you, you have the strength to make them your own. They are hunters and tenders of goats and sheep. Before I was taken prisoner by Kez, their leader was Gibb. He came from somewhere deep in the mountains. To become the leader of my people you will have to kill him."

"I will think on it," Aton responded, pulling the horse hide over him as he stretched out.

By morning it was snowing and Aton said to Zell, "We will look for your people if for no other reason than to find shelter from the snow and cold."

"You will find a people, Aton," the story-teller responded, "and you will also find your purpose: to be *a man amongst men, a beginning*."

Aton did not answer, but as they began to search for Zell's people Aton suddenly realized how close the story-teller held him. He brooded on it for most of the day. In the evening, when they stopped to make camp for the night, he asked, "Did you know from the very beginning that I would not find my father or his people?"

"No," Zell answered quietly, "such a thing was not mine to know. I put my trust in Yahweh."

"Let us hope," Aton said, sullenly, "that your Yahweh puts His trust in us." Again he felt Zell had used him as a hunter used a bow, and he shrugged to throw off that unpleasant feeling.

Later Aton built a small fire, and Zell held the spitted carcass of a rabbit over the flames. The smell of roasting meat filled the air and quickly drew the company of a small pack of wild dogs, who prowled like shadows beyond the circle of wavering firelight with only their eyes gleaming yellow in the deep darkness of the night.

"It would be well to take them with us," Aton said, gesturing to the dark moving shadows of the dogs.

"They will follow us," Zell told him, "if you throw them the bones of the rabbit."

"Nempie's dogs," Aton commented, "were good hunters."

"Perhaps," Zell offered, "this pack will be as good."

Aton took the guts of the rabbit and threw them into the darkness. The dogs sprang on the bloody offal with a sudden burst of barking and snapping jaws, followed by angry growling. "They will stay with us now," Aton said, "unless I drive them off with fire."

Zell lifted the rabbit from the fire and handing it to Aton, he said, "Eat first, Aton. I will have what is left and the dogs will finish what I leave."

"Why that way, Zell?" Aton asked, since he always cut the meat for the story-teller.

"Because," Zell answered, "I am less than you are. You are *a man amongst men, a beginning*, while I am only Zell, the story-teller."

"You tell me one thing," Aton said, "but I know another. I am no longer angry. I will cut the meat for you as I did before. But do not play me, Zell, do not bend me as you would a bow."

Zell nodded and in a low voice that was only slightly louder than the hiss of the falling snow he said, "I can bend no one, Aton. If you are a bow, then you are in Yahweh's hands and who can escape His hold?"

The pack of dogs followed Aton and Zell as they searched for Zell's people in the sequestered valleys of the foothills that lay before the mountains.

Often the sky was so filled with clouds that the sun could not be seen and the star figures remained hidden at night. The wind howled and whipped the falling snow around them or pelted them with rain and bits of ice. Sometimes the cut of the wind was so bruising that it opened their skin, causing blood to flow.

To Aton each valley had its own characteristics, and almost as soon as they would enter it, he would turn to Zell and say, "There are no people here," or he would wave his hand and say, "The people left here before the coming of the snow."

Zell always answered, "Perhaps we will find them in the next valley."

Aton would call to the dogs, ranging closely behind them.

The bite of the wind lessened and the snow stopped. Warmth came into the air; the sky cleared.

By the time the first buds began to show on the limbs of the trees, Aton had tamed the dogs and had brought to his side the leader of the pack, a brownish colored beast with only a left eye, like his master. The dog sat close to Aton at the fire but never near Zell. Aton had trained the pack to obey his commands.

The days became warmer and the trees and bushes were in full leaf. The horses enjoyed the luxury of fresh grass and the stallions mounted the mares. When the mares were filled with the spirit of a new horse, Aton took milk from them.

Then one afternoon, as they came to a valley in the foothills that lay to the north of the mountains, Aton said, "There are people here."

"Are you sure?" Zell asked, unable to keep the excitement out of his voice.

"There are many signs," Aton answered. "The grass here is enough for their goats and sheep."

Zell wanted to ride up the valley immediately, but Aton said, "I will go with the dogs. If I am killed by Gibb, or whoever their leader is, you can come to them with the horses and the grain. With such gifts they will not refuse to take you to them."

Zell nodded and asked, "Is that why you wanted the dogs?"

"They will help me do what must be done," Aton answered.

"When will you go?"

"When there is thunder on the mountain and lightning in the sky."

Zell gave him a questioning look, but Aton only smiled at him.

They rode out of the valley and made camp for the night. Using a rough stone Aton sharpened the blade of his sword until he was able to slice through the long strands of his hair. Then he hefted his spear. Satisfied that his weapons were the way he wanted them, he cut meat for Zell and himself.

Later, when the fire was low, Aton said, "I have often wondered where Dahsan's people found Yahweh."

"He never told me," Zell responded.

Aton uttered a soft chuckle and, stirring the fire, said, "At least your Yahweh has brought us this far. I was beginning to think that, like Nempie's people, we would never find yours."

"Yahweh will make you leader——"

"My trust is in Pula, the black boar, whose tusks I wear and in the sword I took from Kez."

"In the end," Zell said, "you will come to know it was all Yahweh."

"Who knows what will be in the end," Aton answered with a sigh. "What often seems so certain becomes nothing. I never thought that I would be a slave, and I was. I never thought that I would be here with you, and I am. And I had always thought that some day I would kill Nempie and claim his people for my own, but I could not even find him."

"It is Yahweh's way," Zell commented softly.

Aton sighed and said, "And who knows where this will end?"

Zell shook his head but did not speak.

For a long time Aton stared at the fire as if the flames themselves were something that the sight of his one eye could brush aside and allow him to see into the future. All he could see were ashes and glowing embers. Whether they were a good or a bad omen he could not decide.

"Did you know," Aton questioned in a low voice, "that Kez knew of Pula, the black boar?"

"I thought he must have," Zell answered, wondering how much more Aton knew about the man he had killed."

"It is strange that he should come into my head now."

"He is with you," came Zell's ready answer, "because you will do as he has done. He challenged the leader of the Horse People, killed him, and made the people his own."

"They were never really his," Aton said. "He held them with his sword, with his strength, but they were never really his."

Aton's words were like strokes of a knife and they cut close to the bone of truth.

"Sometimes," Aton continued, "when I looked at Kez, I could almost see Nempie, my father."

Zell began to cough.

251

"They did look that much alike," Aton affirmed, lifting his face toward Zell. "And many of the things that Kez did along the march, after he took me captive, Nempie would have done. They possessed the same kind of cunning and hunting skills."

"Perhaps that was why you hated Kez so much?" Zell offered, clearing his throat.

"That would have been reason enough," Aton agreed with another chuckle.

To avoid the risk of betraying what he knew about Kez and what Aton only sensed, Zell said that he was very tired and wanted to sleep.

Aton sat at the fire awhile longer and then, putting his hand on the dog next to him, stretched out and slept.

Many days passed and the dark clouds that held the thunder did not come to the mountain.

Zell became impatient.

Aton told him, "It must be done my way, Zell."

"But what if we are found here?"

"Then you will know that Yahweh has failed you," Aton said.

"My trust is in Him," Zell responded.

"If it is and I am His voice," Aton said, "then heed me."

Zell did not answer.

The summer heat lay over the land. Each afternoon more and more dark clouds gathered over the mountain. Then one day the air was very still. It was very hot and though the sun had not yet reached its highest point in the sky the dark clouds gathered around the top of the mountain.

"If no one comes for you," Aton said to Zell, "wait here until three days pass before you return to your people. You have enough meat to eat and water to drink."

"Will the thunder be on the mountain and the lightning in the sky?" Zell questioned.

"When the sun begins to drop into the pit at the edge of the great desert," Aton answered. Then he called to the dogs and, taking his weapons, he walked slowly toward the valley.

"Yahweh will stand with you," Zell shouted after him.

Aton did not bother to answer.

The dogs ranged behind him with the one-eyed leader at his side. They seemed to sense that they were being used for a special purpose and uttered low throaty sounds.

"We must be swift in what we do," Aton said, speaking to the dog beside him.

The animal growled.

Aton broke into a trot and the dogs matched his pace. He watched the clouds on the top of the mountain become darker and darker until most of the sky was covered by them.

And then he saw the camp of Zell's people. It was on the far side of the valley. The smoke from the cooking fires hung above the camp like puffs of white clouds.

The sky was black.

From the shouts ringing out, Aton knew he had been seen and the people were being warned.

He began to run and the dogs ran, too. He was wet with sweat. His chest heaved with each breath.

The drum in the camp sounded. Its booming filled the valley and seemed to go up to the very clouds.

Suddenly many men were running toward him from the camp. The rest of the people followed close behind them.

The dogs began to bark and the leader of the pack ran slightly in front of Aton, who added his wild blood cries to the sound of the dogs.

The men coming toward Aton suddenly stopped and he slowed down long enough to find one for his spear.

253

He loosed the weapon and it whirred through the heavy air.

The men broke and ran but the spear caught one in the back, pierced his body, dropping him to the ground. His screams were louder than the barking of the dogs. He tried to crawl but only managed to wiggle his feet and arms.

"I am Aton," Aton roared, "Aton, son of Nempie." Pointing to the black sky above the mountains, he told them, "I come from Yahweh. I speak with His voice and His voice is the thunder." Then he shouted to the dogs and, obeying his word, they stopped and crouched.

One of the men came forward. He was tall, muscular, and in his hand he held a spear.

"I come for you, Gibb," Aton bellowed.

The man stopped.

"I come for you," Aton shouted.

His words were followed by the deep roll of thunder. Gibb glanced over his shoulder at the mountains.

"Yahweh speaks," Aton yelled. "I will let you live, Gibb, if you throw down your weapon——"

Gibb hefted his spear.

"I will kill you," Aton shouted. "Yahweh calls for your blood!"

Gibb charged Aton.

"Now!" Aton yelled. "Now kill!" The dogs rushed at the man.

He hurled two of them to bloody deaths but the leader of the pack sank his teeth into Gibb's thigh.

The man howled with pain and tried to fight off the dog.

Aton rushed forward.

Gibb tried to fend off the stroke of his attacker's weapon, but the blade slicked off the spear's shaft.

Aton pulled his sword up and, thrusting it in Gibb's chest, shouted, "I am *a man amongst men, a beginning!* I am Aton!"

Gibb dropped to his knees.

Another roll of thunder boomed out.

"Yahweh is satisfied!" Aton yelled to the people.

The sky suddenly became emblazoned with streaks of lightning.

Gibb screamed.

Aton pulled his bloody sword from the man's body and let the dogs have him.

The other men saw what had happened and cowered from the one-eyed stranger and his dogs.

"Hear me!" Aton shouted. "I am your leader. I want what is mine to take. You were his people. You are now my people."

More lightning flashed across the sky.

"Yahweh will soon speak," Aton said, pointing with his sword to the top of the mountain where the clouds were darkest.

And then the thunder came.

The people dropped to their knees and begged Aton to spare their lives.

"I came only to become your leader. Yahweh did not want blood. But Gibb wanted to fight. Yahweh stood with me against him."

Each time one of the dogs tore a chunk of flesh from his body, Gibb screamed.

"Kill him," shouted a woman. "Kill him!" She rushed to Aton and threw herself at his feet. "I am yours as I was his, but kill him."

Another streak of lightning slashed the dark sky.

"Yahweh will answer you," Aton said.

The thunder came again.

Aton went to Gibb and drove his sword into the man's heart. Then he said, "Such was the will of Yahweh!"

The lightning came again, and the thunder followed quickly.

When it stopped Aton told the people, "This blood was necessary. I come with gifts that will give you more than you ever had. I come to do all that can be done for a people. Yahweh stands with me, I am His voice to Zell, who is one of your own, and he will be my voice to you."

When the people heard the name of Zell they remembered the story-teller and how he had been taken in a raid by the men who rode on the backs of animals.

"I have come to be your leader," Aton said. "To bring you to Yahweh!"

One of the men shouted, "We are your people."

Another uttered the same cry and soon they were all shouting, "We are your people Aton. We are your people."

Aton held up his sword; suddenly it was sheathed with a white glow that soon covered him, too. "I am the voice of Yahweh," he shouted. "I am *a man amongst men, a beginning.*"

The people echoed his words, and as the first flood of rain gushed from the clouds Aton became the leader of Zell's people.

He walked slowly toward them and, seeing a young woman with green eyes and long black hair, he pointed to her. "I will take her for my woman," he told them. "I do not want what Gibb used."

She did not shrink away from him when Aton took hold of her hand.

"How are you called?" he asked.

"Tua," she answered.

Aton repeated her name and said aloud, "I take Tua for my woman!"

"She was promised to me," a man called out.

Aton lifted his sword and answered, "Then fight me for her?"

No one answered the challenge.

Three times Aton repeated it. Then he said, "Tomorrow I will bring Zell back to you, but tonight I will spend with Tua."

23

EXCEPT FOR TUA, the people feared Aton. They considered him a fierce looking man made even more terrifying by his damaged eye and scarred lid. But from the moment he embraced Tua, she knew there was a part of Aton that only a woman who lay with him could ever know.

By the passing of the late summer moon Aton and Zell had become familiar figures in the camp. They took Zell to them because he was one of them and, afraid of Aton's Yahweh, they quickly accepted the man as their leader and, through him, Yahweh, whose thundering voice spoke only to Aton.

The people, Aton found, were weak as Besop's people had been and were better at tending goats and sheep than at hunting. Though, as his first gift, he gave them the horses he had taken with him, they were more interested in the mare's milk than in the strength that a mounted man had over a man on foot.

To make his people strong enough to defend themselves, he took the young men and made riders out of them, taught them to use the spear from the back of a horse, and how to use the bow and arrow when they were at a full gallop. He put guards around the camp so that no other people would surprise them and carry off their women.

Aton seldom spoke to the people about Yahweh but he was aware of Zell's efforts. Zell gave credit for everything that happened to Yahweh, even for the things that Aton accomplished himself.

When the planting season came again, Aton brought his people to a field near the camp. He ordered them to clear it of grass. Taking a planting stick, he showed them how to put seeds in the ground. Later when the grain was harvested he taught them to pound the grain into flour and from the flour mixed with water, he showed them how to make the slave food.

It was soon winter again and the days were filled with snow, wind, and rain.

To Aton's surprise Zell approached one day as he walked toward one of the guards and said, "It is the custom of the people for one man from all of the men in the camp to challenge the leader of the people and fight him until he is either slain or slays the leader and becomes the new leader. Sometimes the challenger is from the outside, as you yourself were, and as Gibb was. Often it is one of the men from the camp. That way the people are assured that their leader is always the strongest of the men."

Aton understood and, nodding, asked, "And when does the challenger make himself known?"

"Usually on the longest night of the year," Zell answered.

"I will meet him," Aton said but added, "tell the people that he who slays me will become me."

Zell did not understand.

"Tell them," Aton said, "that it is Yahweh's will."

Zell was about to object but an angry look from Aton was enough to silence him.

The night was cold and the sky filled with all of the star figures when Aton killed his first challenger. The contest was brief. Driving his sword into the man Aton shouted, "I am *a man amongst men, a beginning.* He who would become the leader of the people first become me!"

The people were transfixed by his astounding ferocity and they feared his words, knowing no man could become him since they had already been told many of his amazing exploits by Zell, the story-teller.

More years passed and on the longest night of each of them Aton met, fought, and killed the man who would become the leader. As each challenger came, Zell took the opportunity to relate to the people the wonders of Aton, so that they could understand the immense power of Yahweh, whose voice was the thunder on the mountain.

The people thrived and though they were the strongest in the land they raided only the camps of those who threatened them or for women.

Aton eventually led them down from the foothills of the mountains to a place where there was a river and more grass for their larger herd of goats, sheep, and horses.

Aton's camp soon became a stopping place for those people who used camels as he used horses.

These people came like windblown leaves and like windblown leaves left, resting for a few days to fill their water skins before continuing their journey. For fresh meat and bread they gave salt, chunks of black rock that Manlo, the arrow-maker, was able to fashion into sharp arrows and knives.

The sons that Tua dropped quickly grew into boys and almost before Aton realized it they were old enough to ride with the men. He was filled with pride.

To him, as to all of his people, life was more fruitful than he or they had ever known it.

"Surely," Aton's people said, "Yahweh stands with Aton." For by now none of them doubted Yahweh's power or Aton's ability to use it against his enemies or for his friends.

They had heard him call upon Yahweh to bring rain and the rain fell, or they had seen him lift his sword to the dark clouds and make it and himself glow with the light of Yahweh. And they had heard Zell tell of the miraculous things that Aton had done before he became their leader, even to going to and returning from the House of Set, the lord of the Underworld, who was there by Yahweh's will.

Many seasons passed and it was once again the time for Zell to spin the tale of Aton's exploits and the time for Aton to face another challenger.

Zell was very old; so old that very few of the people remembered his summers. There were those who said Zell had been witness to all of the events in the stories he told. But they had forgotten that the story-teller had been born and raised in the camp before Kez had taken him captive. There were some people who could recall the day Zell and Aton had ridden into camp, and a few of these even remembered seeing Aton when he challenged Gibb, slew him, and claimed Tua for his woman.

All the years had bent Zell, but when he stepped into the circle of those who came to hear Aton's story his body straightened, grew tall in the wavering light of the fire, and, casting his wooden staff from him, he spoke in the rich full voice that, like some wonderful bird, wheeled in the cold night air above the heads of the people.

Both his hair and beard were white and each curled in its own way; his hair around the side of his face, in ringlets, and his beard in waves, like the water of the river when the wind blows. His brow was seamed with so many lines that it was impossible to discover where one ended and another began.

Zell was always led by one of the younger boys in the camp—except, of course, when he was in the center of the circle telling his stories of Aton. There he always stood alone and though he moved very close to the fire he was never burned by it.

Zell stood very still. The boy who had brought him into the circle of people had left him standing close enough to the fire to feel its heat and though he could not actually see the red of its flames they did become gray wavering shadows against the otherwise altogether dark of his world.

To gather some warmth to him, Zell moved closer to the fire, parting the flames—as he knew it seemed to those who watched him—with movements of his hands. When he was warm enough he cast down his staff, straightened up, and in a loud clear voice announced, "I am Zell, the story-teller. Listen to my words and you shall know the wonders of Aton. Listen to my words, oh my children, and through them you will come to know Aton."

The fire burned low. Where but a short while ago there were leaping flames, now there were glowing embers, some the color of the western sky when the sun dies at the end of each day and some covered with a gray ash.

Zell paused again, for the weight of all his years was a heavy burden for him to carry and Aton's story taxed his strength. If the people were patient with any man, they were patient with Zell.

That night was only the beginning. Even Zell, great a story-teller as he was, could not encompass in a single night all that had happened to Aton. Many nights were needed, which was why those nights were set apart from all others and gathered together when the sun journeyed quickly through the sky, beginning with the longest night of that season.

The people murmured with pleasure. The night's story was at an end and Zell waited for the small boy to come and lead him out of the circle, where only the embers of a dying fire remained.

The boy who led Zell from the fire was the one who had taken him inside the circle. His name was Dubi, the youngest son of Aton.

With his left hand hard on the boy's shoulder and his right grasping his wooden staff, Zell was escorted to the far end of the clearing, where Aton's tent stood.

It was the custom of the story-teller to abide with the leader for as many nights as it would take him to tell Aton's story. Otherwise, he lived in a tent set away from the others where he was tended by two crones who always squabbled, much to the amusement of everyone, about which one of them would share his pallet, though he had long since ceased to want the pleasure of a woman.

Sensing the boy's impatience with his slowness, Zell said, "Do not strain so, Dubi, or you will have me running at your heels."

The boy laughed.

"That tickles you, eh?"

"I am very fast," Dubi said proudly. "Tomorrow I will run in the races."

"May you have wings on your feet," Zell responded, and then asked, "Do you know the story of the tortoise and the hare?"

The boy shook his head.

And Zell said, "You have spoken so low that I could not hear you answer."

That made the boy laugh even more.

"Suppose I tell you," Zell said, "that when they raced it was the tortoise who won."

Dubi stopped laughing and asked, "How could that be when the hare is so much faster?"

"You think on it," Zell told him, "and when you have the answer, come and tell me."

The brief conversation lessened the boy's impatience and brought them practically to the door-flap of the tent where Aton waited with a torch in his hand.

Aton was now a tall, broad-shouldered man of forty years. The muscles in his arms and legs were corded. Some of his people claimed he looked like a hawk but almost everyone agreed that he was as strong as a beast. He had three women in his tent and children came from them. Tua was his favorite.

"Welcome, Zell," Aton called out in his deep voice.

"Thank you. I am honored to be your guest," Zell responded, and he released his hold on Dubi, telling Aton of his conversation with the boy.

"You have invited a plague worse than locusts," Aton said as he led Zell into the tent. "That boy will give you no peace."

"He will provide me with some diversion," Zell told his host.

The two men seated themselves on thick sheepskins.

Though he could not see it, Zell felt the heat of a nearby fire. And from the sounds in the tent, he knew the women and children were gathered at the other end, where they would stay whenever he was there.

"Drink?" Aton asked.

"Yes," Zell answered, putting out his right hand to receive the gourd of goat's milk.

"There is honey in it," Aton told him.

Zell drank noisily. When he was finished he set the empty gourd down at his side.

"You told the story well tonight," Aton said. "The people were pleased."

"It is Yahweh who speaks when I speak," Zell answered. "And it is he who gives me the strength I need."

Aton leaned very close to Zell and whispered, "I do not want to die."

Zell nodded.

"Then you will help me to live?"

"I can only tell your story," Zell answered.

Aton leaped to his feet and stalked away. But almost immediately he came back and asked, "Who demands my death? Tell me, Zell."

"He who will slay you."

"No!" Aton shouted. "No!"

Zell heaved a weary sigh and said, "I am very tired, Aton, too tired to talk any more."

"Old man," Aton growled, "you have too many summers to know how sweet life is. For you there is nothing but going down under."

"I am not too old to remember how sweet life was," Zell answered, "nor have I forgotten why you came."

"I am not Pula, the black boar. I am I, Aton!"

"We are what Yahweh wants us to be," Zell responded with a wave of his hand.

"I will not die."

"The choice is not yours," Zell said.

"I will not die," Aton repeated in an angry growl.

"The choice is not yours."

Because darkness was already in Zell's eyes he had no need to close them as other men did to find sleep. Yet sleep, like a troublesome woman, would not embrace him, and he was past wooing her.

He did not understand Aton. Zell shook his head. He truly did not understand!

"And what can I do about it?" he whispered.

Uttering a ragged sigh, Zell rolled over on his side. Aton was not afraid to face his opponent. He had killed all those who had tried to wrest his leadership from him. One by one his challengers came and he smote them with his sword. There were some who caused him to fight long and hard before he vanquished them but most fell very quickly. Even the one he would soon fight might fall to his sword unless Aton knew that he would be the one to fall.

Zell pondered that possibility. He had known men who had presentiments of their deaths and they had indeed died.

"How can I change what has been and what must be?" Zell muttered. "I am only Zell, the story-teller, nothing more."

He was annoyed now that Aton had spoken to him. It might even be taken as a bad omen? That Aton was no longer willing to serve Yahweh was in itself a sign that something was wrong.

A man became the leader of the people knowing that some day he would have to die. So it has been and so it will always be.

"Change that, Aton," Zell grumbled challengingly, "and you will be able to turn night into day and day into night."

The pile on the sheepskin was not as thick as Zell thought it was and he felt the ground press against his hip. He rolled on to his back and placed his hands behind his head.

"I am not complaining," Zell whispered into the darkness. "It was Yahweh who chose me as He chose Aton, as He chose all of us."

Zell moved again and with his head resting on his right arm he sensed the nearness of sleep.

He nodded and said, "I knew you would come." Then he gave himself up to her embrace.

Aton stood on the bank of the river. The water, darker than the night, flowed past him with a soft swishing sound, softer than the rustle of leaves in the twilight of a summer's day.

Frogs croaked. Dark wings whirled in the air while rats and other small animals scurried to the water's edge to quickly drink and then run to the shelter of the thick foliage growing along the riverbank.

These sounds to Aton were the sounds of life, and as each summer came and passed he found them more and more pleasing to his ears; yet the things he saw also gave him pleasure, for some of them he had brought forth.

He looked back over his right shoulder at the encampment of his people. Beyond the circle of tents, where the earth was rich and black, the fields lay fallow now, waiting for the season when the men would come with their planting sticks to set the seeds.

The fields, ripe with grain, gave him pleasure. He had led his people to them and had told them that the earth was good and would yield a bountiful harvest. And it was good, as he had told them it would be.

Since he had become their leader the people had never been without bread and meat. He had made them a strong people so that none of the other peoples who lived about them could fall upon them and take what was theirs.

Aton's brow furrowed and he faced the river again.

Yahweh had favored him and had always stood at his side, giving him the strength to kill all those who had come in the hope of becoming the leader of his people.

He crossed his arms and with his fingers touched the thrice-circled boar tusks that he had taken long ago. Those now-brown-stained tusks were the only sign on him of his authority. And those tusks were now banded so tightly around his forearms that nothing would remove them short of——

A sudden tremor coursed through his body and, letting go of his arms, Aton would have said aloud, *"It must not happen."* The sudden sound of footfalls stopped him.

Aton whirled around. The night was filled with spirits. Perhaps Kez's spirit had come to set upon him or perhaps it was some other one of the men he had killed.

A form materialized out of the darkness and by the clothing Aton knew it was a woman.

"It is I, Tua," the woman called out before Aton offered a challenge. "You left the tent and stayed away too long for me to sleep comfortably," she explained.

Aton nodded. Tua had at least as many summers as he. Her hair was gray, her face wrinkled, and her body no longer gave him pleasure, yet she was his favorite woman of those in his tent. She had given him two fine sons, Barda and Sendor, now each with a woman of his own; Barda was even thinking of taking another woman into his tent.

Aton could not explain to himself or anyone else what he felt about Tua. The strange thing to him was that he knew she had the same feelings for him.

He enjoyed immensely his other women, Gitta and Boonpa. Boonpa was the youngest of the women. She always laughed. Even when he took her to him she found something to laugh about. Gitta did all of the cooking because she was better at it than either Tua or Boonpa. She was favored by Yahweh to drop more children than his other women. Dubi had come from her. It was the wise Tua who managed everything—the other women, and all the children.

Aton slipped his arm over her shoulder and drew her close. She still smelled sweet to him. "Come," he said, "we will go back to the tent together."

"Zell brought you to us again," she said.

He agreed.

"Did you speak with him about——"

"Yes."

"And what was his answer?" she asked, pausing to look at him.

"That I must fight."

"And will you?"

"I do not know, Tua," he whispered.

"Are you afraid?"

"I do not know that either," Aton answered.

Tua touched his face and placed her head against his chest.

"When I came here, so long ago," he whispered, "I came looking for my father, Nempie, and his people. Had I found them, I would have tried to kill Nempie, and if I had I would have claimed his people for my own, giving them what I gave to your people after I slew Gibb."

She tried to speak but he said, "Listen to me, Tua. I have never spoken about this to anyone."

She nodded.

"I gave your people horses, grain, and Yahweh. The horses and the grain were to win you to me, but Yahweh, was to bind you to me. People fear what they can not see. Zell taught me that when we were both slaves in the camp of the Horse People. Yahweh was always more Zell's than mine. I put my trust in the tusks of Pula, the black boar, the sword I took from Kez, and that I was *a man amongst men, a beginning.*"

"And Yahweh?" she questioned in a low voice. "You thought nothing of Him?"

"I am not sure," Aton answered. "There were times I did but more often I felt I had made happen what happened. If others saw it as Yahweh I saw no harm in that. Now I am not sure. Looking back at all that has happened to me, I see things that I have never seen before. Not as Zell sees them, but in such a way where there is some sort of meaning to them, as if someone had moved me. I almost believe that Yahweh was responsible for all of it."

"But He will stand beside you as He always has whenever you have met a challenger," Tua said.

"It is because of my feelings about Yahweh that I do not want to fight. Tua, I do not want to kill any more. I looked at the grain after the last harvest and my heart was full of life. It still is. I have killed many who sought to gain my sword and become me. I do not want to kill anyone else. I do not want to die now, when I am close to knowing Yahweh."

She clung to him and asked, "Have you told Zell all this?"

"No," he whispered. "He is past understanding any of it. I am not even sure I understand."

"If you do not fight," she said in a tremulous whisper, "they will tear you apart and then the young men will fight to wear Pula's tusks. Long before you came I saw such a thing happen."

"People still speak of him in whispers," Aton said. He had heard in bits and pieces over many summers what had happened when the leader of the people had refused to fight. It was the way of all people. They expected their leader to kill or die. It hardly mattered which occurred as long as blood was shed and a life taken.

Tua took hold of his hand and, pressing it to her shapeless breasts, said, "To all of us, Aton, you are the leader of the people."

He did not answer.

24

THE FOLLOWING DAY the sky was covered with gray clouds. The wind tugged violently at the tents. The smell of snow was in the cold air.

On the far side of the encampment, where the games took place, the people made fires around which they gathered to keep warm while they watched. Every man, young or old, took part in one or more of the games. Some ran, others used their spears or bows, and some even showed their strength by grappling with his opponent. Those games in which Aton took part interested the people. In them he matched his skill against the younger men in camp. And from these bloodless encounters came one man who, at the end of Zell's storytelling, would suddenly seize the sword and challenge Aton. During the games his opponent would make the decision to fight. That much he had learned, regardless of what Zell might claim about Yahweh's part in the encounter.

To Aton, Zell seemed more sullen than usual and

even when Dubi won the race in which he ran against other boys in the camp, he was restrained in his praise of the boy, saying only, "Having won favor with Yahweh, abide by His word."

Aton was quite certain that Zell was speaking to him, more than he was praising the boy.

After the games of the old men, the women brought bowls of hot stew to the field, rich with a peppery taste and filled with chunks of tender meat. And with this they gave the men freshly-baked loaves of bread and large cruses of grain water.

Zell complained about everything. The meat was too tough, the bread not baked long enough, and the fermented water, he claimed, "tastes like piss."

Aton said nothing.

"I hope," Zell commented, "that you will show more skill than your women have shown." He purposely spoke loud enough for the men at the nearby fire to hear.

Aton, aware of what Zell had done, answered in a loud voice, "I will let you beat them until they beg your forgiveness." And then in a much lower voice he said menacingly, "Do not harry me, old man. You are not a hawk and I am not a hare. I told you last night I am not Pula, the black boar."

"The games," Zell shouted, drumming his staff on the ground. "Let us have the other games."

And the people, too, cried out for Aton to take to the field.

Quickly he won the first contest. Against five men, all of whom had half as many summers as he, Aton matched his spear and hurled it farther and with more accuracy than the others.

The people cheered when he won.

Zell knew by the sounds that Aton had won the match and he cheered, too, hoping that each victory would bring Aton back to Yahweh and make him willing to die, should that be his dessert.

Aton won the next contest, too, running far in front of the five young men who had tried to prove their prowess with the spear.

Again Zell knew from the sounds of the people that their leader had proved himself.

Of all the contests, the game of the sword was the most meaningful, and for it Aton returned to the fire, where his sons Barda and Sendor dressed his arms and chest with thick padding for protection against the blows of the wooden sword.

"You have done well," Zell told him.

Aton said nothing. His throat was parched and he poured himself a bowl of fermented grain water, wet his mouth, let some of it wet his throat, and then spat most of it out. Then he announced, "I am ready."

"Let the sword game start!" Zell shouted.

His call was enough and Aton and his five opponents walked slowly out into the field. The people were still, and only the voice of the wind was louder than the thump of his heart.

He moved his hand over the hilt of the sword, gripping it tighter. The young men were very close now, circling around him like wild dogs, moving around their prey.

Suddenly he saw an opening and, rushing through their line, slashed violently at one of his opponents, knocking him to the ground. There were four now and they closed the breach left by the one who had fallen.

Aton worked his way close to the man at one end and in a sudden shift of tactics dashed to the other end of the line to drive his sword into the man's chest. Had he been using a real weapon he would have driven through his opponent.

The remaining three tried to attack him simultaneously and he stuck one in the throat, taking a slash on the arm from another.

Of the two left, Aton realized that only one was any good and that was Nissen, the son of the arrow-maker,

Manlo. He dispatched the other one by pretending to give him an opening and then moving so quickly he knocked the weapon from his hand.

Now there was only Nissen facing him. From the look on his face Aton knew that he was going to have a hard fight.

The two men circled each other. As each of them struck at the other, the people could no longer keep silent and shouted encouragement to one and then the other.

Wet with sweat and breathing hard, each man skillfully avoided the other's weapon. The wind became colder and blew harder and still they continued to fight. The sky darkened and snow began to fall. Though they were half blinded by the swirling flakes, each sought to deliver the one blow that would end the game.

From the far side of the field, where the falling snow obscured the rise of the earth, came the sound of metal striking metal.

Nissen seemed not to hear. His youth made it possible for him to pursue his goal with oblivion to all else for already he had the stunning vision of himself becoming the leader of the people.

But Aton heard the sound and, thinking it might be visitors, called out, "Someone comes." He turned and pointed to the far side of the field with his wooden sword.

"I see nothing," Nissen shouted back.

And before Aton could face him again a blow crashed down on the back of his neck, darkening the world for him.

When the people saw Aton fall they gasped as one and then were silent. Never in all the summers that Aton had been their leader had anyone ever felled him.

"What has happened?" Zell asked, hearing only the wind-driven hiss of the snow and the crackling of the fire. "Tell me, tell me, what has happened?"

"Aton has fallen," Barda answered in a low voice. "He is defeated."

"Defeated!" he shouted shrilly. "Defeated how?"

"The snow was too heavy to see," Barda said.

Zell pounded his staff on the snow-covered ground and demanded to be taken to Aton.

"He is on his feet," Sendor, Aton's second son, said, "and walks slowly toward us."

"Who was it who felled him?" Zell questioned.

"Nissen," Barda answered.

Zell repeated the name and said, more to himself than to Aton's sons, "I will speak with him later."

"He has not yet become the leader of the people," Sendor commented.

"To look at his strut," Barda said, "it would be difficult not to believe the sword in his hand is only wood and not a spear wet with Aton's blood."

"Where are they?" Zell questioned impatiently.

"Almost here," Dubi answered.

And then Aton said, "I need a drink of grain-fermented water. And pour one for Nissen, too. He has fought well today."

Barda handed his father a bowl and Aton proffered it to Nissen, saying, "Never have I received such a blow. Go ahead and drink."

Nissen grinned and pulling his shoulders back responded, "I am less than you, Aton. You are the leader of the people. Drink first."

"Well said!" Zell exclaimed.

A bowl of grain-fermented water was passed to Nissen and, raising his bowl, Aton said, "Let us drink together."

Nissen only sipped at his drink, while Aton drank all of his, hoping that it would dull the tendrils of pain that folded themselves around the back of his neck, growing upward into his head and spreading out along his shoulders.

"I must go to my father," Nissen said, handing the bowl back to Sendor.

"I will go with you," Zell told him.

"No," Aton said. "Zell, you will remain with me awhile longer."

Nissen's eyes went to slits and Zell complained that Nissen's father Menlo should be spoken to with congratulatory words.

"You will remain here," Aton said, hardening his voice so that there was no misunderstanding of his will.

Nissen nodded and left Aton's fire.

"Leave us," Aton told his sons. When they were gone he said, "We will soon have visitors."

"Visitors at this season?" Zell questioned.

"The caravan is somewhere over the rise, at the far end of the field."

Zell shook his head.

"I heard the striking of their bells," Aton said.

Zell strained to hear the bells. "There is only the hiss of the snow and the crackling of the fire," he told Aton.

"They will come."

"For them to come at this season," Zell said, "is unnatural. They come when new buds are ready to open."

Aton agreed and explained how the sound of the caravan's bells had caused him to turn and how Nissen had struck him from behind.

Zell drove his staff into the mounting snow before him. This was not what he had expected and he asked, "Why would Nissen do something like that?"

"I do not know," Aton answered with a shrug.

"Are you sure you called out——"

"Yes," Aton said. "I told him about the bells."

Zell thumped on the snow with his staff and asked, "Do you see the caravan yet?"

"No," Aton replied. "But they will come."

"Do you hear the bells now?"

Forgetting that Zell's eyes were sightless, Aton shook his head.

"Well," Zell demanded impatiently, "do you hear them now?"

"No."

"Where are they, Aton?" Zell asked.

"I heard them."

"Great is the power of Yahweh," Zell exclaimed, suddenly comprehending what had been incomprehensible. "He has seen fit to warn you, Aton, and take heed of his warning. He has shown you a strength equal to yours and to whose you might well fall, should you lose favor with Him."

"I tell you, Zell, there were bells."

"I hear none, you hear none. Call to your sons and ask them if they heard the jangle of caravan bells. You do not, eh? Take heed of Yahweh's warning lest He desert you, Aton, when you most need Him. Now call one of yours and have him take me to the fire of Nissen's father Manlo."

Aton lay back on his pallet. His whole body was wracked with pain. The feeble yellow light from a wick burning in an earthen cup of oil looked like a single glowing eye. The tent was relatively quiet, though there was a murmur from one end where the women and children gathered. To give him a chance to rest, Tua had drawn a line in the tent and threatened to beat anyone who crossed it.

Aton caught Tua's sweet scent and opened his eyes.

"Something to make you feel better," she said, proffering a small earthen bowl filled with steaming brew.

He looked questioningly at her.

"Drink it," she told him.

He took the bowl from her and felt the heat of the brew on his palm.

"Will you go to hear Zell tonight?" Tua asked.

"Yes," he said between sips of the pleasant tasting

broth. Then he asked, "What was I like when I first came to these people?"

Tua smiled and told him, "Like some wild beast and dressed in skins. Fierce looking, especially with your scar the way it is."

"And when did I take you to my tent?"

"After you slew Gibb," she said.

"But what of Gibb's women and children?" he asked.

"You would not have them. You took me instead."

"What happened to Gibb's women and children?" Aton asked.

"The women were claimed by other men and the children went with them. That was the custom."

"Strange," Aton said. "I recall none of it."

"Why should you?" Tua asked. "Then you did not know our ways."

"Are any of Gibb's women still here?" Aton asked.

"Yes," Tua answered. "Nissen's mother Bilot is still alive. She was the youngest of Gibb's women."

Zell sat in Manlo's tent. Nissen was close to him and Manlo was on the other side of the fire. He sensed that Bilot was close by. The warmth of the fire drove the chill from him.

Manlo, a short man whose muscular arms and strong hands were seared in practically all their parts from the flames that were his constant companion, offered Zell a bowl of grain-fermented water "to give heat to the insides," he said.

Zell drank slowly. He was deeply troubled by what had happened. That Aton had heard the jangle of caravan bells when there was none to hear was an omen of uncertain meaning. That Nissen had, according to Aton, struck him from behind was a serious offense against Aton. But it could also be taken as an omen, since no one was ever certain whether Nissen had come from Manlo's seed or from Gibb's. If he were Gibb's spawn, the omen for Aton's fall could surely be read in the outcome of the game.

Ending the silence Manlo asked, "And what did Aton say of my son?"

"That he was the best of those he faced," Zell answered.

"Yahweh favored me," Nissen commented.

"Yahweh does," Zell responded, "what Yahweh does."

"Praised be Yahweh," Manlo offered.

Zell set his bowl down on the ground next to him and asked, "Tell me, Nissen, what did it feel like to fight Aton?"

"More pleasurable than I can find words to tell. More pleasurable than mounting a woman and better than taking meat in a hunt."

"Were you afraid?" Zell asked.

"No," Nissen answered.

"You are very brave," Zell told him.

"Yahweh was with me," Nissen said in a low voice.

"How did you know that?"

"Aton called out and asked me to stop and let him rest," Nissen said.

"And what did you do?" Zell questioned.

"He felled him," Manlo said. "He dropped him there in the snow."

"Where did you deliver your blow?" Zell asked.

"On his right shoulder," Nissen answered. "That bent him low and then I struck again."

"Where?"

"In the chest," Nissen said, "with a thrust that splintered my sword."

Zell nodded and asked, "And you heard nothing more?"

"Nothing more than Aton begging me to stop and let him rest."

"Begging?" Zell questioned.

"Yes," Nissen answered excitedly. "Yes, he begged

me to stop and let him rest. That was the way of it. But I would not stop. I pressed him. I pressed him until I found an opening."

Zell listened.

There was a fire in Nissen that, even to his blind eyes, seemed to glow with the light of Yahweh.

Could Aton have changed what happened to hide his weakness, his fear of even his knowledge that Yahweh was no longer at his side?

"Should Yahweh call me," Nissen said, "to fight for Him, I will."

"And should He still stand with Aton," Zell asked in a low voice, "would you be willing to die for Him?"

"Yes," Nissen answered without hesitation.

"You have raised your son well," Zell said to Manlo.

"Well enough to become the leader of the people," Manlo responded.

"Perhaps," Zell said. "But it is not the winner of games who becomes the leader. He who becomes the leader must first kill Aton. Then he becomes Aton——"

"I will do it," Nissen declared. "I will surely do it."

Zell suddenly felt weary and said to Manlo, "I must return to Aton's tent and rest."

"I will lead you," Nissen offered.

"You have earned your rest," Zell told him and asked Manlo to see him back to Aton's. When they were on their way Zell asked, "Why would you have your son become the leader Aton, when his life lasts only as long as he can defend it?"

"Nissen is young and strong," Manlo said. "He will be able to defend himself for at least as long as Aton has."

Zell shrugged.

"Aton came to us as a stranger," Manlo said, "and became the leader of the people. But there were those who thought that one of us should have become the leader of the people."

"Aton was chosen by Yahweh," Zell replied sharply.

Neither Zell nor Manlo spoke again until they reached Aton's tent. And then Manlo said, "May Yahweh be with you tonight when you tell Aton's story."

"And may He be with you," Zell responded, "when you listen to his story." Then he called for Dubi to lead him into Aton's tent. As soon as he was in his place he asked to speak to Aton.

Tua came to him and said, "He is asleep. He has been hurt and needs to rest."

"Wake him!" Zell demanded, thumping the tent floor with his staff.

"No."

He spoke her name and stopped, remembering suddenly that she had been promised to Manlo before Aton had claimed her for his woman. "Tua!" he exclaimed in a whisper.

"Well, what is it?" she demanded to know.

"Nothing," Zell told her, wondering if she remembered that she had once been promised to Manlo.

"When Aton wakes," she said, "I will tell him you want to speak with him."

Zell nodded.

25

Dubi led Zell to the great fire, around which the people gathered in a huge circle.

Standing alone, Zell let the heat of the fire flow over him, for though the snow had stopped falling, it was bitter cold and the wind still blew hard enough to grab at the ends of his cloak.

He faced the fire. The flames, red and orange to all those who were there, were to him gray tongues licking at an eternal blackness, made blacker still by the dark anger that filled him.

Aton refused to speak to him, saying, "I have nothing more to say about what has happened."

Zell said, "Nissen's account differs greatly from your own."

"Did you think that it would not?"

"Nissen said——"

"I am not interested in what Nissen said," Aton said.

Zell shook his head and muttered, "Sooner or later,

Aton, whether you will or not, you will speak on the matter."

Aton did not answer.

In the warmth of the fire the memory of that conversation between himself and Aton was enough to make Zell tremble with rage and whisper, "Yahweh will bring him to me. Yahweh will bring Aton to me."

Turning away from the fire, Zell tossed his staff on the snow-covered ground and cried out, "Oh my children, I am Zell, the story-teller. Listen to my words and you shall know the wonders of Aton. Listen to my words and through them you will come to know Aton. Hear, oh children, the words of Zell the story-teller!"

A hush came over the people and Zell began to tell them how Aton was taken captive by Kez, the leader of the Horse People.

Zell rested again, and with his blind eyes he searched the night sky. A few snowflakes touched his forehead and the wind still tugged at his cloak. His breath steamed in the cold air and all around him he could hear the movement and whispers of the people.

They, like him, were filled with the spirit of Yahweh and though he took little pride in anything (for he possessed none of the things that made other men boast) he was filled with the certain knowledge that he had brought Yahweh to them, as he had done so many times in the past. In that accomplishment, there was a strength greater even than that of Aton's, who must inevitably lose it to another, while his would continue until Yahweh called for him to give up his spirit.

"To serve Yahweh," Zell mumbled, "is all any man can do." Turning from the fire, he faced the people, cast down his staff, and called to those around him. "Hear, my people, the story of Aton, from Zell the story-teller. Listen my children and learn what next befell Aton."

The snow had ceased but the wind, still not spent,

whirled the snow in hissing spirals in different directions at once. The clouds raced across the sky and huge gaps revealed a sky full of stars.

Zell's words vanished in the cold night air and, reaching down, he lifted his staff to him. His throat ached and his body was tired beyond describing, but the night was still full and after a brief rest he would again speak to the people of Aton.

Some of the men brought more wood from beyond the circle and laid the huge pieces across the fire pit, building, as it appeared to those who watched, a shelter for the fire. They frequently looked toward the place where Aton sat with his family, or turned their eyes to Nissen and his father and mother.

As always, Aton appeared deeply interested in Zell's telling of his story. Though he saw others look at Nissen, he did not.

Nissen could not keep his eyes from reaching out across the fire-lit circle to where Aton sat.

Though Aton still ached from the blow he had taken on the back of his neck, he himself brought Zell another gourd of grain water and as he gave it to the old man, he said, "I am sorry I angered you."

Zell nodded.

"Nissen eyes me," Aton said, "as though I were a fat sheep."

"He feels Yahweh is close to him," Zell responded.

"I can not say what he feels," Aton told him.

Zell drained the gourd dry and tossed it into the fire. "I must rest a bit more before I continue," he told Aton.

And Aton answered gently, "Rest, old friend, rest, and may Yahweh come brightly to you."

Nissen grew restive over Aton's brief conversation with the story-teller and whispered his concern to Manlo.

"I would do," Manlo said, "as he has done."

"Take him grain water?" Nissen asked, the very tone

283

of his voice questioning the wisdom of his father's words.

"You have already done," Manlo told him, "what no man has ever done."

Heartened by his father's answer, Nissen poured grain-fermented water into a gourd and, leaving his father's side, proceeded across the open space to where Zell stood.

Everyone there saw him, and a low murmur rose from the people, swelling out into the night until it was louder by far than the hissing sound of the wind-driven snow.

Zell, hearing the people and the sound of footfalls coming toward him, turned to face Nissen; but even before he reached the story-teller, Aton was on his feet and roaring, "Go back, Nissen! Go back!"

Nissen stopped.

"It is not your place to give Zell a gourd of grain-fermented water."

Nissen glanced over his shoulder at his father.

And Manlo stood up and said, "He does no more nor less than you yourself did, Aton."

Aton stepped away from his sons and, grabbing a spear from one of them, shouted, "Go back, Nissen!"

Zell knew that Nissen acted foolishly. Furious with Aton for threatening to shed blood while he was telling Aton's story, he trembled with rage and tried to find words to rebuke both of them.

"Kill Nissen now," Manlo yelled, rushing to his son's side, "and the people will know why. They will know that you fear him, fear his strength, fear that a new leader might soon come to us."

The murmur became a hush. The people waited to see what would happen.

Zell suddenly screeched, "Enough! Enough! Manlo, take Nissen back with you. I do not want any more water. And, Aton, move away from me. May Yahweh forgive this intrusion and seek no punishment for either of you."

Aton put up his spear and, still breathing hard, sat down again, though his eyes never left Manlo and Nissen until they were back in their place at the far side of the circle.

Zell sighed wearily and his breath smoked in the cold night air. Tossing his staff to the ground, he began once more to speak of Aton.

Zell fell silent. This night of story-telling was at an end and his strength, too, was at an end. He waited for Dubi to come and lead him from the circle of the people to the warmth of Aton's tent, where he would be given warm goat's milk and a good skin on which to sleep.

After awhile the boy came to his side and Zell put his hand on the child's shoulder and said, "I am ready to go with you."

Dubi led him away from the fire and out of the circle of people. When they were still some distance from his father's tent the boy asked, "Yahweh still watches over Aton?"

"Yes," Zell answered.

"Then He will watch over my father?"

"Yes," Zell said, "as long as he is Aton."

"But he is Aton," Dubi asserted.

Zell did not answer. Such a mystery would be incomprehensible to a small boy, as it often was to a grown man. That was the way of Yahweh.

Aton bid Zell welcome and, taking the story-teller by the arm, led him into the tent to the place prepared for him.

Settling down with a weary sigh, Zell said, "It was good of you to bring me the grain water."

Aton handed him a bowl of warm goat's milk and asked if he wanted to have some bread with it.

"No," Zell replied. "I am too tired to bother with

eating." He drank the milk with the loud sucking noise a baby makes at the teat of its mother.

"I did not mean to become so angry with Nissen," Aton said.

Zell stopped drinking and, setting the bowl down, told his host, "He is anxious, Aton, even as you are."

"Anxious to become the leader of the people."

"Do not sneer at it," Zell said, "lest Yahweh desert you when you most need Him."

Aton remained silent.

Zell moved his head toward that part of the tent where the women and children were sequestered for the night. In a low voice he asked, "Do you remember that Tua was promised to Manlo before you claimed her for your woman?"

Aton looked questioningly at Zell.

"Did you remember that?" the story-teller asked.

"No," Aton answered. "I knew nothing of that. I claimed Tua for my woman because she was the one who——"

Zell waved his hand and said, "Do not tell me what she did to you. I know what the sight of a woman can do to a man."

"But all that was so long ago," Aton commented.

Zell nodded.

"As the leader of the people," Aton said, "I had the right to claim the woman of my choice. Even then I understood that much."

"As Aton," Zell told him, "it would have been fitting and proper for you to have taken all that was Gibb's, and then Nissen would have been your son and by the laws of our people unable to become the leader."

"I know there is a question about whose son Nissen is. But how does that question affect me?"

Zell shrugged and said, "The ways of Yahweh are the ways of Yahweh and only He can understand them."

That was not the kind of answer Aton wanted but he did not press Zell.

"I am tired," Zell told him with a yawn. "Very tired."

"Sleep old friend," Aton said. "Sleep and may your spirit know peace this night."

Zell stretched out his sleeping skin and fell asleep.

Aton crept away from his guest and left the tent. Outside the night was bitter cold but the wind had stopped. He stood with one hand wrapped around a taut support rope and glanced up at the sky. The stars were bright and the last of the night wanderers already far down in the east.

Aton pursed his lips and looked back at the tent. Had he known when he became the leader of the people, what Zell had told him about Tua, he would have still claimed her for his woman. He was certain. To the night he whispered, "I would take her again." And he spat three times in the old way to confirm that he meant what he said. Then he went back into the tent.

Everyone was asleep. Their sounds were as distinguishable to him as their voices. He stretched out on his sleeping skin, closer to Tua than to the other women.

She stirred and whispered, "Boonpa was waiting for you. She hoped to give you pleasure."

He chuckled and said, "What she gives, she also gets."

Tua giggled.

He almost asked her about Manlo but changed his mind. There was no need to blame her for something she could not have changed then, even if she had wanted to. Besides, of all his women, she was the one who suffered when he suffered. He reached and touched her face with his hand.

"Would that I could still give you pleasure," she said, holding his hand to her cheek.

"You give me more, Tua, much more."

"I am like a withered flower," she told him.

Aton felt her tears on his hand and gently said, "I do not see you that way, Tua."

She nodded and whispered, "I fear for you, Aton, I fear for you."

"No more than I do for myself," he answered, remembering how Rika spoke those words, a long time ago.

"What has happened?" she asked.

He uttered a deep sigh and said, "I do not really know."

"Tell me what you feel."

Again he uttered a deep sigh.

"Tell me," she pleaded.

Aton turned toward her and said, "A man can hear the same thing so many times that he does not truly listen to what he hears. Last night and tonight I listened to Zell with a different ear."

"I do not understand," Tua admitted.

"My story," he said. "The Aton who slew Pula, the black boar——"

"But you are Aton!"

"Perhaps," Aton said. "Yahweh meant——" He stopped and shook his head.

"Meant what?"

"I do not know what He could have meant," Aton said. "But I will tell you this, Tua, even from the way Zell tells the story, I know there is something missing to it—something that he alone knows but has never told."

Tua gasped.

"I will have to think more on it," Aton told her.

"The story moves," Tua whispered. "Soon he who will challenge you will make his presence known."

"He has already," Aton commented gruffly.

"If it is Nissen," she asked, "will you fight him?"

"I do not want to die," he answered, and he added

almost as an afterthought, "I do not want anyone else to die."

Tua was silent and then she whispered, "Do you think he is Gibb's son?"

Aton shrugged.

"Perhaps," she offered, "if I spoke to Manlo——"

Aton asked, "And what good would that do?"

"Before you claimed me for your woman," she said, "I was promised to him." She chuckled. "But he did not challenge you again, when you waved your bloody sword, threatening to kill anyone who would take me from you."

"Was that Manlo who objected?" he asked, remembering his own thoughts.

"Yes," Tua answered. "But he must not have wanted me very much because soon afterward he asked you for Bilot, Gibb's woman. I remember it very well because you only knew a few words of our language and I spoke to you with my hands, even to showing you with my body why he wanted her. That you understood and you gave her to him."

Slowly the images formed in Aton's head and recalling what Tua told him, he commented, "So that was the way it was, eh?"

"Yes," she answered. "Manlo was so pleased with you he made you a new knife."

"And what of Bilot," Aton questioned. "Was she pleased, too?"

"It seemed that way," Tua said. "But Nissen was more important to her than Manlo. I think Bilot felt about Gibb the way I feel about you." And she took hold of his hand and brushed her lips over the back of it.

Aton gathered her to him and he held her in his arms until sleep came to both of them.

Sleep left him suddenly as if, it seemed to Zell, she could no longer hold him in her embrace, for what woman would want a man with as many summers as he had?

He stretched. His bones creaked and then he lay still, listening to the low booming of his heart. Then he heard someone stirring at the other end of the tent. He listened very intently. The footfalls were coming toward him. They were too heavy to be a woman's. He was sure they belonged to Aton. He sucked in his breath and wondered what was going to happen.

Aton stood over him. He could feel his presence and heard the soft sound of his breath.

"Zell?" Aton called softly.

Zell pretended to be asleep.

Zell did not move.

And Aton said, "Sleep old friend, sleep." And then he padded away.

"The ways of Yahweh are the ways of Yahweh," Zell whispered with a sigh. "Who but Himself can truly know them?"

26

THE MORNING SUN was warm enough to melt the
snow, though there were places, especially around the
trunks of the big trees and other shadowed spots, where
it remained. In this welcomed warmth the people
gathered before the start of the day's games to speak of
what had happened between Aton and Nissen.

Those among the people who long resented Aton
were quick to see in Nissen's victory a victory for
themselves. To these people even Aton's sudden burst
of anger at Nissen and then at Manlo was another sign
that a new leader would soon come to be.

Many people, who did not harbor any ill feelings
toward Aton because he was not one of them,
maintained that the sword game was no more than a
game. Winning or losing it meant no more than the
movement of a breeze through the rushes on the river's
bank on a summer's day, since such a breeze was not
the harbinger of a cooling wind. To his defenders,
Aton's anger at Nissen and Manlo was more than jus-

tified because Aton was still their leader; his rights surpassed those of anyone else.

All of the people, no matter what they felt toward Aton, eagerly looked forward to the wrestling match between him and Nissen.

The sun crept up to its highest place in the sky and shortened the shadows of the men who watched it. As the shadows began to lengthen again Zell with his long bony fingers on Aton's arm came to the field.

He walked slowly, sometimes faltering in his step; and he mumbled to himself about the sudden alternation from biting wind and falling snow to the warmth that now lay over the land.

The people, seeing their approach, opened a way for them and ceased talking.

Aton said to Zell, "Last night I dreamt I came to speak with you and you pretended to be asleep."

Zell's step faltered and Aton, holding fast to his arm, saved him from falling.

"I dreamt," Aton told him, "that you cried out in your sleep."

Zell tried to speak but could make nothing more than strange gurgling sounds and when he again found his voice he was already in the circle of the people. He looked at Aton and, though he could not see his face, he sensed that the man was smiling knowingly at him.

He might have spoken then but the people were shouting for the games to begin. Once more he thumped the earth with his staff and his voice rose above all the others as he cried out, "Let the games begin. In the name of Yahweh, let the games begin!"

The boys wrestled first. They wrestled well—some with laughter and some with grim determination. All enjoyed themselves.

Then came the contests between those young men whose chins were beginning to sprout hair and who had already hunted with their fathers and older brothers.

They laughed less and were serious about how they grabbed and pinned each other's oiled bodies.

Zell paid little attention to the matches, though he was kept well informed about what was happening by Aton, who stood by his side. Zell's interest lay elsewhere. Deeply disturbed by what Aton had said to him, he tried to understand its importance.

Had he feigned sleep before Aton's spirit?

If he had, then he had probably missed the opportunity to learn what had happened to Aton's belief in himself.

If it was actually Aton who came to him, why would he speak of it as a dream?

Perhaps, Zell thought, Aton knew he was shamming and his intention was to make him realize that for all his protestations of devoutness to Yahweh, whom he served, he took, like an ill-loosed arrow, a faith that fell far short of the mark. But what indeed would have been the mark that Aton would have wanted him to strike?

These questions sorely troubled Zell and made him twitch impatiently. Like any other petulant old man, he complained a great deal about the unusual warmth of the sun, and that his feet hurt from having to stand so long.

When all the competitions save one were over, the people fell silent, waiting for Nissen to challenge Aton. Their silence throbbed with expectation that seemed to mount even as they waited.

"He comes," Aton whispered.

"Nissen?" Zell asked in a raspy voice.

"Yes."

Nissen came through the ring of people on the far side of the field. He wore a white woolen cloak over his oiled body that glistened where the sun touched it.

"What does he look like?" Zell asked, wetting his lips.

Aton told him, adding, "He is a handsome youth."

"As you yourself were," Zell answered, "before Kez scarred you."

Aton did not answer. To him it seemed that he could never have been as young as Nissen was, or as foolishly eager to fight, and yet the thrice-curved tusks of Pula, the black boar, on his arms were proof that in his younger days he was, indeed, as foolish.

Nissen strutted across the field. There was confidence in his bearing and almost a teasing smile on his full sensuous lips.

Aton suddenly wondered what would become of his women should he fall to Nissen's sword? Perhaps Nissen would reject them, even as he had declined to take Nissen's mother Bilot? He thought of what would be meted out to Tua and suddenly felt his anger rising.

Nissen was almost in front of him when he stopped and, dropping his white cloak to the ground, he stood silently before Aton.

The people from every part of the field craned their necks to see what was happening.

The youth and the man faced one another.

Then Nissen, as was customary, raised his right hand and, pointing to the leader of the people, shouted so that all on the field could hear, "I, Nissen, son of Manlo the arrow-maker, challenge you, Aton, to a game of wrestling."

Never before had anyone offered that summons to Aton since no one had felled him in the game of swords.

Aton stood still. As he looked at Nissen his anger was fueled by the foolish confidence of his challenger.

"Answer him," Zell prompted, his voice edgy with anticipation.

Aton said nothing.

Nissen shouted again, "I, Nissen, winner of the game of swords, claim my right to challenge the leader of the people to a wrestling match."

Aton took a deep breath and in a deep voice, rumbling far louder than that of the youth standing in front of him, shouted, "There will be no contest, Nissen."

Nissen's jaw went slack and a murmur arose from the people, while Zell, the story-teller, uttered a wordless shriek, coming to the understanding of Aton's dream after it was too late.

"It is my right," Nissen cried.

The people quickly echoed Nissen's words, shouting them until their words sounded like the roar of the river as it tumbles from the distant mountains. Even those who found no fault with Aton could not feel comfortable with his refusal to wrestle Nissen and they, too, cried out.

"You must wrestle him," Zell screamed.

Aton did not move.

"Then I am the winner," Nissen shouted. "I am the winner."

"No one," Aton thundered, "has won or lost. There has been no match. There will be none."

"You can not change the law," Zell cried. "The law demands that you——"

"As long as I wear these," Aton answered, touching the thrice-curved tusks of Pula, the black boar, "I am the law."

"Then I say," Nissen roared, "they should be taken from you, Aton, even as they were from the one whom the people tore apart because he would not fight."

Such words brought a sudden silence to the people. Once more there was the throb of expectation in the people. It hovered above them, pushing out and up like a huge flat-based cloud that heralds the coming of a sudden summer storm.

Aton left Zell's side and, walking past Nissen, went to the center of the circle. "Let those who would take the thrice-curved tusks of Pula, the black bear, from me come to me." And with his right hand he gestured toward himself as though he would cull them from those who watched.

No one moved.

"So be it," he said and strode back to Zell.

"You shamed me," Nissen shouted.

Aton looked at him and in a voice loud enough for only him to hear, he answered, "No more, Nissen, than you did yourself."

"I will not forget this," the youth cried.

But Aton paid him no more attention and to Zell said, "It is time for us to talk."

Zell shook his head and stamped his foot. "I do not have anything to talk about to you." Calling to Nissen, he asked to be led to Manlo's tent.

27

THE PEOPLE WERE as angry as they were confused by Aton's actions. They had looked forward to watching the wrestling match between him and Nissen. Denied that, they were not given anything else in exchange. Most felt wronged; they were left with nothing.

Aton left the field with his sons. They did not understand what their father had done, but because of the challenge he had leveled at the people, defying any of them to take the thrice-curved tusks of Pula, the black boar, from him, they dared not question his actions. Despite all the angry looks put upon Aton, he appeared strangely unaffected. His brow was neither furrowed in anger or concern, and there was even a lightness in his step which for a long while Barda, his oldest son, had noticed was missing.

Zell was escorted by Nissen to the tent of Manlo. The anger of the old man and the youth was greater than the anger of all others on the field.

Nissen raged, saying, "He has shamed me before everyone. He has brought shame to the tent of my father. He lacks even the courage of a hare. Who but an un-manned man would have refused to wrestle. I am the winner of the match, whether or not Aton admits it since he was the one who refused to wrestle. The people saw it. They know."

The youth continued, oblivious to the furious mutter-ing of Zell, who was affronted by Aton's actions and who saw in them the portents of some enormous disas-ter.

A flood, perhaps, when the budding season begins and the river runs so full that it overflows its banks and puts down its burden of black earth?

There were other seasons when Yahweh let Set bring the river not only over its banks but to the tops of the trees. Then the land became a watery death for both men and animals.

In other seasons Set stopped the river from flowing and the land became full of dust. Then man and beast died from the swollen bellies of the starving.

Such calamities, or one much worse, would come upon them if Aton did not do what he must do, for Yahweh's anger was terrible, once it was aroused.

Zell was as mindless of Nissen's complaints as the youth was of the old man's fears. Each spoke to him-self and did not expect the other to answer. When they came to Manlo's tent they fell silent.

Manlo greeted Zell, giving him a place on a thick sheepskin, near the cooking fire.

They drank goat's milk and ate bread together before Manlo said, "I am sorry for Aton. He was a brave man."

Zell grunted. He did not want to speak about Aton. He was still fearful of what might be put on the people if Yahweh let Set have his way, for it was known that between the two, Yahweh and Set, there was always the people. Yahweh demanded that He be served through Aton, but Set was always there to tempt the people away from Yahweh, who had dominion over all, even over Set.

"The people are angry," Manlo said, feeding the fire with a few sticks of wood.

"And they should be," Nissen said.

Manlo glared at his son. Nissen, who was about to say more, clamped his mouth shut and gnashed his teeth.

Again Manlo said, "The people were angry. Their anger is like a summer fire that starts small but grows large, consuming all before it, with the slightest breeze that fans its heat."

Zell nodded and his sightless eyes filled with the sudden leaping grayness of the flames as they chewed voraciously on the dry wood Manlo had added.

"Aton," Manlo said, speaking the name with a sigh, "is not the same Aton who came to us so long ago to slay Gibb and become the leader of the people."

Zell lifted his head questioningly.

Manlo, responding to the unspoken question, said, "Then he was truly, as he claimed, *a man amongst men*, and all who saw him knew it. But now ..." He purposely did not finish saying what he had begun to say.

"And now what?" Zell pressed.

"I do not know," Manlo told him. "There are some who claim that Aton no longer stands with Him."

Zell made a sucking noise but did not speak.

"If Yahweh no longer stands with him, Zell," Manlo asked, "where then is He, whom we serve through Aton?"

"The ways of Yahweh," Zell whispered, "are the ways of Yahweh. Who but He can understand them?"

Manlo nodded and looked knowingly at Bilot, who, like a shadow at the coming of night, hovered close by to listen to the conversation. She returned the nod, and Manlo said, "I am not so wise as you, Zell, for surely your summers are already many more than I will gather to me, but if Aton does not stand with Yahweh, then the People will anger Yahweh if they continue to look upon Aton as the leader."

Zell agreed with a silent nod.

"You can tell the people that," Manlo said. "You can tell them that Yahweh no longer stands by Aton."

"We do not know that," Zell replied. "We do not know that."

"From everything that has happened," Manlo said, his voice suddenly hardening like the rock he worked, "we have the signs. All the signs are there. Tell the people that——"

"I can not do that."

"Nissen will become the leader of the people," Manlo told him. "He will become the new Aton."

"Except for Yahweh, who can know that?"

"It can be made to happen and if it does, will you put the thrice-circled tusks of Pula, the black boar, on my son's arms? Will you make him the new Aton?"

"I am only the story-teller," Zell said.

"You can be more," Manlo told him.

"We are what Yahweh wants us to be."

"Yes," Manlo agreed. "But perhaps Yahweh has wanted you to become more than what you are. Perhaps He has chosen Nissen to accomplish it. In the years left to you, Zell, you should have more than what you have—more than two old crones who squabble all day. Why not two young women between whom you can lie to warm your old bones and from whose breasts you can suck milk that will bring new strength into your tired body?"

Zell trembled and managed to say, "Aton has treated me well."

"It was you who brought him to our people. It was you who told us about Yahweh. It was you who told us about Aton. It was you who gave him more than he ever gave you or anyone else."

"Aton is *a man amongst men, a beginning.* He was

promised by Yahweh. I was told that by someone a long time ago. Someone who brought me to Yahweh."

"Nissen will make more out of you than Aton ever did. You are more than a story-teller, Zell. You are the keeper of the word."

Zell nodded.

"I will give you all you want," Nissen suddenly said. "I will give you two women who have never known a man for you to do with as you want!"

"Zell," Manlo told him, "none of this would happen if Yahweh did not want it to."

Zell could not speak for his trembling, and he let his tongue wash over his thin, dry lips.

"Will you think on it?" Manlo pressed.

Zell nodded.

Then to Nissen, Manlo said, "Let him touch the sword. Let him feel what you will use when you go against Aton."

Nissen withdrew the burnished metal blade from under several horse hides and handed it to Zell, who ran his trembling fingers over its cold surfaces.

"It took many, many years to make," Manlo said.

"How long?"

"From the day that Aton slew Gibb and took Tua for his woman," Manlo answered. "Bit by bit I gathered the metal and learned how to work it. Each time the caravans came I managed to trade something for some metal and now the sword is finished. Nissen is old enough to use it."

Aton stood alone on the high bank of the river, a distance from the camp. The sun was low in a sky streaked with fire; the warmth of the day was past. A cold wind tumbled down from the mountains behind him, forcing him to gather the robe he wore closer to his body. Where the wind touched the river, the water was waved and crested with white.

Aton came to this place after he left the field with

his sons. He went only as far as his tent with them and then said, "Stay with the women and children. I must be alone now."

The two young men looked at each other, and Barda spoke for the both of them. "It is you who are in danger now, Father, not the women and children."

"No one will harm me," he assured them. "I am still the leader of the people. I have a great need to be alone."

Again the two young men exchanged looks and Sandor said, "Then go armed, Father."

Aton shook his head. "To do that," he told them, "will be taken by anyone who might see me as a sign that I am afraid." He paused and looking at each of his sons in turn he said, "I am not afraid."

Neither Barda nor Sandor spoke as Aton went his way.

That had been when the sun had passed its high place in the sky but had not yet gone so far down in the west that Aton's shadow had lengthened behind him.

Now, though, his shadow was long. Aton could not understand why he had not accepted Nissen's challenge.

He had intended to wrestle the youth and bring him to such an extremity of pain that he would have cried out for mercy. Then he would have forced from him an admission of his trickery.

That way Aton had hoped to avoid open combat between them in which one or the other would have to die.

But when Nissen had stood before him and had offered his challenge, Aton could not have either accepted it with a nod or have spoken any words other than those he had. Those words had come to his lips, so it had seemed to him, without ever having been in his head. Yet when he had spoken them, they were undoubtedly his.

Aton pursed his lips and ran his hand over his beard. How could a man ever know what was his or what was given to him by Yahweh or whispered to him by Set?

Such a question was beyond answering; even Zell with all his years had not yet gathered enough wisdom to him to be able to say whether it had been Yahweh or Set who had given him the words to refuse Nissen's challenge.

Then there was the dream.

Aton was as much troubled by it as Zell was, especially when he had realized from his telling of it to Zell that the old man had experienced it.

What had his spirit tried to tell Zell?

Aton shrugged and uttered the sigh of a man perplexed by what he sensed but could not see, touch, hear, or smell. Yet it was always with him, something that lay across his shoulders with a heaviness greater than all the summers that rested on Zell.

Aton turned and walked slowly back to camp. A long night of listening to Zell tell more of his story lay ahead of him. He now would take his son's advice and carry his sword with him wherever he went.

28

ONCE MORE ZELL WAS LED into the center of the circle. To the astonishment of the people and the anger of Aton, it was Nissen, rather than Dubi, who took the story-teller to his place at the great fire.

There was no wind. The flames stood straight up, growing into the blackness of the night like enormous red flowers that quickly bloomed and just as quickly died before the eyes of those who waited for Zell, the story-teller, to speak and tell them more about Aton.

The people shifted uneasily, whispering to one another about the events of the afternoon and why Nissen had brought Zell to the fire rather than Dubi. Some said Zell knew that Yahweh had already deserted Aton; but these were the few who were anxious to see someone else take his place. Most of the people did not understand what was happening and all of them could not remember such things happening before.

Zell faced the fire. He did not move as the grayness of the flames wavered in his sightless eyes.

The promises of Manlo and Nissen filled his head, even more than the words with which he would soon tell the people about Aton.

For the remaining summers of his life the two offered Zell much of what he had longed for in his youth: food that was not the leavings from someone else's fire, and two young women, between whose supple bodies he could warm his own withered one. Their gesture was certainly enough to make him wonder if indeed Yahweh had chosen to stand with Nissen?

Zell also feared that such words could be prompted by Set, and if they did come from him and he did accept them, then when his spirit separated from his body and he was put down under, his spirit would dwell forever in the house of the Underworld, where Set would be his lord and master.

After serving Yahweh for most of his life, Zell could not allow himself to be tricked by Set.

Before he did anything to help Nissen become Aton he would have to be sure Yahweh no longer stood with Aton. There could be more nights left before he would be finished with Aton's story, several more nights before Aton would have to fight the challenger, who would become Aton and then the leader of the people.

As Zell turned slowly from the fire and faced the people, their whisperings faded away until there was no other sound but the crackling of the fire and yelping of wild dogs in the distance.

He cast his staff from him and called out, "Oh my children, listen to Zell, the story-teller, and from him learn the wonders of Yahweh. Hear my people of what next befell Aton. And from what you hear, gain strength and wisdom for all that you encounter."

The people leaned forward and Zell, after taking a deep breath, spoke again of Aton.

Zell told the people of Aton's journey to the House of Set, lord of the Underworld. "Only then," Zell said,

"Aton did not know where he was. To him and to all his people it had always been down under, a place where the spirits of the dead dwelled. But let me tell you, my children, for Aton, a living man who entered the House of Set through a large crack in the wall, it was a terrifying place. Who but Aton would go there to seek the spirit of the mother he never knew? And who but Aton could make his way through all the spirits that were waiting to tear him apart."

Aton listened to Zell's words and watched the old man move in the wavering light of the fire. He saw his breath steam in the cold night air each time he opened his mouth or sent it whistling through his nose. He had heard Zell tell this part of his story many times. Until now he did not realize how much of what had happened to him was changed by the story-teller.

There was no crack in the wall; the darkness had a certain glow to it, and none of the spirits had tried to tear him apart.

"Aton found his mother," Zell told his audience, "playing a game of stones with Set, for it was Yahweh's will that nothing happen without His hand. Think on it, my children, and know that it was Yahweh's hand that made possible her victory over Set so that she could return her son to the world of the living and fulfill his purpose to be *a man amongst men, a beginning*."

"But she lost," Aton whispered to himself. "My mother lost."

"What?" his oldest son asked.

Aton looked at him and shook his head. Why had Zell made such changes in the story?

He turned his attention once more to the story-teller.

"Imagine, my children," Zell said, "Aton's flight from the House of Set in darkness so heavy that it almost crushed the life out of him. Imagine the wild screams of the spirits who pursued him and where suddenly in the depths of the darkness Aton turned and struck out at the spirit nearest him. They wrestled there in the House of Set, rolling over each other until Aton was almost too exhausted to continue. But then summoning his last bit of strength he hurled the spirit from him. Before he was able to free himself the spirit stabbed Aton in the right eye and slit the lid and brow with his longer finger nail."

Aton shook his head. Had Zell always told his story this way? He glanced at the people around him. None were bothered by what the story-teller was saying. But that was because they could not know how much Zell had altered the story.

Aton sighed deeply. The changes he realized had come about over the years, moving subtly through the story. He had heard them with little regard. They were not important. He even remembered having spoken to Zell about the differences between what actually had happened to him and what the story-teller told the people.

And Zell said, "I have fitted you to Yahweh, Aton, with my stories far better than the realities of your life. Do not chide me for something I have done far better than anyone else could have."

Aton agreed and they began to speak of other things.

"Yahweh," Aton whispered, drawing Barda's questioning look again.

That he had to be fitted to Yahweh disturbed him now. He would have thought that all the exploits of his life had joined them together from the moment his mother had dropped him and had said to Nempie, *"I have brought forth a man amongst men, a man better than all other men."*

"Aton," Nissen shouted. "Aton, I, son of Manlo, challenge you!"

Zell's words were halted on the gasp of the people. He stepped back and another child ran into the center of the circle with the story-teller, and, picking up Zell's staff, led the old man to a place in the circle.

"Aton," Nissen called, "I, son of Manlo, challenge you to fight me!"

Aton blinked. Nissen's words slashed into his thoughts. He stood up and answered, "I would end the killing before it begins."

Nissen tossed away his robe, and, bare-chested, leaped from his father's side, brandishing his metal sword so that the blade flashed in the glow of the firelight.

The instant Aton saw Nissen's sword he understood the meaning of the sound he had heard when Nissen struck him from behind, the sound of metal striking metal, of bells. He walked slowly toward the youth and in his deep rumbling voice called out, "Put down your weapon, Nissen, and I will put down mine."

The people sucked in their breaths and with one voice shouted, "Blood must be shed. He who is our leader must prove himself."

"We will fight," Nissen answered.

Aton stopped, slipped the cloak of skins from his shoulders and with the old blood cry of Nempie's people on his lips, leaped toward his challenger.

Nissen held his ground and smashed his blade against Aton's, making the night ring with the sound of metal clashing against metal.

Aton moved back. His chest was heaving and his body was wet with sweat. He, too, drove his blade against Nissen's.

Blow followed blow until each man withdrew and paused to suck air into his lungs.

Nissen bolted toward Aton who locked his blade with Nissen's. The two struggled, trying desperately hard to bring the other down.

Aton twisted his sword down and suddenly broke free. With a sudden movement his blade sliced across Nissen's left arm, opening it with a deep wound.

His arm covered with blood, Nissen backed away.

"Throw down your weaon," Aton called, breathing

hard. "Throw down your weapon and I will not kill you."

"One must die!" the people shouted.

"Zell," Aton called. "Zell, tell them."

"Yahweh's will must be done," the story-teller answered.

"I am His voice——"

"And I will become you," Nissen suddenly shouted, running at Aton.

Again they traded blows, shivering the blades in their hands and filling the air with the din of metal striking metal.

Suddenly Nissen's sword slipped down the blade of Aton's and cut him across his fingers, severing them at the knuckles.

Blood spurted from the wound and Aton could not hold his sword.

Nissen leaped forward and drove his weapon deep into Aton's stomach.

The people started to shout.

Nissen pulled his blade free.

Still holding his sword in the bloody stumps of his fingers, Aton dropped to his knees. There was fire in his stomach. He shook his head and tried to gain his feet.

"Take the tusks," Zell shouted. "Take the tusks and become Him. You must take the tusks, Nissen, to become Aton."

Nissen rushed at Aton and with one swift downward stroke severed his arm at the elbow.

Aton screamed.

Nissen cut the other arm away too and from each place where a limb had been now poured a fountain of blood.

"Yahweh's will has been done," Zell shouted, going forward to the victor and the vanquished.

"I am Aton," Nissen shouted. "I am your leader."

"Pula," Aton cried. "Pula!"

Aton pitched forward. *He stood in the rushes waiting for Pula, the black boar, to come out of the willow grove. He came with a snort. He was enormous and his black back hid the vastness of the night sky. Aton nocked an arrow to his bow. Pula swung his head, snorted, and charged. His thrice-circled, spear-pointed tusks pierced Aton's body before he could loose the arrow. "Pula," Aton whispered as blood poured out of his mouth, "Pula, we have slain each other."*

"Aton lives!" Zell shouted. "A new Aton has come to us by Yahweh's will. A new Aton has come to us!"

THE BIG BESTSELLERS
ARE AVON BOOKS!

- [ ] **Creative Aggression** Dr. George R. Bach and Dr. Herb Goldberg   24612 $1.95
- [ ] **Aton** Irving Greenfield   24844 $1.75
- [ ] **Chief!** Albert A. Seedman and Peter Hellman   24307 $1.95
- [ ] **Endgame** Harvey Ardman   24299 $1.75
- [ ] **Alive: The Story of the Andes Survivors** Piers Paul Read   21535 $1.95
- [ ] **The Rosemary Touch** Lois Wyse   23531 $1.75
- [ ] **The Wall Street Gang** Richard Ney   23549 $2.25
- [ ] **Teacher and Child** Dr. Haim G. Ginott   24414 $1.75
- [ ] **Watership Down** Richard Adams   19810 $2.25
- [ ] **Devil's Desire** Laurie McBain   23226 $1.75
- [ ] **Having a Baby Can Be a Scream** Joan Rivers   23234 $1.50
- [ ] **Autopsy** John R. Feegel   22574 $1.75
- [ ] **Shifting Gears** George and Nena O'Neill   23192 $1.95
- [ ] **Working** Studs Terkel   22566 $2.25
- [ ] **The Loo Sanction** Trevanian   19067 $1.75
- [ ] **Final Analysis** Lois Gould   22343 $1.75
- [ ] **The Eye of the Storm** Patrick White   21527 $1.95
- [ ] **Jane** Dee Wells   21519 $1.75
- [ ] **Theophilus North** Thornton Wilder   19059 $1.75

Available at better bookstores everywhere, or order direct from the publisher.

AVON BOOKS, Mail Order Dept., 250 West 55th St., New York, N.Y. 10019

Please send me the books checked above. I enclose $_____ (please include 25¢ per copy for mailing). Please use check or money order—sorry, no cash or COD's. Allow three weeks for delivery.

Mr/Mrs/Miss _____

Address _____

City _____ State/Zip _____

BB 7-75

NATIONWIDE BESTSELLER!

THE RIVETING TRUE STORY OF
A HARDNOSED NEW YORK DETECTIVE WHO SOLVED
SOME OF THE MOST DARING CRIMES OF OUR TIME!

AVON
24307
$2.25

ALBERT A. SEEDMAN AND PETER HELLMAN

CHIEF!

Al Seedman . . . hard-boiled, city-wise, smart as a whip, and as tough as they come. As Chief of Detectives in the biggest, roughest American city, he cracked the notorious Kitty Genovese stabbing, the Black Liberation Army cop-killings, the "Crazy Joe" Gallo murder, and many others. Cases that thrilled and horrified millions of newspaper readers . . . cases that baffled everyone but Al Seedman.

Now he tells it like it was—giving all the facts, and all the details, plus sixteen pages of photos.

"THE BOOK'S GUTS
HAVE A .38 CALIBER KICK!"
Publishers Weekly

"I WAS ENTHRALLED! TRULY A GREAT
COP STORY ABOUT ONE OF THE
GREATEST DETECTIVES IN THE
WORLD'S GREATEST CITY!"
Robin Moore, Author of
THE FRENCH CONNECTION

CC6-75